M.E.N. B X

NEB

In the Way

In the Way

by
Grace Livingston Hill

The American Reprint Company

MATTITUCK

Originally Published 1897
by A. J. Rowland
Philadelphia, Pennsylvania

International Standard Book Number 0-89190-040-3

To order contact
AMERICAN REPRINT CO.
PO Box 1200
Mattituck, New York 11952

IN THE WAY

CHAPTER I

THE kitchen looked unusually dreary that
night. It was raining and the two young
men who called it home had thrown down their
wet coats on chairs to dry before the fire when
they came in. Their heavy boots also had been
drawn off and looked out of sorts and out of
place in a dark pool by the door. The stove
needed blacking and the fire was sulky. In the
sink were piled the dishes of the entire day, still
unwashed. They were not many to be sure, but
they added to the general air of desolation.
Two blackened pipes on the mantel-piece lay in
the one cleared space, the rest of the shelf being
occupied by a miscellaneous collection of years.
On a hook behind the cupboard door there hung
a faded checked gingham apron. The owner
thereof had been dead nearly a year, but the
apron had never been taken down, either because
it had never been noticed, or because the boys
had not known what to do with it. It could

5

scarcely have been a pleasing object to them, but they had not been accustomed to much that was pleasant in their lives so far, and hardly thought to try and make it for themselves.

The table was set for the evening meal without table-cloth or much regard to the fitness of things. A baker's loaf of sour, puffy-looking bread lay on the bare table. A paper containing a slab of cheese was on the other side. A knuckle of ham on a plate and the molasses pitcher completed the array, with some miserably made tea in a tin teapot. It was a very uninviting-looking table, and yet these two preferred it to having their premises invaded by hired help, or to going out to board. They shrank from any more changes. They ate in silence, for they had worked hard all day and were hungry.

At last the elder of the two shoved his chair back from the table and sat thoughtfully gazing across the room.

"Joe, she wants to come here!" he said, still looking thoughtfully about the dismal room.

"Who're you talking about?" said the younger a little crossly, helping himself to another slice of ham. He had been working all the afternoon in the rain, mending the cowhouse roof, and the supper tasted good to him. "I wish you'd ever begin at the right end of a thing, Dave," he went on; "you always plunge into the middle, and it takes half an hour to get at your idea. Where have you been this afternoon, and who are you talking about?"

"Ruth," said David.

"Ruth?" said Joseph, showing by his tone that he was scarcely enlightened.

"Ruth," said David again.

"Oh, Ruth!" said Joseph, a kind of dismay and consternation in his voice. He laid down his bread and molasses and sat back in his chair. "What in the name of common sense does she want to come here for?" he asked after a minute.

"Because Aunt Ruth is dead," answered David, like a lesson he had been saying over to himself to be sure he had it right; "and because she is alone and is our sister and we are her brothers."

"Well, where's all the money that was going to be left her? Is it dead too?"

"I don't know about the money; she doesn't say as to that."

"It must be gone or she wouldn't want to come here. Why doesn't she do something and stay where she is? After being away from home all her life, she can't expect to be taken care of now."

"Joe," said David rather sharply, bringing the front legs of his chair down with a thud, "she's our sister. What would father say to hear you speak like that? She doesn't say anything about money, but I don't believe she was thinking of that. She seems to want to come to see us. Maybe it's only a visit she wants, but anyway she is coming. She isn't even going to wait to see whether we want her. She is going to start to-night and will be here to-morrow morning."

Joe answered this announcement with a long whistle of astonished disapprobation.

He reached for the letter David handed him, and drew the smoky kerosene lamp nearer him to read it. His face grew dark as he read it slowly. It was a letter fair and dainty enough for any brother to be glad to read. Written on heavy, creamy linen paper, in even, graceful lines and curves, a sort of initial of the lovely writer herself.

But Joseph threw it down angrily when he had finished, and flung back his chair roughly from the table.

"I guess I'll clear out of this ranch for a while, and let you enjoy your company to yourself," he said, rising as if to carry out his threat.

His brother rose also, and laying a rough hand kindly on his arm said: "No, you won't do any such thing, Joe; you'll stay here and behave yourself, as you promised father you would do, or at any rate as I promised father I would see you did. She is our sister, and you have got to do your duty toward her, whether you like it or not." Then David took one of the two dirty pipes from the mantel, and lighting it sat down by the stove, with his stockinged feet on the hearth. Joseph followed his example, and for a few minutes there was silence, save for the sound of wind and rain outside.

"Pretty place this is for a girl," said Joseph, taking the pipe out of his mouth to speak; "she'll come around messing up everything, and the way she's been brought up she won't know how to do a thing."

David looked about the room again in a troubled way. It was the same room he remembered in his boyhood, aye, even his babyhood, away back where that shadowy memory of his mother moved about; but the old kitchen had a brighter look in those days. What made the difference? Then when mother had gone and Aunt Nancy had come, the room had seemed well enough; father had lived there and seemed contented. After father had died, Aunt Nancy had kept the room about the same, until her death, nine months ago, and nothing had been changed since.

His eyes wandered to the gingham apron behind the door. He slowly brought his feet down from the hearth, and going over to the cupboard took the apron down from its hook,

and carefully rolling it up put it in the stove.
Then he sat down and went on smoking. The
action stirred up something in the younger
brother's memory which made him uncomfortable, and in spite of the rain he announced his
intention of going down to the store awhile.
David said nothing, and Joseph went about some
noisy preparations, drawing on his boots with a
heavy thud. Then he threw open the door, and
was greeted by such a gust of wind and torrent
of rain that, after scowling out into the darkness
for a minute, he slammed the door and came in,
pulling off his boots and sitting sulkily down
again by the fire.

David roused himself to wash the dishes. So
much he could do toward clearing up. " I suppose I shall have to get some one to fix up here,"
he said, looking hopelessly around.

"What for ? " said the irritable Joe. " If she
don't like it, let her go home. We don't want
her, anyway. There's other rooms in the house
besides this ; she can stay in them and keep out
of here. As for eating, let her get her meals
over to Barnes'. We can't cook for her, and
'tain't likely she knows how herself."

' Look here, Joe," said the elder brother turning slowly around, the cold greasy dishwater
dripping from his great red hands ; " you are
hard on her. She never knew she wasn't Aunt

Ruth's own child until after Aunt Ruth died, three weeks ago. It was part of the agreement, you know. Father thought it best for her to have a mother. Aunt Ruth said she wanted her to grow up loving her as her own mother. I never could quite see how it was right and fair not to tell her, but Aunt Ruth made a good deal of it, and father thought it would be just as well, for she would have everything money could buy—you know Uncle Hiram was pretty rich awhile before he died, until he lost a good deal in a failure of some kind. She was a pretty little thing when I saw her."

Here the dishwasher folded his arms and leaned back against the sink. " You know father sent me there with a message the year before he died, and he told me not to tell any one who I was, but Aunt Ruth. I wasn't to let Ruth know I belonged to her, if I should happen to see her, because he said she had never even heard of me. I didn't kind of like the idea, then, for it seemed as though she would feel ashamed of me if she knew I belonged to her, and I went there feeling all out of patience with a girl that was letting herself be fooled in that way; but you know she was a baby only a few days old when she went there, and how was it her fault?

" Besides, I don't believe they brought her up

near so stuck up as I thought, for while I waited
in the great big hallway she came flying down
the stairs just like a robin, and asked me to
please sit down till her mother could come.
Then I heard some one call her Ruth, and so
I knew who she was, and she answered, yes,
she was coming, and went away. But before
she went she smiled at me, and said it was a
cold morning outside. It seemed sort of funny
to think she was my own sister, and if mother
hadn't died, or things hadn't turned out as they
did, she would have been here instead of there,
and like as not she'd have been washing these
very dishes now, instead of my doing it."

"Well, you needn't count on getting her to do
them to-morrow night, Dave, I can tell you.
City girls never do those things. They're afraid
of their hands. She'll be a precious nuisance;
that's what I think. How old is she now?"

"'Bout a year and a half younger than you."

"H'm, they're always silly at that age. I
wouldn't let her come if I was you, Dave."

"She's on her way by this time, so I can't
help it," said the elder brother imperturbably.
He stood still, the dishcloth in his hand, thinking of the bright little figure in blue and white,
with flying golden hair, that had tripped down
the stairs and given him the chair so graciously;
and then he looked hopelessly about that room

and wished he knew how to make it pleasant for her coming.

The brothers did not sleep well that night. David had an uncomfortable sense of responsibility upon him which he was in nowise able to discharge, much as if an elephant had suddenly found himself inheritor of the proverbial china shop. What he, a quiet, awkward farm boy, was to do with a full-fledged young lady sister, fresh from the city, was more than he could fathom.

He arose early the next morning, as was his custom, and went about his usual duties, or "chores," as he called them, with the problem still unsolved. Joe, meantime, was angry and dismayed. Though it was by no means a pleasant day for such work, he announced his intention of "gettin' the timber off that upper wood lot," which was at some distance from the farm proper, and would require all day. Therefore, he took a cold bite in his pocket, shouldered his axe, and was off before David had realized that he would be left alone to receive their guest, when he had entertained some thought of sending his younger brother to the train to meet her.

Her letter had been a brief one and to the point, with an undertone of eager sisterly love and longing for some one who belonged to her, in her loneliness; and this on the second reading reached her elder brother's heart and made him wish that their father was alive to give her what she wanted. He felt himself utterly unable to do so.

Out of deference to the expected guest he forebore, as his brother had done, to eat his breakfast from dishes, this morning, but took a cold hurried lunch from the pantry shelf. He tried to think as he ate, what his father would have done, but it seemed impossible; and again, as he had done many times before, he decided that it was a bad business to give up one's children to some one else to bring up, even though that one was the rich wife of your own brother and the mother of the child was dead. Doubtless Ruth had had a much pleasanter life in her luxurious city home than she would have had in the old farmhouse with only her rough father and brothers and old Aunt Nancy for company; but now that those who had guarded her life were taken away, what was to become of her? He gave it up and went out to his work again. There was a certain amount of work about the farm that must be done every day no matter what happened, and he was glad that it was so.

When this had been done he harnessed the old horse to the light spring wagon; smoothed his hair; put on a coat—an unusual addition, except in cold weather, for merely a ride to the village—and drove slowly toward the town and the railway station. It did not occur to him to put on a collar. That was an amount of dressing not indulged in, except on Sundays or extraordinary occasions, by the people with whom he had been accustomed to associate. Half-way to the village, and almost overcome with his sense of the nearness of the station and his expected guest, he halted the old horse suddenly, thinking of his collarless condition, and half turned the wagon around again toward home to make it good; but the color mounted to his cheek as he remembered the crowd that would be at the station—always, to meet every train—and he turned the astonished horse's nose back again with a jerk, going on more rapidly toward the station.

It was bad enough to have the gaze of those curious eyes, and the ridicule of the lazy tongues leveled upon him while he met his city sister, without having a collar on. A collar was always an embarrassment to him, and for that reason alone he had several times meditated giving up going to church on Sabbath mornings since his father's death; but the power of habit and his father's steady example still held him to that when there was no reasonable excuse.

There was no need to fasten Old Gray lest she

should be afraid of the cars. She was not afraid of anything in this world now, and so David drew up in front of the long, low station, that had done duty for many a year, and swinging one leg over the wheel to the platform, which was about on a level with the floor of the wagon, he sat surveying the crowd of loafers assembled for their daily excitement of watching the New York train come in.

He had sat in just that way many a time waiting, with no particular end in view except that he happened to be there at that time, and it was interesting to see who would come and who would go. Now it was different, and the commotion in his breast made him wish himself at home. In a few minutes all the eyes would be leveled at him, and the wonder and surprise would be about him and his sister. How strange that word "sister" sounded to him, anyway! He had never really thought of her as belonging to him, and he was conscious of almost wishing at that moment that she did not. Then the distant whistle sounded, and he lounged out of the wagon and stood waiting with the others.

There were not many passengers to alight at the small village. One or two drummers, a merchant returned from a trip to New York, and an old grandmother come to visit a swarm of grandchildren, who were all down to meet her.

After these, preceded by an obsequious porter from the parlor car carrying her immaculate luggage, came a dainty young woman. She had golden hair, which escaped from the imprisoning shell combs into little sunshiny rings about her temples, and her eyes were large and blue, keen and bright, yet tender. David's eyes were blue too. She was dressed all in brown, very plainly indeed, and yet it seemed extraordinary to Summerton, for they seldom saw a dress or a coat so perfectly made. The oldest grandchild, who was herself approaching young womanhood, wondered what in the world there was about her simple hat that looked "so awfully stylish," and began studying it, if perchance her last year's might be made to serve in somewhat similar fashion.

Ruth Benedict walked the entire length of the platform to the dingy station, and had her baggage deposited on the grimy, much-cut benches, paid the porter a shining quarter, and then looked about for her brother. She had not discovered him in her walk down the platform.

He meantime had been sure that this was his sister, but he could not bring himself to speak while that important black porter was in attendance, and the blood mounted in rich waves to his face as she passed him. He turned his eyes the other way lest she should divine who he was and speak. She meanwhile, knew not what manner of person to look for. She knew he was a farmer, but at least she expected a collar, and so she passed him by at the first glance; but something in his face, as he turned during the bustle of the moving train to slip around to where she stood, attracted her attention, and she looked again, a smile lighting up her sweet face, the same smile he remembered of her childhood. That smile enabled him to get over the embarrassing ground between them and reach her side without the painful interval he had expected.

"Are you David?" she asked eagerly before he reached her, and then without waiting to give him time for more than a nod in reply, she put up her pretty lips and threw one arm simply and gracefully about his neck and kissed him.

David felt as though he never had been through such a trying experience in his life, and would rather be killed outright than go through it again. He was painfully conscious of the watching eyes. He dared not turn toward them to see what they thought. He had a faint hope that the outgoing train had attracted the attention of most of them, but it was only a hope. Ellen Amelia Haskins, the eldest granddaughter, was taking notes with undivided attention, and she immediately began to give abroad news.

All Summerton knew that away back in the years somewhere there had been a baby sister in the Benedict household, who had been adopted by the father's rich brother, but they had almost forgotten the story. Now, even as David hurried his sister to the waiting wagon behind the station, it was revived, as Ellen Amelia's excited voice proclaimed in tones which might have been heard by the occupants of the wagon, had it not been for their absorption in themselves, that she "just betted Dave Ben'dic's sister had come to make a visit, 'cause she kissed him," and she added, "and he looked real kind of handsome and majestic bendin' down to encircle her slight form," and she giggled softly to herself and remembered the last week's story in the "Fireside Companion."

David Benedict did not stay to hear what might be said. He whipped up old Gray as that animal could not remember to have been whipped since the last hired man got married and went away, and the wagon was soon hidden down the road behind the great elm trees at the corner.

CHAPTER II

RUTH felt not a little dismayed to find her brother present so unpolished an appearance, but she tried to remember that it was early morning and she knew nothing of farm life. Doubtless he had left his morning work to meet her. Her artist's eye decided that he was handsome in spite of no collar. The Summerton girls had not known enough to discover this as yet. They looked more upon the outward adornment than upon the true man, and could not recognize him except accompanied by well-oiled hair, flashy necktie, and perfumery on his handkerchief, which was to their nostrils a perfect cover for a barnyard odor on the boots or onions on the breath. Besides, David was shy and awkward and never gave them any attention. Joseph, the younger brother, was much more to their liking.

Ruth, sitting beside her silent brother trying to get acquainted and feel her way into his heart, felt her own sink in a lonely, homesick way, and began to long again for the dear ones who were gone, whose constant care had made her life so bright. But she turned her attention to the country about, frankly admiring the river views and the waving fields of grain. It was indeed a lovely drive to the Benedict farmhouse, and Ruth began to dread its ending.

She had been curious to know what her old home was like, but something began to warn her that she would be disappointed. She had read of and seen some beautiful old farmhouses, painted white with green blinds and with lofty columns supporting the front roof. She had imagined that her home would be something like this, with a velvety lawn in front and a dainty white hen here and there walking carefully over it, while at the back there would be a row of shining milk cans, and some peaceful cows musing not far off. That was her idea of farmhouses in general. Now she began to feel that there might be some mistake about their all being like that. Since they had left the station they had passed no such homes.

They presently came in sight of some spacious barns, well coated with red, and a little farther over a large old-fashioned rambling house, of color so dingy that no one might tell what it had been in former days. The front part of the house seemed to be closed, at least the weather-beaten blinds were shut. There was no smoke coming from any chimney except the back one. The front porch had a fallen-down appearance, which gave an expression to the house of a person with the corners of his mouth drooped sadly. This porch was an old-fashioned " stoop," with a narrow seat on either side too, instead of a wide, airy piazza stretched across the front of the house. The front dooryard was overgrown with tall grass and a few straggling pinks and bachelor's buttons here and there, while the rose and lilac bushes had tangled their branches across the path to the steps, according to their own sweet will.

Ruth wondered idly how the people could ever reach the front door, and felt sad at the air of abandonment and desolation. Then she saw Old Gray turn in at the great unpainted gate of many bars, and knew that she was at home. Somehow the tears were very near her eyes, but she bravely pressed them back and tried to be cheery and find something to admire. Strangely enough the old flat stone in front of the worn, much-chipped old green kitchen door with the quaint brass knob, was the first thing that caught her eye.

" What a beautiful flat stone that would have been to play on when I was a little girl," she said impulsively, feeling that she must say something or break down ; and then she realized what a silly remark that was to make. But some One wiser than herself was guiding her words that day. She could not have said anything that would so have warmed David's heart to his sister as that. He had a feeling that she must of course consider her life and her bringing-up as above that of her brothers, and when she actually spoke as if she would have liked to share their childhood joys in the old plain home, he felt as if he loved her at once. The old flat stone was dear to him for memory's sake. He could even remember so far back as when he used to sit on it, in his little gingham apron, and his mother would come to the door and give him a large piece of warm gingerbread, standing there a minute to watch his enjoyment as he ate, and saying in soft tones, "Mother's dear little boy."

His heart was so soft over Ruth's words that when he awkwardly helped her out of the wagon he had an impulse to kiss her. He restrained it, of course. All his life training since his mother died had been to restrain any such sentimental impulses as that, but the impulse had made his heart warm, nevertheless. It is a pity he did not give way to that impulse, for Ruth, suddenly ushered into that dreary kitchen, and left alone with the injunction to sit down and rest herself until her brother put out the horse, felt such a rush of desolation come upon her as almost overpowered her.

She sat down in Aunt Nancy's old rocking chair and buried her face in her hands. What did it all mean? Was there nobody left who cared for her? Did her brother not know what to do with her? Was she an unwelcome guest? That had not occurred to her before. Now it brought a sickening loneliness. She had been rash, after all, as her old lawyer friend had told her, in rushing off to brothers she did not know without any warning to them or any chance to hear from them. Yet she had thought when she prayed to be guided that her direction had been to come here. Could it be that she was mistaken? Perhaps her own desire for the love of some one who belonged to her had made her mistake her desires for God's guidance! Then came another thought. Perhaps he had wanted her to come here after all, and though there might not be comfort for her, still he might intend that there was something she could do for her brothers. Perhaps they did not know Jesus Christ.

Her heart went out in great longing for them. She wanted to be sure that they were Christians. If they were Christians, then surely there would be a tie between them even stronger than blood. If they were not, then she must stay and try to lead them to Christ. She slipped down on her knees beside the old calico-cushioned

rocker and asked her Saviour for help and guidance, promising to try to do whatever he wanted
her to do here in this home, no matter how hard
it might seem, if he would only stay with her
and help her. Then she got up, resolutely
wiped away the tears, and looked about her.
She forced herself to take in every detail of that
room. It did not take long, for the kitchen had
not much in it. She even walked over and
looked at the chromos of bright red and pink
roses framed in pine cones, hanging on each side
of the little high clock shelf, and took in the
fact of the smoky kerosene lamp, realizing that
there would be no gas in this house.

Then with a glance out of the window, to
make sure David was not at the door, she went
over to the pantry with swift determination.
David had told her during the drive that Aunt
Nancy was dead, and that they were living
alone, and she began to wonder how they lived.
Did they board, or what? She stood in the
door in wonder. The great piece of ham, the
half-loaf of bread, the broken cheese, and bag
of crackers, told a pitiful tale to her. She applied the tip of her nose to the baker's bread,
and then straightened up suddenly with an in-
voluntary "Ugh!"

Something of her amazement, disgust, and
pity, mingled, must have been in her face as she

turned at a slight sound behind her and saw her
elder brother standing hopelessly in the door.
He would not willingly have had her see that
pantry. He had fixed it all, out in the barn,
while he unharnessed Old Gray. He would go
right over to the Barneses and take board for his
sister, and then he and Joe could go over and
call upon her often and keep her from being
lonely. The old house was no place for her,
and of course she could not eat there. It was
all well enough for him and Joe to get along
on anything, but such a dainty bit of flesh and
blood as their sister must have better fare.
Accordingly he had stopped in the process of
unharnessing and come into the house to tell
Ruth his plan for her and ask if she would like
to ride over there with him at once, and have
him take her trunk over with them.

Shame filled his face at sight of her discovery of his awkward attempts at housekeeping.
He would have resented her going to look in
that pantry if she had not been his sister, and
even as it was a kind of anger began to rise in
his heart, and he would soon have been ready to
say with pride, "It's none of her business how
we live. She has no right to poke and pry into
things." But Ruth turned with tears in her eyes
and threw her arms about her brother.

"Oh, you poor, dear David!" she exclaimed.

"How you have needed me! And you have been trying to keep house for yourselves. I see it all now. I am so glad I have come. I was afraid at first that you did not want me; but you do need me, don't you? Tell me you do, for I am so hungry to be loved and needed. And I'm glad I came to make you comfortable. You are glad too, aren't you?" and then she hid her face in his coat and cried.

He stood helpless before her tears. He was really frightened. He had never seen a woman cry before, and began to wonder if he ought to go for a doctor; but just when he felt the most helpless, she lifted a face all smiling through her tears and kissed him.

Somehow David felt as though she were more really his sister after that, as if in some subtle way a sympathy had been established between them. He was willing to let her do anything she wanted to now, and he felt as if he would stand up for her against all the world. He made her sit down while he explained his plan for her boarding, but she only laughed a silvery laugh.

"Now, David, my dear brother, did you suppose I came here to be a summer boarder with the Barneses, and have you come and call on me occasionally? No, indeed! The Barneses are well enough in their places, and I shall be

glad enough to call on them some time in the
future if they don't see fit to call on me first;
but just now I have not time. There's a great
deal to be done in this house before dinner. I
came here to find my brothers, and I find they
need me a great deal more than I supposed they
did. What time do you usually have dinner?
and where is my other brother?"

"But what do you mean to do?" he asked
helplessly. "You can't eat here," and he looked
about on the kitchen which seemed, with her
bright presence in it, to have a great many more
defects for a kitchen than he had ever seen
before.

"Why can't I eat here, I should like to
know?" asked the sister brightly; "I guess I
can if you can. But I must go to work, or
there won't be anything fit for either of us to
eat. That bread in there is very sour. I wonder you haven't got the dyspepsia. Do you
mean to say that you and Joseph have been living in this way on such food as that ever since
Aunt Nancy died? You poor dear! Now, let's
get to work. We must have everything nice
and cheery before Joseph comes. That fire looks
as if it was almost discouraged. Can you make
up a good fire for me? I'll have to learn how to
operate that stove; our range was different. But
if you'll fix the fire real rousing and bright, and

bring my trunk in and unstrap it, I'll fix things up all right. Where is my room to be?"

David did not know how to answer all her questions. He felt that some one had come at last who knew what she wanted and his part was only to obey, so in bewilderment he brought her trunk in and deposited it in the room she selected. She had resolutely refrained from looking about her much as she went through a portion of the rest of the house. The kitchen was enough to deal with at first, and too much dreariness would take away her self-control. A room with four walls and a bed was an absolute necessity, and beyond that she would not see anything until she had done all she could in the kitchen. She kept her eyes strictly upon their work, while she rapidly took off her traveling dress and donned a neat gingham, enveloping herself in a large kitchen apron. It was the apron she and her dear adopted mother had made for her to use in cooking school a year before, and the tears came to her eyes as she fastened it, with the memory of all the sweet words and looks sewed into the garment with the dainty stitches.

"Darling, this apron will be with you in many a time of need and stand you in good stead," her mother had said. "You may find times when you will prize it more than any pretty dress you have. I hope this apron will wear to help you do great good and achieve great things in the culinary line." These had been that dear mother's laughing words as she handed her the finished garment. Ruth brushed the tears away and rushed down to the kitchen. There she found a bright fire roaring away in the stove, and David standing by it looking about in a dazed way as if he wondered what was coming next.

" Now the next thing is to find out what there is to work with," said the new housekeeper eagerly. " David, have you any yeast? I want to set some bread the first thing."

" Yeast?" said David; "no, we haven't had any yeast in the house since Aunt Nancy died."

" And David, where do you keep the baking powder and the salt?" called Ruth from the pantry.

" You will certainly have to go to the grocery before we can have dinner," she said, emerging from her investigations. " If you will go to market I will write down a list of things we need right away. I'll try to have some kind of a lunch for you when you come back. I cannot make bread without yeast and I cannot make biscuit without baking powder."

David brought the potatoes from the cellar and saddling the horse made ready to go on his

errand, not much relishing the thought of the
sensation he would make, returning to market
with a basket so soon after the arrival of his
sister. However, he hastened away, and Ruth
locked the door securely and went to work. It
must be confessed that while she was a brave
girl in the city, here in the country she felt the
least bit timid at being left alone in this strange
house for an hour. Who could tell what awful
tramp might come? However, she made up her
mind to be so busy she would not think of it,
and sending up a prayer for help, she went in
search of a knife to peel the potatoes. It was
fortunate that there was so much to be done,
else the desolation of the whole home, without
even an attempt at comfort, might have made
her heart fail her, till she must have returned to
the lovely home in the city she had left behind
for love of two unknown brothers.

The work of setting the table did not progress
so rapidly as it might have done under other
circumstances. In the first place, the table received a thorough scrubbing, as the two young
men had not thought it necessary to wipe off
any stray molasses drops for many a day. They
had supposed a table was an article of furniture
that would clean itself in some way. Then a
table-cloth must be searched for. Napkins she
did not find, but supplied them from a few she

had brought in her trunk. She also placed in
the center of the table a daintily embroidered
bit of linen, and then after surveying the general
effect, decided that it did not fit into its present
surroundings. There would need to be great
changes made in that room before the doily
would belong there. In fact, it seemed to be
incongruous with the immediate proximity of
the cook-stove.

Ruth wondered furtively if there was not a
dining room in the house, but forbore to reflect
much on the subject, resolving to consider the
question at her earliest convenience. Then the
dishes came in for investigation. They were
thick, and some were cracked and ill-smelling.
Up on the top shelf were a few bits of rare old
china, perhaps some of her own mother's wedding gifts. She wiped these off tenderly, and
washed such of the others as she considered
necessary to the meal, not being entirely satisfied with the result of David's dish-washing.
The table at last was set. She stood back and
surveyed it a moment. It did not look much
like the elegant table to which she was used to
sitting down daily, with its fine linen, solid silver,
cut glass, and china, and the various forks and
spoons considered necessary in polite society for
the different courses, but it was neat and inviting looking.

Next she turned her attention to the menu. There was not much variety available until David returned from the store. There were eggs and potatoes, and cheese and crackers, and plenty of milk and cream, and—yes, there was the ham. She despised the very thought of ham herself; but probably David liked it, and she would sacrifice her feelings and cook him a bit, for he must be very hungry after all these months of his own housekeeping. So she toasted some of the cheese, after grating it on the crackers, creamed the potatoes, made a puffy brown omelet, and crisped a bit of the ham by way of decoration. She had everything ready, and was just making a cup of most delicious coffee as her brother rode into the yard.

To understand David's feelings when he opened that kitchen door and saw that table, you must be a man and keep house for yourself for a few months. In spite of the fact that many of the so-considered necessities of a good meal were missing, and that there was no bread, the young man considered it the best meal he had eaten in years. In fact, he was not sure but things tasted better than they ever had in his life, except perhaps that gingerbread his mother used to make.

He told Ruth so, and her eyes grew bright and her heart beat fast with the pleasure. She felt well rewarded for her efforts. She resolved also, if possible, to have some warm gingerbread very soon for David, and meanwhile she started some bread with the yeast which he had brought, which she was sure would be delicious. She was an expert in the art of bread-making.

But the work of regulating that kitchen was by no means more than begun, so though she had been somewhat weary before lunch, she went to work again as soon as David had gone out.

The washing of the dishes proved to be not so 'rapid as she had intended it to be. She unceremoniously dumped the ill-smelling dish-cloth into the fire, and washed all the others out in scalding water before beginning. Then when the dishes stood shining from their bath in boiling water, dry already, because allowed to drain scientifically, she attacked the china closet. It would never do to put the dishes back into such a state of hubbub. She stood a moment reflecting, and then put all the remaining dishes into the hot suds and washed off the shelves. Of course boys could not be expected to know how to clean house, and evidently this one had not been cleaned since Aunt Nancy's death.

When that cupboard was cleaned and the dishes in shining order, her excitement had reached such a point that she felt she could not rest till the mantel and clock shelf were also cleaned of their rubbish. And it was while she was engaged in cleaning off that same mantel that she came on something which made her heart almost stop in dismay, and for an instant she felt as though she must turn and flee out of that house and away from that place as fast as she could go.

CHAPTER III

IT was not dirt, nor insects, nor a revolver, nor a serpent, nor a whisky bottle. It was only David's black, ugly pipe. But it gave her such a throb of disappointment and disgust, that she found herself trembling and weak, and obliged to sit down to regain her strength.

She had been brought up very rigidly with regard to the questions of temperance and tobacco. Her adopted father had never smoked, and her adopted mother had taught her that it was a vile and filthy habit, not only making the persons addicted to it disagreeable nuisances, but making them dishonor and defile their bodies, the temples of the Holy Ghost. Ruth had thought and read a great deal on the subject. She had tried and succeeded in turning every member of her large Sunday-school class of boys against the habit. She had been an enthusiastic member of a club of young Christian women who were banded together pledged not to select their friends from among the young men who smoked, and never to consent to walk the street with a young man who was smoking. It was in her eyes a disgrace. Now to find that one of her own brothers—perhaps both—smoked, was terrible. The blood rolled in waves over her fair neck and cheeks at the disappointment and shame and disgrace of it, and the tears would come in spite of herself. To have her brother wear no collar had been a surprise, but a collar was not a vital matter. This black pipe was.

It required a moment's prayer before she could calmly return to that mantelpiece. What to do with that pipe was a serious question. She hated to touch it. She had never touched a pipe or cigar in her life. After some consideration she got a newspaper, and by help of a burnt match, shoved the pipe to the paper and laid it on the floor in the corner where no harm could come to it. She would have liked to destroy it, but she knew that would do more harm than good, and besides, it was not hers, and she had no right to do any such thing. However, during the remainder of her work that afternoon, she was reflecting on what course she should pursue with regard to it, and many were the prayers for guidance that she sent up.

As she worked and prayed her heart grew calmer. Perhaps, after all, it might have belonged to some hired man; she would try to think so for the sake of her own peace of mind, at least for this afternoon. Happily it did not occur to her to think that it might have belonged to

her own father. There was too much to be
done for her to dwell upon details. She had
set her heart upon having a cheerful room for
her two brothers to come home to that evening.

She viewed the contents of the pantry with utmost scorn, and doubtless gave those two young
men more pity than they deserved, for they had
fed upon such fare so long that it was not the
hardship to them to eat such things that it would
have been to their dainty sister.

It may have been her compassion which led her
to plan a rather elaborate supper, considering
her recent arrival and the state of the kitchen.
For though she was somewhat weary with traveling, her nerves were keyed high to accomplish
what she purposed. She arose from her knees
where she had been washing the oilcloth under
the stove by the door, and stood thinking a
moment. Then she shut her lips firmly and
rapidly went to work making a custard and
some gingerbread. After all it did not take long
to do things when one had the will. When
they were in the oven she went back to her
housecleaning with renewed energy. Given
nerves, a quick brain, and a pair of deft and
willing hands, great changes can be wrought in
the course of an afternoon. David came to the
door once, from his work, to ask if she was lonesome and if there was anything he could do,

and looked about helplessly on her work and
went away bewildered. He had a dim idea that
this was not exactly the way to entertain a city
young lady on the first day of her arrival; but
she seemed determined, and what could he do?

She had promised to call him if she needed
anything, and by and by she did open the door
and ask for his help a moment. She had ventured into one of the unused rooms on the
ground floor; it seemed to have been a bedroom,
and she called David to know if he would mind
if she took the large rug made of rag carpet,
from the center of that room to spread in the
kitchen. He was entirely willing she should do
anything she pleased in the house, and awkwardly helped her to shake it and arrange it
under the kitchen table. Then he stood a
moment irresolutely by the door wishing he
knew something else to do, but finally went out.

Ruth worked hard. It grew late before things
were in the order that pleased her fastidious
taste. It was growing dark. She wondered
why Joseph did not come, and yet was glad he
delayed, and finally she stood a moment and
gave a last look at her completed task before
she slipped away to her room to smooth her hair
and remove the traces of toil from face and
hands and dress.

Everything was immaculately clean. The

lamp chimney shone with cleanliness, and the light glowed through a rose-colored crape paper shade she had hastily improvised from a roll of paper in her trunk. The table was set decently and in order, as nearly like that of her city home as she could compass with her present material. There was a plate of delicate, puffy white biscuits suggestively near the golden honeycomb David had brought in that afternoon from one of the hives. The bread had been started so late that it was just now beginning to send out a wholesome odor from the oven, so the biscuits had been made in a desperate rush at the last, when the cook found that the bread could not possibly get itself ready for supper. The roasted potatoes had their brown coats just ready to crack open, and covered closely on the back of the stove was the meat, which had been gently simmering all the afternoon, till it was tender as could be, and browned to a nicety with a savory gravy about it. The coffee gave a hint of its aroma also.

It is necessary to understand the details of this first supper of the united family in the old home, that you may be able to enter into the feelings of the young man who entered by the back kitchen door not two minutes after the fairy who had wrought all this change, had departed to her toilet.

Joseph had toiled hard all day doing work

that might have waited until his brother could help him. Gloomily he had eaten his dry, solitary lunch on a log, glaring at the brightness of the day with a fierce expression of dislike. Occasionally he wondered how David was managing at home. That he would get rid of the unwelcome young lady sister in some comfortable way Joseph never doubted. The old farmhouse was no place for her. What could they do with her there? David would either send her back where she came from, or get her a place to board near by at some house in the village until something could be done with her.

Life had been hard and disagreeable enough before without this rude breaking in upon the poor comfort of their solitude. Joseph felt a fierce rebellion at the unfairness of Providence in so ordering things, and said to himself two or three times that it wasn't of much account to live anyway. He had indeed reached a stage of his life where he was dissatisfied with his surroundings. He did not know that his restless, unhappy feelings came from a longing for a higher, richer life. He had been brought up to this; how should he know there was anything better? To work hard all day he did not grudge, and in a way he enjoyed the evenings he occasionally spent in the down-town grocery; but David kept a pretty steady watch on his evenings, and

the ones he spent in the village were not so
many as he desired. No other avenue of amusement was at this time open to him, unless indeed he went to church. There had been a
time when he haunted the church steps during
the progress of any meeting or entertainment or
supper, but since he had outgrown his Sunday-
school class at the time of the death of his first
and only teacher he had dropped that amusement.

Life on the whole looked dull and uninteresting to him. He had fierce, wild thoughts of
plunging off into a city somewhere and doing as
he pleased, though that was impracticable, for
he had no money aside from his share in the
farm, and his early training had at least given
him a horror of tramps. He worked doggedly
on in the gathering shadows until the darkness
put a stop to his labors. Even then he was as
slow as possible about gathering up his tools.
He would not go home until every possible
chance of seeing the intruder was gone. David
would surely have disposed of her by this time,
he thought, as he dragged his weary, unwilling
feet homeward.

He was growing very hungry, for his hasty
lunch had been meager and his day long and
filled with hard work. Fortunately he did not
approach the house from the side where the

kitchen windows shone bright in the rosy light
of crape paper and clean window-glass, else he
might have disappeared into the darkness again,
who knows where? and for how long, who can
tell? Instead, so sure was he that David had
managed things somehow by this time, that he
came in as usual through the back kitchen door.
He paused in the shed a moment before he laid
down his heavy tools, and listened. He heard
nothing. All was quiet. Only the sound of
David's voice in the cowyard not far off, as he
spoke to the cow he was milking, and the ring
of the milk-pails as something hit against one of
them.

The light under the crack in the kitchen door
guided him as he hung up his old coat and put
away his tools. He was glad David had lit the
lamp before he went out. Strange he was so
late at milking, but probably he had been so
busy getting their sister off somewhere that he
had only just come home. Now that she was
fully disposed of, he thought to himself perhaps it had been a little mean of him to go
off and leave everything to David in that way.
Not that he would do otherwise now, but he felt
a little compassion for his brother. It was the
penalty he paid for being the elder brother.

Then Joseph pulled off his heavy, mud-covered
boots, set them by the shed door, and walked

on to where the crack showed a little cheer.
He threw open the door and stepped in. Coming from the darkness into the unusual brilliancy
of the room blinded him, and for a moment he
stood winking and trying to see. Gradually the
changed room dawned upon him one corner at
a time. He noticed everything, even to the details of the delicious supper prepared. He was
dazed. Could he have made a mistake in the
dark and gone out of his way into another man's
house? Was he in a dream? What was the
matter? Had David gone and hired a housekeeper, and was the obnoxious sister then in the
house, and were they waiting supper for him?

Before he had time to think further or even
to move from where he was standing, the opposite door opened and the sister came in. She
was a trim little figure in a plain, dark-blue
dress and a white apron. She saw her brother
at once. Some women are gifted with being
able to read men at a glance. Perhaps too, some
words that David had spoken, or more, the words
he had not spoken, about this brother, had helped
her to know what to expect in him, and she had
made up her mind to win him if possible. Her
greeting was as sensible and sweet and winning
as could be desired by any brother, no matter
how crusty he was feeling.

"Oh, this is Joseph, isn't it? I'm so glad

you've come, for supper is all ready, and the potatoes are horrid if they are not eaten the minute they are ready." And she reached up and kissed the bewildered, embarrassed, uncomfortable young man just as if she had been accustomed to kissing him every day all the years of her life.

He was painfully conscious of his old brown jean shirt and his stockinged feet, especially as the weekly darning had been neglected for many a long week. But she, with a cultured woman's instinct, understood his embarrassment and covered it by cheerily bustling about at her supper, telling him to hurry and get his hands washed, and asking if she could not find his slippers for him. David came in just then, the full brightness of the room bursting upon him for the first time, and his heart leaped with a new kind of joy he had not imagined was possible. Was it going to be a happy thing after all to have this high-bred sister live with them? Was it possible there was in the world for them as much brightness as this kitchen contained, to be lived in every day in the week, all the year around? He had supposed it was only rich city people who had things so kind of comfortable and cheery looking.

Then presently they sat down to that supper

table. The meat and potatoes vanished rapidly, for the two young men were hungry. Only the cook did not partake very freely, but her nerves were too highly strung, and she was too weary to eat much. The Benedict boys discovered that their sister could cook. She was so lately the pupil of a famous cooking school that it had been easier for her to prepare this somewhat elaborate repast under the circumstances, than it would have been for most city girls who had indeed been taught to cook, but who had not had the opportunities for every-day practice which her wise foster-mother had given her. So Ruth thanked God for her ability to cook as she watched the great pile of puffy biscuits disappear rapidly. For the brothers did justice to the supper, the like of which they seemed never to have tasted before.

There were embarrassments connected with the meal, and Ruth was glad that they were hungry, in order that they should not feel quite so awkward. Instinctively she felt that she was on sufferance with her younger brother, and perhaps to some extent with the elder also. She dared not stop to think of it, or she would have broken down and cried. It seemed too dreadful to have come all this way to find brotherly love, and to be all alone in the world, and then to find that one was not wanted. Her better sense told

her that she was needed there, and some heavenly
influence seemed to say God had a work for her.
She tried to remember that she had but just
come, and they did not know her nor know what
to do with her.

She must make a place for herself in their
hearts first. She must at least show them what
she was and had to give them, and then if they
did not want her she could go away; and so
she put aside the pride which kept coming up
to trouble her at the thought that she was not
wanted, and calling to her aid all those winning
ways that were hers by nature, as well as of
grace, she set herself to win her brother Joseph.
With glowing cheeks and bright eyes, looking
first at one and then at the other brother, and
with well-chosen, pleasant words she told bright
bits of things that had occurred on her journey.
She made them laugh several times, which was
a great help.

They forgot for the moment that she was
city bred, and that they must have a care for
the way they managed their forks, articles
which had sorely oppressed them during the
beginning of the meal, for Aunt Nancy's training in table etiquette had seldom included the
use of the fork in preference to the knife. David
even ventured to respond to her bright talk occasionally, and secretly voted her unusually jolly

for a girl. Joseph seemed silent, almost shy, watching the new sister furtively, enjoying the good cheer, but wearing an air that said as plainly as words could have said, "I'm not to be fooled into liking you by all this."

At last the evening was over, the preparations made for the morning meal, and the weary young woman was at leisure to rest and think.

It was in the quiet of the bare room upstairs, whose dull ingrain carpet, helped out on one end by a breadth of faded rag carpet, seemed to intensify the dreariness. The only other furniture was a plain old bed of the kind known as a cord bedstead, two wooden chairs, a wooden table, with wash-bowl and pitcher, and a small, cheap, gilt-framed looking-glass hanging over it. There was a closet in the room, and a green paper shade at the window, and the lamp which she had brought up with her and deposited on a rude wooden shelf over the chimney shed a dull, desolate light over all. Ruth's tired nerves gave out at last, and she sat down in the wooden chair by the door and cried. Why had she come here after all? Her lawyer had begged her to write and find out about things, or let him come on ahead and survey the land. Her many friends, and her foster-mother's as well, had opened their hearts and homes to her. A dear old friend of her mother had offered to

make her home with Ruth, in case she preferred
remaining in the old home, which was hers to
do with as she pleased. But she had refused
them all and had come here, stubbornly perhaps,
but feeling that it was what Christ would have
her do. It was what her own father and mother
would have had her do, as well as what would
please the dear ones who had for so many years
occupied the places of father and mother in her
heart. Had it all been a mistake? Ought she
to have waited? Did she then have no call from
God to come? Should she have stayed in the
city?

There were many things she might have done
to feel that she was of use in the world. Not
that she needed to earn her living, for she was
amply provided for as far as money went, but
she might have gone into city mission work.
She could have given her time to church work.
She was a graduate of a school for physical culture. She could have given some time to teaching and helping poor overworked girls to a better
physical life, and so have led them step by step
to a better spiritual life through this influence.
She might have organized classes in cooking, or
dressmaking, or millinery, among young women
who were too poor to afford to go to the schools
where such things are taught. She had delighted in all such things herself and was one

of those people who can turn their hands to almost anything. The father and mother who now were gone had made it their pleasure to see that she had the best instruction in any line which seemed to please her. She thought now of the many words of praise she had received for this or that little service which she had performed well, and how others had envied her varied skill. She had not thought much of it then, because anything she tried to do always seemed easy to her. Now Satan came to tempt her with the thought that she ought not to bury these talents up here in the country, when they might be reaching hundreds, instead of just two young men who really did not want her to stay. Then something seemed to say : " But they are my brothers, and if I have any talents I can use them here as well as in the city. Jesus Christ knows what is best for me to do, and he will show me what I must do next. I will ask him."

She knelt beside the ugly bed and told all her troubles, asking that she might be guided in the way he would have her go ; that she might be humble, and not seek to do work he did not want her to do ; that the Lord would bless her brothers, and if possible give them some love for her. Then she rose and went about her preparations for the night with the tumult in her heart stayed. Even the creaking of the cord bed did not serve to rouse the evil thoughts again, though it certainly was not pleasant. She fell asleep wondering whether she would always care about little things and be so annoyed by them, and if eating with one's knife and wearing no collar would be barriers of the true love that ought to exist between brother and sister, supposing that there was no way to get rid of these little annoyances. She was distressed with herself beyond measure that she noticed these things. Why was it that she noticed them so much more than if they had been in some of her Sunday-school scholars? True, these men were her own flesh and blood— her brothers. Yes, it was pride after all. But the others were her own brothers and sisters in Christ. She was God's, and he would take care of it all, she thought; and then she fell asleep.

CHAPTER IV

JOSEPH spoke but little at breakfast, and went off to work soon after the meal was completed. David seemed to Ruth much changed. He had had time to reflect and get himself out of the maze of unexpected problems into which he had been plunged by Ruth's letter and arrival. He showed great kindness, even tenderness and thoughtfulness, with regard to her comfort. He said at once that they must have some help in the house, and spoke cheerfully about his desire to have things bright and pleasant for her. He even went so far as to tell her that he had never dreamed there could be so much comfort in any home as she had brought to theirs during the few short hours since her arrival.

Ruth flushed pink over his praise, for she recognized that it had been hard for him to say these things, and that to him, hardened and roughened by his outdoor work, she seemed a very dainty, fashionable creature, more to be looked at than used, and that, in a way, he was afraid of her. Still she felt that this feeling was wearing away with him and that they

would presently be as frank and friendly as
though they had always known one another.
She decided that David was a true gentleman,
and she divided the word into two parts when
she said it softly to herself while she washed
the dishes, and she put an emphasis on the word
"gentle," with all its ancient, courtly, noble
meaning. Yes, it was going to be very easy to
love him as a brother, she felt. As for Joseph,
he was very interesting, and she felt sure the
love would come. No need to worry about that.
They were brother and sister, and all the tenderness of that relationship would surely come by
and by. Her troubles seemed to be lightened
by the morning light and she felt more hopeful
of the future, and thus fell to planning.

She had discovered in her talk with David
that the idea of hired help had been a great
bugbear to the brothers on account of the extreme familiarity with the family which all the
Summerton girls who "lived out" expected.
They dreaded it. David in particular seemed
to stand in horror of having Eliza Barnes or
Jane Myrtilla Fowler sitting at the table at
every meal and speaking to him as "Dave Benedict." He had also tried in a helpless kind of
way to explain to his sister how utterly unlike
her these girls were and how incongruous
would be to see them sitting across the table

from her. David had an innate delicacy about him which was more than mere worldly pride. Ruth laughed brightly at the idea that there would be anything out of the way in her eating at the same table with the said Jane Myrtilla if need be, but secretly she saw exactly how unwise it would be for them to try to have another element in their already mixed household. Matters must be simplified as much as possible if they were to find a common level for all three to live upon. It would not do to have a stranger always about who might possibly report to the entire town anything which was said at the table by any one of them. Ruth sat down perplexed. Something must be done. She must talk it over with David. The house needed cleaning. There would be hard work to which she was unaccustomed, which even if she felt competent to do might end by making her ill.

A bright idea suddenly occurred to her. Sally, the cook, of whom she had taken a sorrowful leave but four days before, had been in her foster-mother's family for twelve years. She had been rescued from a life of trouble and taken in by Mrs. Benedict, and she felt a gratitude which knew no bounds. She had clasped the young girl in her arms in a reverent kind of way as she bade her good-bye and said, " Yeh dear little thing, yeh! Miss Ruth, if ye'll jist

say the word ony time and wroite me, I'll folly
ye to the inds of the earth." Now, it was but
four days since she had left and she was going
to her sister's to stay till she had found a suitable place. Perhaps it was not too late to secure
her. Ruth thought over all the possibilities,
pictured Sally, used to large rooms, elegant furniture, and fine cooking, placed in the plain farmhouse, and decided what she would do. She
would put the matter before her plainly and let
her decide for herself. Ruth ran to the door
and called David. He came quickly from the
barnyard, where he was busy about some work,
thinking to himself how very pleasant it was to
have some one there to call him.

"David, isn't there some woman who will
come in to clean house and go home to her
meals for a few days? Or can we get along for
a few days almost anyway, you know? I have a
plan."

David thought a moment and finally decided
on a good, strong colored woman who might be
induced to go out by the day for a short time.
Then Ruth unfolded her plan. David was somewhat dubious about introducing another unknown quantity into the household, but he was
already beginning to have unbounded confidence
in the young woman who was at the helm, so he
gave his assent to her proposition. Ruth then

went in to write to Sally, while David prepared
to "hitch up" and take the letter to the office.

After Ruth had dinner well under way she
took a survey of the house, trying not to feel
the chill of desolation as she entered one after
another the great bare rooms. It made her
shudder to feel the cold air that struck her even
on this warm day in late summer as she opened
the closed rooms. She threw open all the shut-
ters and let the sunlight stream in from garret
to cellar, even over the sacred haircloth furniture in the well-guarded "front room" which
Aunt Nancy had carefully kept just as it had
been when she came, and which, since the mother's death, had not been used. There was a wax
cross with clambering, impossible flowers, under
a glass globe on the marble-top table. There
were several thread tidies in elaborate patterns
on the haircloth chairs and sofa. The small
box stove that was supposed to heat the room
had a grim, leering effect, with a few cobwebs
draped across its front. The yellow paper
shades had stiff baskets of fruit pictured on
them by way of decoration. The ingrain carpet was a bold attempt in crude reds and greens.
Beside the glass globe on the center table, there
was a large old-fashioned family Bible, and on
it lay a red plush album with a looking-glass on
the upper cover. It looked absurdly new and

out of place amid the old-fashioned atmosphere
of the room. It had been Aunt Nancy's purchase of a traveling agent for whom she felt
sorry, and she had excused the unwonted ex-
travagance by saying that "the woman needed
help, and an album was a handy thing to have
in the house, anyway." It was about the only
luxury that Aunt Nancy had ever permitted herself to purchase in the whole of her lifetime, for
she was of a saving disposition and had been
brought up to economical habits.

There was a framed wreath of hair flowers
under glass and there were some portraits on the
wall, queer old-fashioned photographs and da-
guerreotypes in oval gilt, or frames of ancient
pine cones and varnished coffee berries. The
faces were faded and the hair and dress were of
years before. It made them seem unreal. She
wished she knew which were her own father
and mother. It was so strange a position, hers,
not to know the look of the faces of those who
had been the source of her being. With a
sinking sensation as if everything were slipping
away from her, she reached out her hand to the
Bible and read a part of the ninety-first Psalm :

"He that dwelleth in the secret place of the
Most High shall abide under the shadow of the
Almighty."

There came a warm thrill of joy to her heart,

and it was as if her Master were speaking sweet words in her ear. Here was a message for her, and perhaps then she was wanted just here to live and work for him. If she were under the shadow of the Almighty, then surely no earthly shadows could ever fall upon her. It was hers to dwell in the secret place of the Most High if she would. She dropped upon her knees and asked for strength to dwell in that sweet secret place, and then again for guidance in this her much-hedged-about path.

Then Ruth deliberately sat her down to face the question of this bare, old-fashioned, unattractive house—almost uninhabitable it seemed to her refined taste, used to having everything arranged in comfort and harmony. In the first place, the furniture was not abundant, and what there was, was of the stiff, hard kind. How could she ever make this home attractive and comfortable for her brothers and pleasant for herself? Some of the furnishings had suffered through much use and some through neglect. The boys had not been careful housekeepers. How could they have been expected to be? The rag carpets were musty from long dampness and lack of air in the rooms. Ruth leaned her head against the hard haircloth back of the only arm-chair the room contained and closed her eyes, thinking wearily and hungrily of the

soft carpets in rich harmonious colorings which
covered all the floors of the home she had left,
and of the easy-chairs and pretty curtains, and
oh! all the pretty belongings of a comfortable,
even luxurious, city home. She had helped to
select many of those home furnishings, and her
heart ached for a sight of them even after one
day's absence. If she only dared bring them
here, or some of them, but no—and here she
sat erect. Was it possible that she was so bound
down to mere things that she could not give
them up for a time? Her brothers might be seriously offended if she should propose such a
thing. Besides, she had put the house, furniture and all, into the hands of her agent to rent,
and it was doubtless by this time rented. She
had burnt her bridges behind her and must not
look back.

David's step as he came through the hall from
the kitchen in search of her, roused her effec-
tually. Had he returned so soon? She smiled
as she heard his hesitating voice calling her by
name. He scarcely felt that he had a right to
speak to her so familiarly. A thought of sorrow
that it should be so between own brother and
sister came to her, and then she met him in the
hall. He had brought her a letter, and as she
took it a swift hope passed over her that maybe
the Lord was calling her in other directions, that

this letter contained an answer to her prayer.
She tore it open hastily, while David stood
awkwardly by, watching her, not knowing
whether to go or stay, and half fearing himself
that this letter might in some way snatch this
new-found sister away from the gloomy house.
He was beginning to be thoroughly glad she
had come, even so soon.

But no, she found that there was no call for
her to come back to the city. Instead, it was a
letter from her agent saying he had an opportunity to rent the house at a good rate unfurnished, if only she were willing to have her
goods stored. He desired to have an immediate
reply as to whether she wished him to close
this bargain or not, and awaited her orders
concerning the furniture, in case she chose to
have the articles taken from the house. He
added in a postscript, that as they had so often
talked over the matter of renting unfurnished,
and decided it was best to rent furnished under
the circumstances, he feared she might consider
that he had taken a good deal upon himself to
consider the matter at all; but the fact that the
parties wishing to rent were such exceptionally
fine tenants and willing to pay so high a rent
had made him feel that possibly she would wish
to change her mind.

Ruth read the letter through twice, standing

there in the hall, and then sighed and wished
she had some one to advise her, and so looking
up met the clear admiring eyes of her brother
fixed upon her. Why, to be sure! David could
advise her, and was it possible this letter was in
answer to prayer for guidance? Was it put in
this way that it might be easy for her to bring
her own furniture here without offense? Without more ado she handed the open letter to
David and sank upon the lower step of the
staircase saying, "There, David, tell me what to
do?"

Surely God's Holy Spirit was guiding her
every action. She could not have done anything which would have more completely and
quickly won the heart of her brother than to
thus freely and frankly give him her entire confidence. It changed the face of matters quite
materially in his mind. He was no longer being
condescended to by an angel who had suddenly
dropped down and might as suddenly and mys-
teriously disappear, but he was being looked up
to as a brother by one who needed help, advice,
and protection. His heart warmed instantly with
the thought that he would protect her always
from everything just so long as she would let
him. Then he read the letter. Ruth watched
him as he read and decided again that he was
handsome. There was a look and bearing about

him which reminded her of his Uncle Hiram,
who had been known to her all her life as her
father. She wondered if he did not resemble
their father.

David had a few questions to ask. Did she
know what the rates of storage in the city were?
Were they not very high? Was she attached to
the furniture? Would she like to have some or
perhaps all of it about her? Would it not make
the old farmhouse seem more homelike to her?
He had a dim recollection of rich blendings of
color and soft luxury of which he had caught a
glimpse on that memorable visit to his Aunt
Ruth's, and a fine instinct told him that the
haircloth furniture and rag carpets must be a
decided contrast. Her face flushed and her eyes
grew bright with eagerness as he asked this last
question.

Oh, she would like to have her things here;
might she? She clasped her hands in her eagerness and came and stood shyly by his side, looking up at him. Was he sure they would not be
in the way? Would he mind having her put
them in place of some of the present furnishings? She did not want to do anything which
would hurt his feelings or Joseph's, and if he
was attached to the things he had been used to
all his life, she was perfectly willing to live just
as they did. (At this instant she made up her

mind to really like that red and green ingrain
in the parlor, if it was necessary in order to
win her brothers' love.)

But David was in no wise offended. He was
pleased at the idea of pleasing his sister. He
knew their things were old and ugly and that
probably if she had lived at home they would
have been different; but Aunt Nancy's taste had
been severely plain and they and their father
had never thought, if they had known how, to get
better. It did not matter anyway for just men,
he said a little sadly and added: "But if you
will stay and brighten up this old place for us—
if you think you can stand it here and not get
lonesome—why we'll do everything we can to
make it pleasant for you. Joe is a little backward and he'll hold off for a few days, but he'll
be acquainted with you in a little while, I guess,
and then he won't seem quite so shy and sullen.
He's not much but a boy anyway, you know, and
he's always been inclined to be stubborn and have
a way of his own. Maybe you can help make
him different. I think father always had some
idea of giving him a better education than could
be got here, but things didn't go so well on the
farm the last few years before he died and he
couldn't. There was an old mortgage to pay
off that kept him down all his life. But Joe
and I paid the last cent on that two months ago,

and I guess we can afford to paint the house and fix up a bit if you can stay with us. Things need to be different for a woman. Do you think you can stand it?" he asked wistfully.

"Of course I can," she answered, brushing away happy tears that his words had brought to her eyes. "David, I came here to find my brothers. I don't care about things. But I should like to bring the furniture here, for I think I could make it cozier for you and Joseph, and so if you are sure you don't mind I'll send for them to-day. But see here, David. I have not come here to be a burden on you. I am not penniless. I'm to bear my full share of everything if I stay."

It was then that David sat down upon the stairs beside his sister, and they had a talk that was more like what a talk between brother and sister should be than Ruth had been able to hope for. She went back to her dinner-getting and David to his farm-work, with happy, light hearts. Ruth sang about her work :

"Wherever he may guide me,
  No want shall turn me back,
My Shepherd is beside me,
  And nothing shall I lack.
His wisdom ever waketh,
  His sight is never dim,
He knows the way he taketh
  And I will walk with him."

CHAPTER V

RUTH stood in the doorway of her brother
Joseph's room. She was trying to plan
what changes she would make, and what articles
from the city home should be put into it. She
felt like a fairy about to wave her wand and
bring beauty over everything, and she was as
excited and happy over it all as a child with a
new toy. The bare room had given her a
heartache. That any human being should have
so dreary a place for the only spot which he
could call his own, seemed very pitiful to her
brought up amid a wealth of beauty. She would
delight to make it all different. Joseph had
been told that his sister was to bring her furniture to the home, but he had not seemed to mani-
fest much interest in it. He was still very reti-
cent with his sister, to say the least. Indeed, he
sometimes seemed harder to win than ever.
Ruth could not understand it. She wondered
about it now, as she stood in the door of the
desolate room and planned how she would
change it. Perhaps David might have explained his brother's actions if he had thought
about them at all. In a measure, Ruth herself

had had a hand in bringing about a dogged determination to have nothing whatever to do with
her more than was absolutely necessary. It had
happened in this wise.

During the frank, free talk which Ruth had
held with her brother David, after the arrival of
that letter about her house and furniture, the
brother and sister had opened their hearts to one
another in a way that each would have thought
impossible an hour before. Ruth, as the talk
concluded, made up her mind that she would
find out the truth about that horrid pipe.

"David," said she at last, lifting her clear,
sweet eyes to his face, "I found something when
I was clearing up that troubled me very much.
I was so afraid it belonged to some member of
my family. I do hope it doesn't. Do tell me
it was the property of some hired man. I can't
bear to think either of my brothers uses it.
Wait! I'll get it," and she slipped out to the
back kitchen where she had deposited her paper,
and brought it with very gingerly fingers.

David took it anxiously and opened the paper.
Then the rich red blood rolled from neck to
forehead. He was ashamed before this sweet
sister. Never before had the old black pipe
seemed obnoxious. He had always looked upon
it as a friend in his loneliness, a thing as pleasant as anything which came into his life. But

suddenly, without ever having heard an argument against smoking, without even reasoning
on the subject, he seemed to see this little bit of
filthy clay through the eyes of the young girl
who stood beside him, and he felt a disgust for it
and for himself that he had ever had to do with it.
David's was a fine nature. It is not many men
who would have felt this instinctively; others
might have come to the point through reason
or conscience or reverence for another's protest
persistently made. This man saw in a flash, by
the revelation of the curl of disgust in the delicate lips, and the eager pleading in the earnest
eyes of his sister, how a more refined being such
as she was might look upon this subject, and before his reason grasped it he had surrendered to
what seemed grandest, noblest, and best in life
to do. He might have a struggle with himself
afterward to carry out his purpose—doubtless
would—but certain it was, he would never willingly smoke again. He answered very little.
His downcast eyes convicted him. He folded
the paper together with a hasty movement.

"I am sorry about it. This shall not trouble
you any more," he said, and strode away to the
barnyard; but the look he gave his sister as he
said those words made her feel glad and proud of
her brother, though she could not explain why.

But this was not the end. When Joseph

came home that night his elder brother was on
the watch for him and called him to the shelter
of the barnyard. Now David was not so wise
in his dealings with the brother but four years
younger than himself as he might have been.
Perhaps it was because he felt the load of anxiety so heavy upon him as he remembered his
dying father's request : "David, you look after
Joseph. He's not so steady as you, you know.
Don't you let him get astray." And David had
tried to carry out his father's request ; but Joseph
bitterly resented being interfered with, and it
was not always easy to keep him in the straight
path.

"Joe," said David severely, as they came in the
shadow of the great barn, "don't you go to smoking around the house any more. She don't like it.
She'd be perfectly horrified if she saw you with
a pipe in your mouth, and if you dare so much
as bring out a pipe to light it around where she
is you'll be sorry, that's all. You had better give
it up. She'll be sure to smell it on your clothes,
and I know by the way she looked when she
brought mine to me that she hates it. She'll
never think anything of you if she finds out you
smoke."

David wanted to make his speech very intense,
and so he had gone on saying the most unwise
things that could be thought of. By the time

he had come to this climax his younger brother was exceedingly angry.

"She needn't trouble herself," he replied angrily. "The less she thinks of me the better I am pleased. If you think I am going to give up my rights in my own house, you are mistaken. I'll smoke as much as I please, and light my pipe in the kitchen if I choose. You've sat in that kitchen and smoked whole evenings yourself. You needn't be so holy all of a sudden. It is just as I expected. The minute you get a woman in the house everything has got to be turned upside down to suit her. If you're going in for that sort of thing I'll clear out. There's places enough I can smoke, if the house gets too hot for me." Here his brows were drawn in an ugly, threatening scowl. "And as for my part, I shall do all in my power to make it uncomfortable for her, for the sooner she gets out of this and back to her city home the better I shall like it."

With this parting hit he had betaken himself to the house where he had eaten his supper in silence and then departed to the village grocery. He meant to carry out his intention of smoking in the kitchen if he chose, but he preferred to think it over in the pleasant jovial atmosphere of the village grocery before he decided what line of action he would pursue. The supper had certainly been a good one and he had been hungry after the long day's work. Neither had he quite the face to carry out his threat that night; the new sister was so bright and smiling and ready to do anything or get anything for him. There came too an almost irresistible longing to give up and be a part of all this coziness which had come to the old farmhouse, only he was too stubborn to relent. At the grocery he was accosted by various welcomes born of curiosity. "Hello, Joe," said some of his intimate friends who helped him to smoke the evening away. "Got company at your house, ain't you?" and in the question many things were expressed: curiosity, a decided wish to know how the land lay, eagerness for a bit of gossip and willingness to join in laugh or ridicule of the new guest if that was the mind of the brother. But Joseph did not give them much satisfaction.

He did not quite understand himself and so was not ready with his usual caustic sarcasms at the expense of anybody for them to laugh at. He said "Yes!" short and sharp and the company of loafers, young and old, understood that the door to that conversation had been shut; nay, rather, slammed and decidedly locked in their faces for the evening. They set to work to study Joseph in their dull way to find out what mystery of like or dislike there might be behind his manner, but could not determine. He was silent for the most part, unless there was opportunity to turn a joke against one of them and then his words were sharper than usual, fairly making some of his victims writhe.

He had come as yet to no conclusion except that he would do as he pleased; but the days went by, two or three of them, and he still continued to work in that far-away wood lot. He smoked a good deal during his lonely morning and on his homeward road, taking a fierce delight in thus defying his brother's urgent advice, but as yet he had not attempted to bring out pipe or match in the presence of his sister. If it were necessary in order to defy David he would have done it, but unless provocation should arise he would hardly have the face to do it. Nevertheless, he came to the table with the strong odor of tobacco about him and Ruth understood that her younger brother smoked, and thought and pondered how she might win his love that perchance she might get him to give up this habit some day.

And she stood in the desolate room. It was large and square and bare. To one not used to beautifying empty places it would have seemed a hopeless task to make it other than it was, but Ruth enjoyed the thought of what a change she

would make. She puzzled her brows at first
over what should go into it. There were rooms
of various coloring in the city home. They
had all been thought out with the exquisite
taste that belongs to refinement and carried out
as only those who have a well-filled purse can
do. Perhaps just as beautiful effects might
have been reached by a much less expenditure
of money, but in this case there had been
money and everything had been good, enduring,
and beautiful. There was a room in sunset tints
of rose and mauve and cream, whose carpet of
soft coffee and cream color was scattered over
here and there with tiny rose-pink buds and
leaves. The furniture was curly maple and all
the dainty accompaniments were pink and
white. Ruth tried to imagine these things
occupying the empty desolateness before her,
but Joseph with his heavy muddy boots did not
seem to fit into the delicate colorings. It might
seem too fancy for him. She must choose something quieter. David said he was working in
the woods; then maybe the woodland colors
would seem more homelike to him. She did
not want to startle him with a vivid contrast
between his present room and the one she meant
to make; no, only to soften and sweeten and
brighten everything and make it a real home
and not a mere spot in which to stay a few

hours. She would choose the fern and moss carpet with all the wood tints blending and a hint of summer sunshine through the green. He would feel more at home with the woods about him. Then the windows should be draped in soft sheer white muslin, fastened back with green, and there should be ferns growing in a pretty green and brown jar. In that corner where the clothespress made a deep nook in the wall she would put the low bookcase that turned a corner and had the queer little niches for favorite books hidden behind the green curtains that had faint shadows of ferns in the pattern of their silk. She would be careful not to put too many fancy things on the bureau, and the pin-cushion should be severely plain and useful looking, and not the much be-ribboned and be-laced affair that belonged to the original room in the city.

She went on planning, seeing everything take its place in the room. She even chose, with great care, a few choice books and a picture or two which she thought would interest him. There must not be too many chairs, else he would feel the room too full if he was used to this bare-ness, and the main object in it all was to give him a spot in which he should delight. Would he, could he, appreciate it all? The tears almost dimmed her eyes at the thought that she might

fail, and she knelt beside the one wooden chair
the room contained and asked the Holy Spirit to
guide her in her selection and furnishing of this
room. What! ask the Holy Spirit of God to
stoop to the selection of a chair or picture, to
trouble himself with the texture of a carpet or
the pattern of a curtain? And yet these things
have more to do than we think with the influencing of human lives. People who live in a
house made beautiful by refinement and taste,
even though they may not have much money
with which to carry out their pleasure in such
taste, are nevertheless, more able to appreciate
beautiful words and high thoughts and holy living, than those who live where harmony is not
and where colors and shapes are forever at vari-
ance. There is an education and an uplifting in
beautiful things and in quiet, peaceful, restful surroundings, which does not count for naught, else
God would not have made the world so beautiful.

Ruth, as she rose from her knees, began to
think she would have to pray in every room in
that house before anything could ever be done
with it. And then she brushed away a tear that
would come from the longing for the dear ones
gone, and a weariness of fear and hope in the
life that was before her. Would she ever win
this brother for Christ? For neither he nor David
was a Christian, she was now certain. She felt

alone in a strange and alien land. David was growing dear to her. Perhaps this work she was undertaking was too great for her, an unskilled girl. She might do more harm than good. Perhaps she had been audacious to attempt it. Should she leave it all and go back where people knew and loved her, and she could work, and not feel afraid of defeat?

These thoughts would come to her almost hourly, when she had met some new obstacle in her task. But indeed, there was so much to be done during the days that she had little time to reflect, and it was only at night in the stillness of the ungarnished chamber that she could ask herself these questions. It was always her Bible then that brought her some answer. Now it would be, "Fear thou not for I am with thee; be not dismayed, for I am thy God: I will strengthen thee; yea, I will help thee; yea, I will uphold thee by the right hand of my righteousness." Again, she would turn to this verse, "Ye have not chosen me, but I have chosen you and ordained you, that ye should go and bring forth fruit, and that your fruit should remain; that whatsoever ye shall ask of the Father in my name, he may give it you."

"And when He has said that to me, why should I not ask him to help me select the right carpet for Joseph's room?" she asked herself.

CHAPTER VI

A T last there came an answer from Sally the cook. Yes, she would come gladly and would be there soon. Ruth's heart was set at rest about her housekeeping. When a few days later Sally arrived, strong, capable, willing, and warm-hearted, Ruth relaxed the high strain she had been under and began to think that things would really settle down into something like order pretty soon. The house had been thoroughly cleaned from garret to cellar by the woman David had secured for that purpose, and a good deal of the drudgery had also been taken from her, but she had felt she must do all the cooking herself, for the woman seemed not to know how to do things in the right way, nor, what was worse, to care to learn. She had a way of her own which she considered was the only way, and Ruth found, like many another, that it was easier to do things herself than to try to teach another.

So with Sally's coming came an opportunity to rest a little and look about this new home of hers. She knew it indoors pretty well now, but had hardly ventured out at all as yet. She began

to wonder how long it would be before she would
go to church and know the people and be known
in the village. Two Sundays had passed, but on
the first she was so thoroughly exhausted by her
unusual efforts at housecleaning, that she did not
feel able to go; and the second it had been so
exceedingly stormy that the subject had not been
mentioned. She did not know yet that it had
never occurred to either of her brothers as a
subject for conversation. They seldom went any
more themselves. She had yet to bear the disappointment of that discovery.

A day or two after the arrival of Sally, there
was some business to be done at the county seat,
not far away, connected with the farm and the
sale of some cattle. Heretofore David had been
the one who had taken these trips, which occurred once or twice a year. It usually kept
him three or four days, or sometimes a week.
This year when the matter was spoken about,
Joseph declared that he would go. He told his
brother quite gruffly that he would not stay there
with those two women, and besides, he thought
it was his turn to go; he could sell the sheep
quite as well as David. Now, David had been
not a little troubled about leaving his sister
alone just now, fearing lest Joseph might make
her uncomfortable by his silent, unpleasant
ways, so, while he was somewhat anxious about

the way in which his brother might perform the business part of the trip, anxious also as to where he might spend his leisure time during his absence and what companions he would choose, he nevertheless saw no other way but to let him go. Indeed, Joseph was so determined, that his brother felt sure he would go away somewhere if he did not consent. So it was settled that Joseph should take the trip.

Ruth upon hearing that he was to start in three days hastened to carry out one of her own plans for which she had been waiting her opportunity. After consultation with David she dispatched a letter to a firm in her old home, which very soon brought her a large package by express. Her orders had been explicit, and she knew well the man with whom she was dealing, so that the contents of the package was exceedingly satisfactory. Joseph started early the next morning, and about an hour afterward there arrived from the village, paperers and a painter.

David seemed as interested and happy over the plan as if it were his own. He hovered near while Ruth talked with the painter, and helped him to mix and match tints, and while the package was opened and the paperers went to work with scissors and paste on the smooth rolls of paper. Ruth had ideas, and was very particular. The village painter declared to one of the

paperhangers that he never did see such a queer
style in paintin' in his life, that he s'posed he'd
got to do the way that girl said, but it would
look mighty queer, accordin' to his notion.
Nevertheless he worked, and so did the others, as
the strange young woman with the sweet voice
and determined mouth ordered, and, behold, by
night there was a change wrought, the like of
which Summerton had never seen before.

It was in Joseph's room where the changes
began. That was the fun of it all, to surprise
Joseph when he should return. If only the furniture would come before his return. David and
Ruth went up to survey after the workmen had
finished and gone. To David it was a marvel.
How could paper and paint make so great a
change? The ceiling was a sunny cream tint,
plain and simple, shading at the edges into a
deeper yellow sunlight, bordered with maiden-
hair ferns, which by some mysterious skill of
designers fitted the ferns in the border of the
paper on the walls. The tint of the walls was
a soft, hazy green, like the suggestion of an
orchard bursting into leaf, and a deep dado, about
which Ruth had been explicit in her orders to
Browning & Co., was massed over with palms, so
lifelike as to almost deceive the eye. Ruth intended when it was all finished to have a real
palm standing in just the right place by this

dado, to increase the distance and make the room look as if it stretched away to endless groves of palm. But to David, whose imagination had not been cultivated, it was sufficiently wonderful as it was. The woodwork had a beautiful blending of the cream and sunny tints, which the reluctant painter had charily acknowledged "Wa'n't so bad, considerin', only nobody in earth ever see the like before. It was somethin' new, certainly, though fer my part I prefer good, solid, substantial color all through." The floor glistened in a border of hard-oil finish, sufficiently deep for the green mossy rug that was to lie over it.

Said David, as he stood spellbound : " This fits you, Ruth. You ought to have this room yourself and let Joe take another. You can't ever get anything as pretty as this for anybody else."

But Ruth laughed in her pleasure, and said she had plenty more plans for the other rooms, that his was to be even prettier than this. And then she wished again the furniture would hasten on its way, and she ran away to give some direction for breakfast.

And the furniture did come the very next morning. They told each other that it was really wonderful for it to arrive from such a long distance, considering how long freight was sometimes on its way. They forgot to take into ac-

count that the man who had sent it on was a
friend, and had spoken a word to another friend
in a freight office, which had hastened things a
little. They forgot also that the Holy Spirit
was guiding the whole affair, and that perhaps
God wanted Ruth's plan for Joseph to succeed
even more than she did. We have a habit of
thinking our nice little plans are all against
God's way, and of asking his help much as if
we expected he would naturally refuse or let
something hinder them. We forget that if we
are letting him guide our lives in everything, it
is very often his own gracious Spirit which gives
us the thought of these plans, and it is God
who has given us the intellect and skill to plan.
Even when he lets our plans fail apparently, it
may be that their very failure has been their success in his eyes.

David had tried to arrange for the freight to
be brought from a quiet little station two miles
up the road, from the village, that the whole
neighborhood might not know everything that
was going on, but it had proved impossible.
For some reason the cars could not be left on
the right side-track. So through the eager little
village the hauling wagons toiled back and forth,
back and forth, an incredible number of times,
emptying the great freight car. Mrs. Chatterton could hardly get her work done that day, so

afraid was she that she would lose count of the
wagon loads, but when the night came her record
was correct, she was sure. Not much satisfaction had she from her watch, however, for everything was so carefully packed by professional
packers that its shape and design were hopelessly
covered. A crowd of boys and older men, and
even a few curious women, had made errands
down toward the station, that they might see
these city things nearer, and some papers were
picked a little just to see the woodwork on a
bedstead or the upholstery on a chair. There
were great stories afloat, and much wonder. But
there was nothing to go on but hearsay and sur-
mise. David was always " close-mouthed," the
neighbors said, and they did not like to ask him
questions, and Joseph had gone to the fair to sell
sheep. If Joseph had been home they felt sure
they might have found out something. One old
man with a ragged, discolored beard, where a
river of tobacco juice ever and anon flowed down,
even said he shouldn't wonder if there was trouble
up there with that highflier of a city girl, or Joe
never would have gone; he never went before,
and this was reported as true by the postmaster
to three friends of his as he sorted over the mail
to go east.

But at the farmhouse there was eagerness and
pleasant hard work. David got his own neces-

sary work out of the way as soon as possible
that he might help. As the loads came in they
were deposited here and there, out of the way, in
rooms that were not to be used immediately, and
Ruth selected the things she wanted for Joseph's
room at once. David opened boxes and helped
to uncover the swathed furniture, and carried up
and arranged. He did not wish to trust the men
with this more than he could help. Some
things he found pretty heavy, however, and was
obliged to have help, so he kept John Haskins.

Perhaps that was a providence too, for John
Haskins was brother to Ellen Amelia, she who
had admired the hat of the city lady at the station the day she arrived, and Ellen Amelia's
heart was delighted, and her life was brightened
greatly by the wonderful account of velvet carpets and downy chairs, which her brother John
gave at the supper table. It may be that John's
vocabulary was hardly suited to convey exactly
correct impressions of all he had seen, and it
may be that where he could not remember he
drew somewhat on his imagination, but on the
whole the account was a good one and eagerly
listened to by the entire Haskins family, including the New York grandmother, who was pleased
to be able to explain the uses of some articles
described, though she was hardly familiar with
them in her own home. But city people have

opportunities, which gives them an advantage
sometimes, and it pleased her to be able to air
her little knowledge.   As for Ellen Amelia, her
" Fireside Companion " had just come, and she
had finished reading " The Disguised Duke ; or,
From Poorhouse to Palace," by the fading light,
when her mother called to her for the fifth time
that the table must be set that minute.   And
now her dreams were being carried on into real-
ities by John's account.   It did her good to
think that there were such beautiful things in
the world, and that they had come as near her as
to be in Summerton.   Thenceforward it should
be her great desire to get into that house and
see all those beautiful things.   Perchance there
might be something there which she could carry
out in cheaper form at home.   For Ellen Amelia
was not all dreams.   She was ambitious, and in
her way she was not unskillful, but the poor
child had few opportunities of any kind.

Meanwhile at the farmhouse things were growing interesting.   Out of the chaos of the morning was evolved a room so beautiful that David
as he went and came, bringing this and that at
his sister's direction, fairly held his breath.   The
old cord bed was replaced by one of white and
brass, and from this and that chest and bureau
and packing box, Ruth brought linen and
blankets and white drapery and made the bed,

all white and lovely. The corner bookcase was
there with a few books and a statuette and vase.
Ruth unpacked in a reckless way. She was
determined to have that room done before Joseph
came, no matter how much she broke all laws
laid down for movers and unpackers. She pulled
a box of books all to pieces to find one which
she knew was there and which she wanted
Joseph to read sometime. She would have a
certain picture for his room. She would have
driven a less interested helper than David dis-
tracted with her searches after certain little
things, which in the natural order of things
might have been waited for till they turned up.
Ruth wanted that room complete, and David
was none the less an eager boy at play than she
was a girl. There was a large, soft, luxurious
couch covered with green plush, which looked
like a mossy bank, and this accompanied by
its many soft silk pillows was established near
a window, and by its side a small flat-topped
desk on which was a reading lamp with white-
lined green shade. The palm was there, for
Ruth had had some of the choice plants from
the greenhouse sent on, and all the windows
were draped in soft white swiss.

David, while he put up the little brass rods for
the curtains and sawed and fixed a heavier pole
in front of the closet door to hang a heavy dark

green *portière* where the door had been missing
for many a year—so long that the reason for its
disappearance had been entirely forgotten—wondered in his heart if he would have been a different being if he had been surrounded by such
things sooner; wondered what Joseph would
think, whether he would be offended or pleased;
resolved to give him a lesson if he were not
pleased; and wondered again what poor, economical Aunt Nancy would have said to all this
luxury in the old farmhouse. He remembered
the dazzling plush album in the parlor and
smiled to think how tawdry and common it
seemed to him now, though in former days he
had looked upon it as an awesome treasure.

They stood back at last and looked at the
finished room. Everything was in its place,
even to the articles of toilet.

"It is beautiful, beautiful!" said David. It
stirred something in him as he gazed at it completed that he did not understand. It made him
long for higher, nobler things. It opened possibilities that he had not dreamed of. It made
life seem rich and sweet, and, did it speak to him
of heaven and his mother? Was not heaven
something like this? It came nearer to his
ideal than anything he had ever seen before.
Perhaps it might stir Joseph with the same
thought and make him want to be better, to

please that mother who was up there, somewhere, among palms and songs. He closed the
door softly as they went out as if they were
stepping from some sacred place. As he lay
awake that night in his own bare room he liked
to think of that lovely spot and know it was
near. It made heaven seem a fair reality and
even a possibility for him. "And now what
next?" he said the next morning with almost
as eager a look on his face as Ruth wore. They
had each been that morning for a silent peep at
Joseph's room, just to see it by the daylight,
finished, but neither guessed it of the other
Ruth had knelt a minute there and breathed a
prayer that the Spirit of Jesus might hover over
that room and influence the life of the occupant,
and David's wish for his brother, unuttered, had
been perhaps no less a prayer for him.

"What next?" said Ruth gayly. She was
growing happy. David and she were comrades,
and they had accomplished one purpose together;
now they were ready for more. It was beautiful work, albeit there was a sad side to it which
her brother had not thought of yet. She was
unpacking and putting about the things which
she had laid away in sadness and tears. Everything was full of associations of the dear ones
who were gone, for whom and by whom and
with whom they had been purchased. It was

hard to keep back the tears sometimes and yet she felt that this was the very work those dear ones would have liked the precious things to be put to, so she went bravely and even gladly on with her work. There might be tears for the quiet of her own room, but she must have only smiles here, for the old house had been gloomy long enough, and she was come that she might help to win home to heaven and Jesus the two brothers, so long strangers to her.

" We will work at the parlor I think, and in there," pointing to the large room adjoining the kitchen, which had been so long a dusty, unused bedroom. " If you don't mind I want to make a lovely dining room out of that, with a library in the front room beyond. The little room adjoining the parlor would make a nice retreat for my piano and a couch for you to lie on and listen to the music sometimes, if you are willing to cut the doorway a little wider so that it will take in the fretwork archway that used to be between the parlors at home. It is in the hall-way at home. This is the only place I can think of where it would fit prettily."

David assented eagerly. He would cut any number of doorways, if she wanted them, though it did puzzle him a little to know what fret-work was. However he held his peace, for he had confidence in the present architect.

"I want to keep all signs of work from the halls and kitchen and the places where Joseph usually goes, so that his room will be a complete surprise. Shall we leave our own rooms till the last? Then we can work at them at our leisure?"

David agreed and they went to work. The painters and paperers were kept close within certain rooms. The transformation in the old house went on, and so did the village tongues.

Mrs. Chatterton ran in to see old Mrs. Haskins and took her knitting. Ellen Amelia hovered about with her paper in her hand and her hair in curl papers. She was going to a church supper that night.

"They say," said Mrs. Chatterton, as she picked up some stitches she had dropped, "that there's great doings goin' on over to Benedicts'. I guess that girl's a piece. That aunt and uncle 't adopted her must have been awful rich. I guess you'd be surprised if you knew how many loads of furniture I counted at my window yesterday, and 't ain't all there yet, I heard."

"Well, I guess she's used to havin' things mighty stylish," responded the New York grandmother. "John, he says she has pictures painted right onto the walls, of trees and things, and she's fixed something in the room, he don't know what, that made the sunshine streak right in on anything she wanted it to shine on, even though 'twas a dark day. I s'pose it's one o' them new kind of Eddysun things you read about. They do most anything now."

"You don't say!" said Mrs. Chatterton, pausing to take in this great wonder and pack it away for further transportation.. "One o' them Edsun machines fer makin' sunshine! Well, I ain't sure but I'd like to have one. Well, she's got some funny idees about paint. My son's wife's brother did the paintin', and he tried fer all he was worth to 'dvise her 'bout things, but she would have her own way, an' a mighty funny one it was too. I wonder what Joseph'll say 'bout it all when he comes back. Strange he went off so sudden, ain't it? I wonder if he knows."

And that night Joseph came back.

CHAPTER VII

JOSEPH was cross. He had not enjoyed his trip so much as he had expected. Somehow everything with which he had come in contact had made him discontented, and as he came in sight of the farmhouse he scowled at it and hated it. Perhaps he added a little hate with the thought that it contained the sister who had come in to interrupt the quiet and have her own way. He did not want to go in but neither did he wish to go anywhere else, and besides, he must make report to his brother at once of the result of his trip.

David met him as he came around to the back door and gave him a hearty welcome. Indeed he could hardly keep the light of the secret upstairs from shining in his face. He had a fear lest his brother should read the story of the new room in his eyes before he went in. He got Joseph's report in a few words and then turned away. He wanted his brother to go upstairs at once, as he was sure he would; so he went to attend to some small unnecessary matter among the milk pans, that he might not seem to be watching him.

Joseph went upstairs. It was growing dusky
outside, and Ruth had taken advantage of the
moment that her brothers had been talking together, to slip upstairs and light the lamp which
shed its soft green glow over the new room and
even shimmered unusually under the crack of
the door. Joseph paused in wonder at it, and
looked up and down the hall to see if in his pre-
occupation he had made a mistake and was
standing in front of the wrong door. Then he
threw the door open and gazed, first in wonder,
then in dismay, and then in anger. What was
all this? the door of a palace open before him?
He made one step across the soft rug and looked
down and then brushed his eyes to see if some
cobweb were across them which hindered the
vision. It was beautiful, it was wonderful, but
it did not belong to him; and in his present
mood he desired to be alone in his own room.
Where then was that old retreat? Had it been
spirited away? Oh! with a flash he understood
it all now. During his absence my lady Ruth
had pitched upon his poor room as the only one
she wished to occupy, and had arranged it with
her own things to suit herself. Their house was
not good enough for her. She had taken his
room without his leave. She might at least have
told him before he left and given him some
notice of where his bed had been moved. He

was intruding upon her room it seemed, when
he had but thought to go to his own. Well, he
should not trouble them further to tell him
where his things were, and he shut the yellow
and cream door with a slam and thundered down
the stairs and out at the kitchen door, shutting
it also with a heavy jar. If they chose to thus
ignore his rights he would show them he could
get along without their help. What he meant
to do he was not sure yet, except that he would
not sleep in that house that night. And he
wished them thoroughly to understand that he
was angry beyond recall. He went with long
strides down the walk and out the gate to the
road, but he turned his face away from the village for once.

David, standing behind the shed door, watched
him with deep dismay. What had happened?
Was Joseph displeased at the change in his
room? Had they then failed after all? Notice
that he classed himself with his sister in the
enterprise. He had gone over completely to her
leadership. He turned and went in the house.
Ruth stood in the kitchen by the pleasant, attractive tea table, with a look of mingled fear
and dismay. Fortunately Sally was upstairs
putting on a clean apron preparatory to waiting
upon the table, for though they had not yet established the dining room, things were beginning

to be served in some sort of order, such as she
was used to in the city.

"What is the matter, David? What has happened? Doesn't he like it?"

There were tears in her eyes and David felt at
that moment as if he would like to go after his
younger brother and chastise him severely. He
had no business to be such a bear.

Ruth went on : "I had just lighted his lamp
and slipped over to my own room as he came up
the stairs and opened his door. He stood still a
minute and then he shut the door very hard and
went downstairs. I came right down after him,
but he isn't anywhere around."

David tried to comfort her as best he could.
He did not quite understand what was the
matter with Joseph, for he had been sure he
would be pleased. But yet, on general principles
Joseph was often displeased. He seemed to be
always out of harmony with himself and with
everything about him.

But Ruth was not easily consoled. She ate
little supper that night, though David did his
best to keep up a show of eating himself and to
talk cheerfully. Joseph did not come back.
Ruth went soon to her room and wept. By and
by she slipped upon her knees and tried to pray,
but it seemed as though she had set her heart so
upon the success of this her plan, and had been

so sure she was being guided by a higher Power
than her own, that she could not rally from the
shock of finding that it had failed. She never
doubted that it had failed, and that Joseph was
exceedingly angry that they had meddled with
his room, and had gone off, perhaps never to
return. She had little creeping thoughts of
doubt as to whether her prayers had not all been
in vain, though she put them aside and would
not give place to them. But it did seem strange
that she should have been living with such a
firm belief in that promise, " Whatsoever ye
shall ask in my name I will do it," and now had
come this failure. Then she remembered the
first part of that verse again, and it became to
her like a rebuke for doubting her Lord. " Ye
have not chosen me, but I have chosen you, and
ordained you, that ye should go and bring forth
fruit, and that your fruit should remain."
Surely she had forgotten. She had not taken
up this work for God, but he had led her to it,
had put her into it, and ordained that it should
be as he wanted it. Nothing could really fail
of what he had planned, and he had promised
that it should bring forth fruit, the fruit he
wanted, and that it should be fruit that should
remain ; not just the kind that blossomed and
formed and then fell off with the first wind or
storm or blight that came along. He was able

to make good come out of even this failure, disappointment though it was for her. She dried her eyes at last and went to bed, first looking out of her window in the vain hope that she might see something moving down the road to the gate. Oh, if her brother would but return, she would replace his old room just as it was, if he wanted it so; she would beg his pardon for having displeased him. Then she turned away from the window and tried to hum

> He holds the key of all unknown,
>   And I am glad ;
> If other hands should hold the key,
> Or if he trusted it to me,
>   I might be sad.

She sighed as she thought of what to-morrow might bring of certainty about Joseph, and then the hymn answered her :

> What if to-morrow's cares were here
>   Without its rest ?
> I'd rather he unlocked the day,
> And, as the hours swing open, say,
>   " My will is best."

Then she laid her soul down to rest saying :

> Enough ; this covers all my wants
>   And so I rest ;
> For what I cannot, he can see,
> And in his care I safe shall be,
>   Forever blest.

Out there, not many feet away from her
window, over in the great hay barn, lay the
young ingrate who had so torn the peace of mind
of his family. He had stolen softly back after
walking about two miles, for the exertion of his
day's trip made him feel suddenly weary, now
that the first heat of anger had worn away. He
would not go back into the house, neither would
he go to the village. He wanted to lie down
and rest. The sweet hay in the great barn was
easy of access by a little side door of which he
carried the key, and so, while his brother and
sister were worrying about him, he was sleeping
heavily from sheer weariness. When the morning broke he rubbed his eyes and wondered
where he was ; and then it all came back to him,
but his own stubbornness came as well. He
was hungry but he would not go in and eat. It
was early. He found some old clothes which
were almost unused, a coat and a pair of overalls
which he had kept in the front of the barn for
occasional service, and with these he arranged a
working suit ; and taking a wash and a drink at
the pump and his tools from their places, he went
breakfastless to the wood lot to work. It did his
angry soul good to have this revenge of feeling
that they had driven him from home and to his
work without food. Of course this could not go
on forever, but while he worked he could think

and decide what should be done. He felt pretty certain that he would go away somewhere, and that at once; but he wanted to think his plans over a little more before he put them into execution. And so he chopped angrily away at the trunk of an old tree and thought and grew hungrier and more stubborn with each hour, and the autumn sun rose high and clear, but it brought no cheer to him. It seemed to him now that all the universe was against him and was exulting in the fact that it was so.

Ruth did not know what to do with herself. To take up the work of finishing the house where they had left it the day before was impossible. Her heart was no longer in it. She would much rather have packed up all her things and sent them back to the storage house, replacing the old plain furniture now. All the plans seemed wrong. David at her earnest request had started out immediately after breakfast to see if he could find a trace of Joseph. Ruth was restless. She wished she were a man and familiar with her surroundings that she might go also. She tried to work at this and that, but her restless spirit would not be put down. She went from one window to another, and the tears were very near the surface. If she could but go out and search and in some way make amends for what she had done. She felt

certain that she would break down and cry outright if the morning went on much longer and
David did not come with word. She would go out
and see if she could not find him. Suddenly the
remembrance of her bicycle came to mind. It
had not yet been unpacked, and was at that moment in its crate in the front room, which was to
be a library, behind all sorts of boxes and chairs
and tables. Could she get it out and uncrate it?
She knew enough about the machine to put it
together, when once she had it out, she was certain. At least she would try, for it would give
her something to do with a purpose. This standing about and waiting was intolerable. Her
vivid imagination through the night had con-
jured up all sorts of things that Joseph might
have done, and she blamed her own sweet services for him for it all.

She went at once to the front room, armed
with hatchet and hammer and screw-driver. It
proved a work of time and strength to get the
crate out of the tangle of furniture, and when
at last this was accomplished she found the task
of uncrating no easy one. But at last the
machine was out and put together, and oiling it
hastily she ran upstairs to put on her bicycle
suit. With a few hasty directions to Sally, who
had learned not to be surprised at almost anything her young mistress undertook, she started

on her way, knowing no way in the whole place and having no fixed idea except to go somewhere and to find her brother Joseph. It was a lovely, clear, cool morning and the roads were perfect for a ride, but she took no thought of that. She rode steadily and rapidly, looking about with eyes which searched but saw not much of what she looked upon. Indeed, so hurried and earnest was she that she did not take her usual care to look about her and take her bearings that she might return without any trouble. She only thought about her errand. Down the road toward the village she started and rode as far as the Chatterton house, but then she reflected that David had probably gone on to the village to search and she would better go elsewhere. A long stretch of smooth, much-traveled road led off to the right just beyond the Chatterton place, so without much thought she turned upon it and flew on.

"For the land sake!" ejaculate Mrs. Chatterton, glancing up from her darning at the front sitting-room window, and dropping her lapful of stockings she hastened to the kitchen windows which looked on the side road to get a further view. Eliza Barnes, who was helping Mrs. Chatterton for a few days while she got the apple butter and mince-meat for the winter out of the way, dropped her dishcloth and went to

the other window to see what it was that so
interested Mrs. Chatterton.

"My land!" said she, her mouth open, her
hands on her hips. "A girl on a bicycle! Don't
she go it though? Who can she be?" Eliza
was not favored by living on the direct road
to the village and therefore did not know who
the young woman was.

"I ain't sure, but I rather suspect it's that new
Benedic' girl. I told 'em I thought they'd find
she was a highflier. The idea! It isn't considered decent; but I s'pose them city folks do
anything they please. She hasn't got no kind
of a ma now to tend to her and you can't expect two boys to hold her in; besides, I heard
Joseph was away from home and I see David a
driving like mad by here an hour and more ago.
She's just waited till they got off, that's what
she's done. Somebody ought to tell David;
such disgraceful goin's on! What would their
poor father and mother say if they could rise up
in their graves and know it all? It's a mercy
they can't, I declare."

"Wal! she don't look any diffrunt from other
folks as I see," said Eliza with admiring eyes as
she watched the lithe, graceful figure disappear
up the road. "I've heard say they dress just
awful for riding, but her dress looks all nice and
proper and she sets up as straight as a needle.

I mus' say I think it would be fun," and Eliza
went back to the greasy kettle she was washing
with a sigh of envy. Eliza was always on the
lookout for fun, and precious little of it ever
came in her way.

"H'm!" ejaculated Mrs. Chatterton severely,
looking over her glasses at the preserving kettle
on the stove. "It's lucky for you you've got a
mother then. Look out that apple butter don't
burn. It seems to me you've got a pretty much
of a fire on," and she shut the door and went
back to her darning.

Meanwhile, all unconscious of the impression
her first appearance was making upon the vil-
lagers, Ruth rode on. She was almost in fever-
ish haste to get somewhere and get home again.
She seemed to feel that she was riding straight
to Joseph, and who shall say she was not being
guided? On and on she went and coming to a
turn to the right and still another she whirled
around them hardly knowing that she did so.
She passed a handsome farmhouse after this
second turn, where some men were working near
the fence, and one called out to her something
she could not hear. But the tone had been unmistakable and she felt sure that the words were
such as she would not wish to hear. She was
frightened; her cheeks burned; and her heart
beat so fast she could scarcely breathe. For the

first time since she started it occurred to her
that perhaps it was not safe to ride alone in the
country, that bicycles might not be so common
here as at her former home. She had been so
accustomed to riding when and where she
pleased that it had not even occurred to her to
ask David whether girls rode here or not, and if
it had, the question would have had very little
weight with her, her wheel had become so much
a part of her by constant use. Now to her confusion, her cheeks flamed crimson. Her nerves
were in a quiver before she started and her hard,
strained ride with the one purpose in view had
not served to calm them. She did not wish to
hasten her speed or to take notice of the presence of the men in the least, but they, thinking
perhaps to have a little fun, added to her
nervousness by sending with a low-spoken word
a great fierce-looking dog after her. He came
with long, low bounds like some wild animal
after its prey and burst upon her with a por-
tentous growl farther down the road from behind a hedge. She had to give a quick turn
here to avoid running into him and her frightened heart beat wildly. She was terribly afraid
of dogs.

She could scarcely manage her wheel. It
was just at the brow of a hill and she put on
all speed and fairly shot down that hill, the

sound of the dog's deep growl seeming to follow
her even after that had become impossible by
the distance between them. But now she kept
on faster and faster, feeling certain that she
was pursued. She heard the sound of the ringing of an axe in a wood she had to pass, but that
only added to her fear. Here was a new danger
to be encountered. She would put on all speed
possible and drive past, and it might be the user
of the axe would not perceive her till she was
beyond reach ; but just as she came to the center
of the very space whence had come the sound
of the axe something happened. What it was
she never quite knew. A great boulder was in
the road. The wheel struck it. The handle
bars which she herself had fastened on, turned
in her hand at this sudden wrench, and the
saddle which she had supposed securely fastened,
turned under her. In vain she threw all her
weight upon the pedals. It was too late. She
had attained a fearful speed. She suddenly felt
herself helpless. She seemed blind with fright
and could give but a little gasping cry for help,
as she was flung violently in the dust of the
road.

It was very strange. She had never fallen before in all her riding, except a little tumble or
two when she was learning. And now to fall in
disgrace before some country loafers who only

wanted to laugh and jeer at her at best—to fall
when there was real peril, when she was far
from home and—oh, that dog! Her mind seemed
in a whirl. Then she lay there as if stunned in
the dust of the road, her eyes shut. She could
faintly hear footsteps crackling over dried twigs
and some one jumping the fence by the road. She
knew that he was coming and perhaps that terrible dog was almost upon her. Perhaps his hot
breath would burn her already hot cheek, and
that awful growl would freeze her very blood
she was sure, if she should hear it in her ear.
She could not help herself now. She would not
open her eyes, let come what might. She remembered that God was guiding her and she
sent up a cry to him for help in her dire need.
Then she felt a touch, a gentle, almost reverent
touch, upon her forehead. She opened her eyes
and looked up. It was her brother Joseph.

Now Joseph had worked hard that morning.
He had perhaps accomplished more in a given
time than he had ever done in the whole of his
life before. It is marvelous how well and rapidly one can work when he feels that he is act-
ing the part of a martyr. He was considering
himself very ill-used indeed. Self-pity, when it is
left to work, getteth to itself thousands more
like unto itself, and Joseph had been having a
real nice gloomy time all alone out there in the

wood lot.   He was cutting a tree quite near to
the road.   Not a soul had passed since his work
began, to interrupt his meditations.   He was
growing very hungry—no supper and no breakfast.   He straightened up and felt his back.   It
was stiff and ached.   Something must be done,
for he did not feel that he was willing to longer
undergo this state of discomfort.   He was certainly not called upon to do so under the circumstances.   He would go away at once, somewhere
—anywhere.   Where?   He paused and leaned
on his axe, looking up the road.

Then had come that flying vision: wheels, a
dark blue dress, soft hair, the waving of a great
dog's yellow tail as he wheeled and gave up pur-
suit, and then the almost immediate catastrophe
right before him.   He did not know who or
scarcely what it was, but he went to the rescue.

CHAPTER VIII

"OH, Joseph!" said Ruth, her pale face lighting up. "I have found you. You'll forgive me, won't you? It was all my fault; David only helped. You won't be angry any more. I really thought it would please you to have your room fixed in that way. We wanted to surprise you; that was why we didn't ask you first; but I see now it was very wrong of us, for of course you were attached to the old room as it was. Say you'll forgive me, do! I wanted so to have you love me!" She was lying in the dry grass at the side of the road, whither her brother had swiftly and tenderly borne her. She was dimly conscious of intense agony in her ankle, but she could think of nothing until she had Joseph's full forgiveness.

There were real tears in her eyes now. Joseph stood staring down at her in amazement, hardly able to take in the meaning of her words. That his sister should suddenly drop down before the wood lot in this unexpected manner was astonishing enough, but that after such a ride and such a fall she should be able to speak was incredible. Her tears melted him at once. He was not used to women's tears. His heart went out to her. Her peril had been so great that it overshadowed everything else, and he did not yet know how badly she was hurt. She made no attempt to rise, but only pleaded with him about that room.

"Bother the room!" he said gruffly, trying vainly to get the huskiness out of his voice. "There ain't anything to forgive. You may have all the rooms in the house, if you want them, and welcome. Are you hurt?" and he stooped anxiously to lift her again.

But she looked eagerly up at him.

"Have all the rooms! What do you mean, Joseph? Was that what you thought? That I had taken your room for myself without asking you? Was that it? Tell me! Oh, you poor boy! I don't wonder you were angry. But Joseph, listen. I never dreamed of such a thing. We were fixing the room up for you. Did you think I would want to take your room away? But I don't blame you; you and I are not acquainted yet. I only wanted to make it just as pretty and pleasant as I could for you, and I had the things and didn't know what else to do with them, and David said they might as well come on and be used; but I'll take them all out and fix it back the way it was if you prefer it that way. It won't take long, and I'm so sorry."

Her nerves had been completely shaken by her excitement and fall. Indeed the poor child had been working beyond her strength for two weeks, in her eagerness to get things done just right, and there had been no one to restrain her. As she talked she could not keep the tears from rolling down her cheeks, she who never cried before people. She remembered it afterward, and rebuked herself for her weakness.

Joseph straightened up and looked at her.

" You fixed that room for me?" he said, such utter amazement in his voice that his sister almost laughed afterward in joy to think of it. She had the pleasure of her surprise after all in thinking of the expression on his face then.

" You never fixed that all up for me," he said stupidly, looking down at her as if she must be a little out of her head. "Why I'm just a—just a—— Nobody ever does things for me."

" Yes, they do, Joseph! David and I do," she laughed, her tears shining like a mist before the sun, and she caught one of her brother's great rough, red hands and kissed it.

He felt a queer kind of a sensation in his own eyes then, and to cover it he stooped once more and said :

"We must get you home. Where are you hurt?" She took his help then and tried to rise, but now the terrific pain in her ankle as-

serted itself, and she turned quite white and
sank back again. "Where—what is it?" questioned Joseph anxiously.

"Oh, it's my ankle, and I suppose it must be
a sprain. I have always thought it was so silly
for people to get their ankles sprained, and now
I've done it. Oh, it hurts dreadfully, and we're
a long way from home, aren't we?"

"Well, not so far but what I could carry you,
I guess, only I'm afraid it 'll be hard on you ; and
what'll we do with this concern?" pointing to
the down-fallen bicycle. "It ain't very safe to
leave it here if you ever care to see it again. I
guess I'd better leave you long enough to borrow
a wagon."

"Oh, don't !" said Ruth, rising again with sudden energy, which sent the pain shooting through
her ankle. "I'm afraid that awful dog would
come again," and she shuddered at the thought.
"If you think you could screw those handle bars
on tight, perhaps I could get on and manage
with your help to ride it home. I suppose it
was very reckless of me to start out when I had
screwed things up myself. I never put it together before."

Joseph stooped and raised the fallen machine.
It was almost as mysterious a thing to have
to do with as a young woman. He had never
seen one save at a distance before. There was

but one in the village, and that was owned by
a youth who spent his time away from home, at
college, almost entirely. He was not a young
man of Joseph's immediate social circle either.

With Ruth's directions he was able to make
all the repairs necessary, and finally, with much
care and not a little pain, Ruth was placed on
the saddle, her lame foot held in as comfortable
a position as possible, while with her brother's
help and her one well foot she was able slowly
to propel the machine. It was a slow and painful ride. They took down the bars of the wood-
lot fence, and went by a little, winding, unused
road, which led among the trees, but straight
across lots to their home. Ruth was at least
shielded from the eyes of the village gossips, and
thus her downfall and untriumphal return were
not proclaimed from the village housetops. Mrs.
Chatterton missed a moral for her sermon on
bicycles, and Eliza Barnes watched in vain for
the spinning figure down the road.

David was just driving into the gateway as
they reached the barnyard entrance, and he
could scarcely believe his eyes to see the prodigal brother steering the despised sister on a machine, which to David's eyes was a very strange
sight indeed.

"You turn right around and go for the doctor," called Joseph peremptorily, as soon as he

was within hailing distance. "She's had a fall and hurt her ankle. No; I'll carry her up," as David jumped from the wagon in dismay and ran to help. "I've brought her this far and I guess I can do the rest. You go quick."

The command was given so decidedly that David turned meekly and obeyed. He hurried the horse as much as possible, but he turned his head once for the astonishing sight of Joseph with Ruth gathered tenderly in his arms striding across the dooryard. Ruth waved her hand to him and tried to smile as she called, " It's all right, he just didn't understand "; but the pain was so bad she had to close her eyes and keep still.

A mother could not have been more tender than those two brothers were during the days that followed. The doctor came and fixed up the poor swollen ankle, encouraging them by saying it might not be so bad as it looked. Then they hovered near her and could not do enough for her, and even neglected their work to stay with her. It would seem as if they were just awakened to the fact that there was something else than work in the world worth living for; for love, the love of a brother for a sister, was growing in their hearts that had been empty so long.

Early that evening Joseph went to the vil-

lage on an errand. The doctor had called again
and recommended some lotion for bathing the
hurt ankle, and Joseph offered to go for it. Ever
since morning he had seemed to take David's
place in ordering about things and in doing all
he could to make his sister comfortable. He had
a feeling as if he had been the cause of her suffering and he must take the responsibility of caring for her. David was quite astonished at him,
and sat down now beside Ruth's couch to talk
things over with her. The large, easy, leather-
covered library sofa had been hastily unpacked
by David and pushed into the kitchen for the
benefit of the invalid, because she utterly refused to be sent off upstairs away from everything. She was quite happy in spite of her
hurt. She was rather glad than not that she had
fallen, now that there was such a change in
Joseph. It was worth a ride and a fall any day
to gain a brother like her younger one, for when
Joseph's heart was once touched there was a
great well of good there, and he bestowed freely
where he chose to do so.

While they talked and arranged some little
matters, going on with their plans where they
had been left the day before, Joseph went with
long, free steps to the village. It was a very
different walk from the one he had taken the
night before. Indeed it never occurred to him

to mark the contrast between himself to-night and twenty-four hours before. His mind was busy over his sister, who, as far as he was concerned, might have just come into his range of vision. Heretofore she had been an imaginary being whom he hated, because he fancied she was in his way and perhaps disliked him. There in the dark on this lonely country road he remembered her words, looks, tones, and her tears. These were things he would not have dared even think about in the daylight or in the presence of others, for he was very much afraid of any sentiment. Indeed the least tendency in that direction was something so new to him that he scarcely believed in it at all. He decided that he had been a fool the night before and metaphorically kicked himself all the way to town for his bearishness and boorishness about that room. It suddenly occurred to him that though he had been about the house nearly all day, he had not yet revisited his room, nor seen it enough to tell what it was like. He tried to recall what he had seen at his first glimpse, but the veil of anger was between and he could tell nothing, except that there had been a green glow and a look like a glimpse of paradise to it. An eager desire to see it at once took possession of him and he hastened his steps. His errand at the drug store completed, he went to

the post office to see if there was any mail. He
and David had not been used to getting letters
nor going often to the office, but since their
sister had arrived there had been something for
the Benedicts almost every mail. They were
growing accustomed to going to the post office
every day as a matter of course.

The grocery, in the front of which the post
office was located, was ill lighted by smoky kerosene lamps. At the back end, beyond the counter
and a little hidden by the dusty post boxes and
the little stamp and letter window, there was a
sprawling box stove and around it at all seasons
of the year, no matter whether there was a fire
or not, was usually gathered at this hour of the
evening a number of loafers, young and old,
spitting, smoking, and talking, with loud guffaws
of laughter interspersed. They were all there to-
night. Joseph recognized one or two voices,
and he drew his brows in a heavy frown. Ruth
had told him of the men who had called to her
as she rode and frightened her so terribly. He
knew at once who they were and that two of
them were at that moment at the back of the
store.

They were talking loudly and laughing as
usual. One of these two seemed to be telling
a story of something he had seen that day.
Joseph, as he waited for the tardy postmaster,

who was interested in the story and came unwillingly with his head turned to hear the rest, could not help but catch some of the sentences. There was something being said about a bicycle and a girl—and—could he believe his senses? He straightened up like a spirited horse that has been angered. Amid the loud laughter that followed the close of the story, there came like a sudden thunderclap a swift, stinging, stunning blow across the grinning mouth of the teller, which caused him to suddenly fall backward into one of the store chairs and made his head ring and his eyes see many constellations. There was startled, utter silence in the room. Joseph, in part by his strange moods, his alternate deep silence and witty, sometimes cutting, sarcasms, and in part by his unusual physical strength, had gained a supremacy over the rest which made them almost afraid now as he stood tall and strong and straight before them, with folded arms and lowering brows looking down at the dazed man before him, waiting until he should come to his senses sufficiently to hear what he had to say. Joseph was conspicuously without his pipe that night. The fact gave him an added dignity.

The young man in the chair was Bill Brower. His brother Ed stood on the other side of the stove. They were two of those who had made remarks to Ruth as she rode by their place that morning. The Browers were rich farmers, and took a good many airs on themselves, though it was whispered about that the father was very " near." The three young men, sons, were rapidly going to the bad. Their mother, poor soul, had never had much control over them, and their father did not care so long as they worked and did not spend too much of his money. He was not over-good himself.

Joseph had never liked these two young men. His sarcasms had oftenest been directed against them, and well he knew they dreaded his tongue ; for they were dull in a way, and not able to make quick reply or get the better of him before others. They hated ridicule as only coarse, weak natures can. Now Joseph stood above Bill Brower and looked down in scorn as the other tried to recover from his blow and show some fight. Joseph placed a firm hand on his shoulder, with menace in his face, and said :

" No, Bill ; don't you dare to stir or answer me back. I have just one thing to say to you. I want you to understand that the young woman you were talking about just now is my sister and that you will be sorry if you ever mention her name in my presence again. You are not fit to be in the same world with such as she. Remember, I mean what I say, and you will be

sorry if I hear of you ever mentioning her again
in any but a respectful manner. And you'd better
look out how you even do that!"

Then Joseph walked away and there was
silence in Summerton grocery till he had well
turned the corner and was out on the pike toward home. Bill Brower managed to pull his
scattered senses together after a few minutes and
talked a little in a threatening way, saying he
would "have it back on Benedic'," but the others only laughed at him. They were easily
turned this way or that and had ever despised
Bill Brower and held Joe Benedict high in their
estimation. It did them good to see a blow well
deserved and well planted.

The records of the remainder of that evening
in the grocery would not be interesting. The
postmaster and storekeeper yawned and shut up
store earlier than usual by a half-hour, for his
usual entertainers and story-tellers had dropped
out one by one. Nevertheless, the story of what
had happened hastened on fleet wings about the
village, a scrap of it here and a scrap of it there,
pieced together by the village gossips who attend
to such affairs, till it got all mixed up and
meant an entirely different thing from the truth.

Meanwhile Ruth was being borne by four
strong arms upstairs, and the brothers and sister
were taking together a complete survey of Jo-

seph's new room. They established Ruth on
the green sofa, while David took his younger
brother about showing him this and that feature
of the new room as though he had been a fancy
house furnisher and upholsterer from the city.
Joseph admired in words stronger than his brother
had ever heard him use before in praising anything. He told Ruth it was too good for him
and she must have it all and let him take some
other room, that it just fitted her; but she, with
happy face, told him all her plans for the house,
and together they arranged to complete the work
begun. Joseph was intensely interested. He
had never been in a room like this before. He
had not had even David's experience of the time
when he went to the city to see his aunt and
take that message before their father died. His
highest ideal of a room was the stiff haircloth
and ingrain of the Summerton parlors to which
he had access.

Ruth selected one of Frank Stockton's incom-
parable stories and read to her brothers a little
while to finish the evening, and they both declared they never had had such a good time in
their lives. They laughed over the book and
made interested comments, which showed they
were no fools, and Ruth enjoyed the reading as
much as they. Then as it grew late they
planned to go at the new work in the morning,

while Ruth should lie on her sofa and direct and read to them.

Ruth, as she closed her eyes to sleep that night, thanked God and took courage. A sprained ankle was not so bad if it was the price of another brother.

CHAPTER IX

THE Reverend Robert Clifton, pastor of a month's standing to the principal church of Summerton, was in consultation with his deacons. He had not really been at work for more than a few days, for though he had preached Sundays in his new charge he had been away during the week most of the time making arrangements to move his mother and young sister to the parsonage from their old home in a neighboring city. Now, at last, the parsonage was habitable and the mother and sister would arrive in a few days. He was anxious to get to work. It was his first charge and he meant to do his best in every way. He must be a good pastor as well as preacher.

They were meeting in the gloomy little room back of the church known formerly as the "lecture room," now in process of being re-christened by the title of "ladies' parlor," at the suggestion of Mrs. Brummel. The Brummels were rich and had their own way. Their only son owned the only bicycle in town until Ruth's came, and was off getting a college education. Mrs. Brummel had given a rocking-chair with one spring broken, a marble-topped table for which she had no use, and a set of "Lives of the Martyrs" in an ancient hanging bookcase, which was apt to collapse at some critical moment if the books were not balanced just so; these to carry out the illusion necessary to a parlor. She also cut up her old piano spread that the moths had eaten, and had her daughter Georgiana embroider crewel sunflowers in Kensington stitch in the corners, to spread over the reading desk when the ladies met to sew.

The minister sat in the broken rocking-chair. It had been given to him out of deference to his office. As a matter of fact not one of the deacons enjoyed the broken spring. The minister was uncomfortable, but he took it as a part of the ills of life. He was trying to get at the boundary of his parish and find out "who was who." He had early discovered that the Brummels, and Browers, and one or two other families, were people to whom the deacons thought it well to pay a great deal of attention, and that the Barneses did not matter so much. It gave him a desolate feeling to find so mercenary a spirit among the chief men of his church. What if the Brummels were worth more money than the Barneses, were not their souls of just as much value in the sight of the Master?

"Now then, there are one or two other places I want to know about, Brother Chatterton. There is a house just a little back from the road, about a mile I should say beyond your house, up toward the Barnes place. Who lives there? Do they belong to us or to the other church? I can't find out about them."

"Why, that mus' be Benedic's," responded Deacon Chatterton, without much interest in his voice. "You needn't trouble about them. Oh, they go to our church when they go anywhere, but they haven't been for a long spell back now, not much since the old aunt died. They're mostly dead, all 'twas any 'count, anyway. There's only the two boys left now and they ain't like other young men. One of 'em's gone to the dogs, I guess, pretty much, and the other might as well be for all the account he'll ever be to the church. Oh yes, they've got a good farm, and I guess they're doin' pretty well at it, but they never go anywhere and they live there alone. You can't do nothin' with 'em. They used to come to Sunday-school awhile back, but they grew out o' that."

"They live entirely alone? Does no one keep house for them?" The minister was curious about them. For some reason they interested him. He had a passion for going after lost sheep and bringing them back. Part of his seminary training had been work among young men in the slums of a city. He would like to try for these two, but he must know more about them before he went.

"Oh well, no, they ain't egzackly alone now," spoke up Deacon Haskins. "There's a sister o' theirs come on from way off somewhere. I don' know how long she 'ntends to stay, but I should say she's set her stakes pretty deep, for she brought a whole raft of things along with her. She's livin' with them and she has a garl to do her work, so they ain't alone now."

"They might a good deal better be, in my opinion," put in Deacon Chatterton with emphasis. "Ef there was any ruin left to 'em, they'll go to it now. From what I hear she's a regular piece. She's one o' those new bicycle girls." He spoke the words in a low convicting tone, much as you would speak of a ballet-dancer in some low theatre, and they conveyed to the new minister a meaning deeper and darker than even the good-hearted, narrow-minded deacon had any conception.

"Yes," said Deacon Hobbs, shaking his head regretfully and sighing a funereal sigh; "I'm afraid she's pretty bad. There's a story come straight from headquarters about her and those Brower boys, and we all know what they are. I'm sorry for the sake of the young women of

this locality—yes, and the young men too—
that she's come among us." And he sighed
again.

"Now, brethren, don't be too hasty. We don't
know her as yet. Let us wait till we see more
of her."

It was Deacon Meakins, kind, sweet-spirited,
always ready with a good word for somebody,
everybody, who spoke. He was a thorn in the
flesh to this body of good men, for they loved a
little gentle gossip as well as did their sisters,
and he was forever putting in with some meek
reminder of mercy, or a word in favor of the one
who was being discussed. They rose and began
to button their coats, for the evening was chilly.
It was time to depart if Deacon Meakins had
begun.

But Deacon Chatterton felt that he was
called upon to have the last word, in this case
especially.

"Brother Meakins," he said severely, "isn't it
enough that she has been an inhabitant of this
town for now over two months, and not once
has she made her appearance inside a church?
I have it on good authority from two or three
members of the other church that she has not
been there."

"Yes," said Deacon Hobbs ; "it is a pity, a
great pity. Her folks were very good, respecta-

ble people. Her father was once a deacon in this church."

"Well, brethren," said Deacon Meakins apologetically, "you know she has been confined to the house by a sprained ankle. Dr. Stormer seems to have a very good opinion of her, so far as I have heard him say. Perhaps she might be helped in some way, you know, brethren."

"Yes, and how did she get her ankle sprained, Brother Meakins?" said Deacon Chatterton with a severity that he evidently expected to be convincing.

"Dr. Stormer never says much about his patients. It is not to be expected," said Deacon Hobbs, and then he turned the lights out and they all went out into the crisp autumn evening.

The minister walked along in the starlight silently. He was puzzled and troubled. Here was this case of the Benedicts in whom he had been so interested. It was complicated sadly by this wild, gay sister. From what these men said, she was evidently one whose influence was to be dreaded, to say the least. It would not do for him to allow his name to be mixed up with hers. He must move very cautiously. It was a case where a woman would be a great help. His mother was a shy, quiet woman, who had always been sheltered, and who had loved to stay at home with her children. She could not help in a case like this. And his sister! He sighed. She was bright and gay and pretty, but she had no wish to help. She was not even a Christian; she must be sheltered from evil influences herself. She must yet be won to Christ, and he had no earthly help apparently. If he only had a wife, one who would love the work as he did, and would know just how to go to work for such a girl as the Benedict sister, one like—here he stopped and would not go on, even in his thoughts. She was far away, and far above him. But how strange that this name should be Benedict! Well, life was a queer puzzle, anyway. It was no use to try to think it out. He fitted his night key to the parsonage door and tried to shut out his troubled thoughts as he shut himself in. He sat down in his study chair and drew his hand wearily across his eyes. He had started out that evening eager and interested, his spirit glad, rested, ready for work, but somehow he had lost his enthusiasm already. What was the matter? He reached his hand to his study table for the Bible and it opened of itself to the first chapter of Joshua, perhaps because that was a favorite place of his. He wanted help and here it was.

"Be strong and of a good courage: for unto this people thou shalt divide for an inheritance the land, which I sware unto their fathers to give them. . . Be not afraid, neither be thou dismayed : for the Lord thy God is with thee whithersoever thou goest."

Surely he was not presuming to take these words to himself, for if he believed anything in life he believed firmly that the Lord had called him to the ministry as much as he ever called Joshua to take Moses' place at the head of the children of Israel. If this were not so he was committing sacrilege to try to preach at all. The words comforted him. The Lord who was leading would provide a way and would keep his promise. He was with him, even if he had no earthly helper. God would take the place of mother and sister and wife if need be. God would care for it all. There came to him the words of a hymn or a poem, he could not tell which, that he had heard recited in a young people's prayer meeting by a sweet girlish voice. He had met the girl once or twice and talked with her for a few moments, and he knew that her life must fit such words, and so they had meant more to him than they would have done otherwise, and when he had chanced to find those words in print he had committed them to memory.

He was not in love with the girl. He had never given time to thinking of such things, nor indeed to knowing girls very much. She was very young, and he had met her only once or twice and talked but very little with her. That was four years ago, before he was through the seminary. He could not tell if she even knew his name. But she had seemed like an ideally happy Christian, and had left a pleasant fragrance in his memory which he had used occasionally for a womanly ideal when it had been necessary for his thoughts to have one to fill in with somewhere. But he was not at all sentimental, nor did he often think of her. The words of the verse were these :

> Bear not a single care ;
>   One is too much for thee.
> Mine is the work, and mine alone ;
>   Thy work—to rest in me.

It was strange—and yet nothing is ever strange that happens to God's people, for he knows the whys and wherefores—that he was reminded of her again the very next morning as he stood at the front window of the parsonage looking idly out at the village street that stretched away into blue misty mountains whose feet were already wreathed with the last autumnal tints. He was wondering whether he should venture to call at the Benedict farm that day or wait until his mother came and try to persuade her to go with him. He had just made up his mind that he would pray about the matter a little while and see if any light came, and perhaps he would be guided to go there that afternoon or the next day. He was sure he would be shown the way.

A lady was walking slowly along the street, stopping now and then to gather a lovely crimson leaf from the flagging. She walked as if she was waiting for some one and was not in a hurry. Now and then she turned her head in the direction of the stores as if looking for something. She glanced up curiously at the houses as if they were new to her; not with a steady stare like a person who had never been there before, but with a well-bred interested glance, that had such a touch of pleasant admiration for all she saw. The minister hardly knew that he was watching her till as she came nearer she turned her face and looked full up at the upper windows of the parsonage. In truth she was admiring the dainty ruffled curtains which the minister's mother had selected with great care, and thinking to herself, " Some little woman with good taste lives there, I'm sure, and perhaps she and I will be great friends," and then she turned her face away and looked for more leaves and walked slowly on and did not see the minister at all.

And Robert Clifton looked at her full face and thought how like it was to that other face he had remembered, in purity of outline and with clear earnest eyes. He made up his mind with the moment's glance he had that the woman looked as *she* would look when she grew up. She had been a girl with floating hair four years ago, and dresses not quite touching the ground in full-grown fashion. By and by she would be a woman, and then she would look like this woman and he would like to meet her then. Would she keep her childlike trust in Jesus, he wondered? And then he began pondering where she might be and what her life was now, and half forgot to wonder who the passer-by had been, so brief had been his sight of her. He noticed in a moment that a surrey went by with a young man driving, and that farther up the road it stopped and picked up the lady and that they drove on. "Some one from West Winterton," he murmured to himself and turned to go to his almost completed sermon. A sermon was still an arduous and serious undertaking with him. He wanted this one to reach hearts. Without knowing it he had written it with the Benedict boys in mind. He did not know them, but he had imagined what they were. He did not expect to have them present, and yet his sermon was an earnest plea for Jesus Christ to just such young men as he imagined they were. But there were young men who were like that, and they would be present in some numbers to hear the new minister preach, and the sermon was not written in vain, in spite of the fact that it did not fit the real Benedict brothers.

Before he took up his pen he settled one matter. He would go and call on those two young men before the week was out. He would do it for the sake of that sweet girl face, a vision of which he had just beheld. She had once said to him that she thought God gave us our fancies and preferences for some real reason, and that if we could disconnect them thoroughly from our own way, we would usually find that they led to some work for him when we were on the lookout for it. She had not expressed it in just that way, but more simply and girlishly. It had impressed him at the time as being a very unusual thing for one who was not more than a little girl to say, but he had heard that her mother was an unusual woman. That might explain it. At any rate he made up his mind to try and follow out this fancy.

Here the minister resolutely locked the door of those thoughts and dipped his pen in the ink.

CHAPTER X

THROUGH many perplexities and prayers Robert Clifton had arrived at a decision with regard to his proposed visit to the Benedict farm, viz., that before another Sunday passed it should be accomplished; and so the first bright afternoon he took his way down the long, dusty country road lit up along its edges with faded autumn tints and a few late, brave, scarlet leaves. He was going in fear and trembling, yet he hoped much from this visit. He had planned it with a view to reaching the entire household if possible, and yet not at a time when there might be danger of his meeting that bugbear of a sister alone. It would be best not to do anything which might make talk in a country village. He had wisely learned that fact early in his career. The two young men he was reasonably sure to find at or near the house at this time of the day. He had been utterly unable to decide what he should say to them when he reached there. He had planned conversation after conversation, but the unknown quantity represented by what the Benedict brothers would probably respond to his first sentences was so uncertain that he finally

gave it up, and with a prayer that his lips might
be guided and that his ears might hear a voice
behind him saying, "This is the way, walk ye in
it," he started on his errand.

Arrived at the place he was surprised to find
as he walked up the front path to the door, that
painters seemed to be preparing to paint the
house. He had understood that things were
somewhat run down and that the young men did
not care to keep them up. Perhaps this sister
had money; and he sighed to think of the possibilities of what that sister might be. The old-
fashioned knocker did not give back the empty
comfortless echo he had somehow expected, but
it sounded forth his arrival as if from cheerful,
well-filled rooms that had no need to shrink and
be sad at the approach of a stranger.

Sally the cook responded to his knock. It
had not been exactly within the range of her
province in the city to answer the door, but
things were different out here, where none of her
associates would know of her condescension,
and besides there were so few visitors. So she
smoothed her hair before the little glass in the
kitchen and tied on a wide, long white apron
which hung on the identical hook which poor
Aunt Nancy's had adorned for so long, and went
with quiet, trained footsteps to the door.

Robert Clifton was somewhat taken aback at

the sudden appearance before him of a city-trained servant. For the instant he thought she must be the sister, though her age was somewhat more advanced than he had been given to suppose Miss Benedict's to be, and he afterward remembered finding something incongruous in the thought of Sally's dignified proportions mounted on a bicycle.

It must be owned that he was somewhat embarrassed, and just escaped addressing Sally as Miss Benedict, but caught himself in time and asked if Mr. Benedict could see him for a few moments.

Now Sally had determined in the depths of her soul that if she was obliged to be door maid as well as kitchen maid, she would make the most of her opportunities and impress this country village with a sense of the high station of her young mistress, so that she really succeeded in quite overawing the young minister with her airs, as she told him that Mr. Benedict was not in, but she would see if Miss Benedict knew if he would be back soon, and would he give her his card? Then from a tiny stand she produced the silver salver, and the Reverend Robert Clifton could scarcely find a card, so astonished was he at the difference between what he had expected and what he had found.

While he waited in the lovely reception room

which had once been the cold and deserted
parlor of haircloth and red-and-green ingrain,
he had ample opportunity to observe the many
evidences of refinement and taste spread all about
him. Everything was beautiful, luxurious, comfortable; evidently purchased by one who knew
how to do such things. Mechanically his eye
took in the fact that the heavy rugs spread in
the wide oak hall were real Oriental. He could
see an upright piano through a veil of fine bead
portières and a glimpse of an inviting couch
with pillows, in the room opening out of the
parlor, and across the hall a pleasant vista, a
library furnished with luxurious leather-up-
holstered couch and chairs, with a large reading
table and shaded lamps, books, a low bookcase
running around the wall. He could hear a
canary singing in the room beyond the library.
He wondered vaguely what sort of young woman
would appear and rapidly began to change his
mental picture of her. She must be a woman
of the world, and if so, she would be doubly
hard to reach and help, and he would need to
take the more earnest care of his own good name.
He began to fear he had done wrong in coming
alone and to wish he had heeded the advice of
Deacon Chatterton. Then there came the soft
rustle of a dress down the stairs, and a light step
at the door, and Ruth Benedict stood before him.

Ruth had looked at the card curiously when it was brought to her. Had her servant been one from the village she would at once have been informed that the visitor was the new minister; but Sally did not move in Summerton society and shunned gossip of all sorts. Ruth recognized the name at once as belonging to a young theological student whom she had met several times at the home of friends during a summer visit. He had interested her because he seemed in earnest, and had also disappointed her in some respects because he had not seemed to have thought seriously about a great many questions which to her were very important ones. Now her quick brain at once jumped to the conclusion that this student had finished his educational course and was a full-fledged minister, and was probably occupying the position of pastor in Summerton. She had heard David say that there was a new minister and that he was a young man, and she had hoped that he would call on her brothers and would have a good influence over them. Indeed she had planned it all out nicely how he and his wife would be such helpers in her schemes, and would perhaps invite them to the parsonage and make friends of them. She was very anxious for her brothers to meet some earnest, Christian, cultured young men. But she looked doubtfully at the card.

Would this young Mr. Clifton be the one to
do them good? He was bright, she knew; indeed some had called him brilliant. He was a
Christian—she had felt sure of that when she
met him—and that he had chosen his profession
because he felt that God had called him to it,
but—she drew a sigh and went downstairs
breathing a prayer. Perhaps after all Mr.
Clifton had changed some of his theories. She
remembered very distinctly how it had troubled
her to know that a young man, who was so soon
to be a minister, had deliberately sat himself
down to read a comic story in one of the current
magazines on his return from the Sunday morning service, and how later in the day, when the
subject had come up for discussion, he had
defended his action by saying that he did not
believe the Lord wanted us to be long-faced, and
that the "sabbath was made for man and not
man for the sabbath." He also said that his
mother and several of his dearest Christian
friends always read whatever they pleased on
Sunday, and so long as it was a good thing it
did not seem to him that the Heavenly Father
could object. He added that their professor in
theology in the seminary told the students that
he had often read novels on Sunday evening
after his most earnest services, in order to give
his mind as entire a relaxation as possible.

Ruth had sat quietly in a corner, a very young girl, not supposed to be taking any part at all in the conversation; but her eyes must have expressed wonder, and perhaps disapproval, for as he raised his eyes he caught her clear gaze, and with his pleasant smile had appealed to her with, "What do you think about it, Miss Ruth? Isn't that a wise position I have taken?"

She had not expected to be asked her position, but, though taken by surprise, she answered quietly as she had been taught to do, just what was in her heart.

"I cannot judge for any one else," she had said simply. "For myself I feel as if God made the Sabbath for me to enjoy him in, and not to enjoy myself. There is a verse in Isaiah that settled the question for me two years ago."

The young theologue was pleasantly interested. He asked for the verse and listened respectfully to her answers to his questions. She had repeated the verse in a matter-of-fact tone much as if she had been reading a bit of a letter from a dear friend. It seemed to have a new light to the young man as she spoke it: "If thou turn away thy foot from the sabbath, from doing thy pleasure on my holy day; and call the sabbath a delight, the holy of the Lord, honourable; and shalt honour him, not doing thine own ways, nor finding thine own pleasure, nor speak-

ing thine own words: Then shalt thou delight
thyself in the Lord ; and I will cause thee to
ride upon the high places of the earth, and feed
thee with the heritage of Jacob thy father: for
the mouth of the Lord hath spoken it." He
had hinted that these words belonged to the old
dispensation and that we were no more under
the law but under love, and she had laughed a
low happy laugh. "Oh, I don't feel that it is a
law at all," she said, "because I love him. It is
merely a statement of what he would like to
have me do. When my mother asks me to do
something or says, 'Ruth, it would please me
very much if such and such a thing were done,'
I don't feel like going around saying my mother
has made me do this thing, or commanded me
to do that. But it is just as binding on me as
if it were a law, for I know it is what she would
like to have me do. Besides it seems to me as
if God had put the words just in that way to
make us see that it is meant for a law of love as
well as that written in tables of stone. It says
not 'if you don't do these things I will punish
you,' but 'if you do them then shalt thou delight
thyself in the Lord.' I should think that must
be the highest, most restful happiness there could
be, to be perfectly delighted in the Lord and have
him delighted in us."

Their conversation had been interrupted just

then and they had not seen each other since, but Ruth had carried away a troubled feeling. Her reverence for and her ideal of the high calling of the ministry had been very great. It troubled her that one who professed to believe that in Jesus Christ alone could true rest be found, would try to rest his own brain from preaching the message to others by reading worldly papers and books, some of which were written by men who did not believe in Jesus at all. It seemed to her that a minister should know the way to find true rest from anything in Jesus, else he could not point it out to others. There had been other discussions too, during those few weeks when she had seen him occasionally, that gave her the feeling that he was worldly in a great many ways. But the Ruler of all was leading and she could trust it with him.

Ruth had the advantage of her visitor, for she was reasonably sure who he was before she saw him, while it had not occurred to him that she and the other Miss Benedict could be identical.

"Mr. Clifton, this is a pleasant surprise, to meet one who is not a stranger when I am in a strange land."

There was sweetness and modest grace in tone and movement. The young minister was utterly bewildered for a moment. She stood just as he had planned she would stand in the years to

come, his ideal of Christian young womanhood.
How had she attained to it so soon? She ought
to be but a little girl yet.

But she was standing there to welcome him
and he must gather his scattered faculties.
All thought of the Benedict brothers, so hard to
reach in hermitage and isolation with their wild,
worldly, bicycling sister, drifted away from him.
The surroundings were such as to make him
forget. He greeted her warmly. He was eager
to know how she came here and what it all
meant, and he must answer her questions about
their mutual friends. It took him some time to
understand the situation, and he began to wax
indignant in his heart at his deacons and their
wicked gossip. Surely some one must be
greatly at fault that such terrible things could
be said. He wondered what her brothers could
be about that they allowed it, and what indeed
could have started it in the first place, and then
wondered again if he had not made some great
mistake and gotten into the wrong house; and
yet it was scarcely possible that he could have
made such a mistake. Presently Ruth gave
some light on the subject, however.

"I am sorry my brothers are neither of them
in," she said. "They told me they had not met
the new minister. I want them to meet you.
I am sure you can help them;" here she

looked anxiously at his face to be sure whether
she was sure. "They are neither of them
Christians," she added sadly. There was an
answering sympathetic light in the minister's
face which reassured her, however, as she went
on. "I have been so sorry not to go to church.
Day before yesterday was the first time I have
been outside of the yard since my accident. I
had the misfortune to fall from my bicycle and
sprain my ankle."

Ah! here was the key to the story. He
would ferret out the rest and have it explained
fully. He asked a few questions about the
matter, and then, that she might not think he
had a special reason for his earnest inquiries, he
changed the subject.

"Miss Benedict," he said earnestly, "I have
always thought I would like you to know that
you once helped me very much on a certain subject, and indeed I am not sure but on more than
one, for I found it reached to many things when
I once began to think about it. Do you remember a certain brief discussion on the subject of
Sunday reading and conversation? And do you
remember repeating to me that verse in Isaiah
as your answer to my question what you thought
about the subject? Well, that verse stayed with
me. I could not get away from it, and in spite
of the fact that I had settled it long before that

I had good ground for the position I then held,
I could not get rid of the feeling that I was
doing wrong and grieving my Saviour every
time I gave myself over to enjoying a secular
book or paper on Sunday. In vain I used my
former arguments. In vain I told myself I
was reading this or that for the spiritual good I
could get from it. I could not help seeing that
that was merely an excuse I was hiding behind,
and that the reading was being done for my
own pleasure, more than anything else. I was
brought to see then that I did not love my Bible
so much as I ought to do, and that my excuse
used heretofore that I had not time to devote to
its study as I ought, was a flimsy one, for I did
have some time on Sunday, if not for study,
at least to read, and get rest and refreshment
and joy and new strength. Then I saw that
the Bible had not been all those things to me at
all, and I set about changing the matter. Now
I stand in an entirely different position from
what I did. I do not say nor think that it is
wrong to read anything other than the Bible or
some strictly religious book on Sunday, but
I do say that I have not time enough for my
Bible now and cannot afford to lose one moment
of the precious rest it brings to me on Sunday,
when I am weary with my work, and I believe
that was what He intended the book and the

day should be to us. I want to thank you for
bringing that message to me."

Ruth's face shone with the joy that comes
with the knowledge of having helped another
human being. Her heart was relieved about
another matter also. There was no mistaking
the true ring to the minister's voice. She felt
sure he would be a helper for her brothers. Before there was time for any answer a step came
across the hall and David entered.

CHAPTER XI

DAVID wore a collar now almost all the time. It had come about through the influence of the beautiful things with which the old house had been filled. He did not feel at home among them without a collar, and so he was gradually becoming accustomed to its stiffness. It is true he always took it off as soon as he reached the solitude of his own room and gave a sigh of relief, but he nevertheless put it on the next time with less reluctance. As soon as his farm work was done and he could come in the house he put on the collar. As for Joseph, he took to collars and the like much more naturally. He had at one time had longings toward a glass scarf pin and oiled hair, but having little use for such things his longings had not met with much encouragement. But David dressed as a distinct mark of respect for the new sister and the new order of things in the house. So Ruth was not ashamed of the appearance of her brother when he entered the room to meet the minister.

He did seem somewhat surprised to find a stranger there, it is true, for visitors at the

Benedict farm had been few in the lifetime of the boys. But David's welcome was cordial, and Ruth noted with pride that he did not seem to be embarrassed by the young minister, but talked well. She thought that Robert Clifton's face expressed some surprise and admiration at David's intelligence. She sat by listening and praying and watching the two. Would they become warm friends and mutual helpers? She saw that they were mentally measuring one another, and that each was at least pleasantly impressed by the other. She wished that Joseph would come in, and excused herself once to go in search of him, but he was not to be found. However, just as the minister was going out the front gate he met Joseph coming in, and with his naturally frank, pleasant impulse he greeted him and introduced himself. It was but a moment they stood together within the fast gathering twilight, but the younger man went into the house with his heart completely won over. He had not been in a state of mind to resist, and the new minister had a very winning way with him.

Joseph was in a softened mood these days. Ever since Ruth had been hurt he had been different. All the repressed child-love that had found no expression seemed to be stored up in his nature, and was seeking an outlet. Now he poured it upon Ruth. They had been a happy

family during Ruth's temporary confinement to
the house, and though they did not know it, the
two young men had been growing in knowledge
of many kinds so rapidly as to astonish any one
who had known them well before. It is wonderful what a refining influence a few pictures
and books can have upon a human soul. Ruth
was delighted, but yet her heart was heavy, for
though she had been able to reach her brothers
in many ways, there had not been one little
minute when she felt she had done anything
toward influencing them to come to Christ. It
is true she recognized that she was gaining an
influence over them that might help her in the
future, but she was anxious to have them one
with her on this great vital question at once,
that she and they might grow together. She
had been pained to discover that the subject of
church-going was very doubtful, so doubtful that
it often did not come up as a question at all.
She knew that they would be willing to accompany her, at least one of them at a time, perhaps
as soon as she was able to go, but she would so
much rather have had them go from love of it, or
at least from habit. She had wondered so many
times what sort of a minister the Summerton
Church had, that it was a great relief to know at
last who he was. Somehow she felt a great deal
more certain of his help for her brothers since

that earnest speech of his about Sabbath keeping. To be sure it was no way to judge a man,
by his theory on some one subject, but still it was,
in a way, an index to his character, and as he
had said, led off into other subjects. Still she
had seen men whose ideas of right and wrong
fitted hers exactly, and who were by no means
fitted to be helpers to young men who were not
Christians.

Therefore Ruth prayed much during the
Saturday that followed the minister's call at
their home, for a blessing on the Sunday with
its services. She had arranged with both of
her brothers to accompany her to church. They
had acquiesced as a matter of course. If it
pleased her to go to church they were entirely
willing. Indeed on Joseph's part there was not
a little pride connected with escorting his beautiful, well-dressed sister to church. He hoped
the Brower boys would be there, and if they
dared once to even so much as look in her direction, and he saw them, woe betide them. David
wanted to amuse his sister in every way possible,
and his only fear was that she would find their
church a dull place. However, there was also
an element of interest in the person of the young
minister with whom both brothers had been
pleasantly impressed. They would like to see if
he could preach. He had talked with them so

well and freely, just as if he had always known
them and had worked beside them. At least
David so put it to himself as he thought over
his conversation with Robert Clifton.

Sunday morning dawned bright and beautiful.
There had been a sharp frost during the night
and the air was clear and crisp.

Ruth somehow felt very happy as they drove
down the long white road, so smooth and hard
and straight. She had just come from communion with Jesus and her face was shining with
the peace in her heart. She had been enabled
to leave all her cares and perplexities to him
who was guiding, sure that he knew the way
and could not make a mistake.

The minister had spent much time upon his
knees that week. It seemed to him that he
could not pray enough. As the week neared its
close and the Sunday services were at hand he
began to realize the awful responsibility of
speaking the word of God to the people. He
was beginning to know some of his young
people now, and to be personally interested in
them for their own sake, and as he had inquired
about this one and that, he had been pained to
learn how few of the younger ones were members
of the church. He had been told that Summerton was a hard field and indeed he feared from
what he had seen that it would so prove itself.

He had laid aside some of his cherished sermons which seemed to him the best fruit that
thought and study could produce through his
brain, and had written a plain, simple, earnest
appeal to sinners from the text, " What think ye
of Christ? " He had written it out fully, but
he felt that he would not have to read it, for
every word of reason and exhortation seemed
burned into his soul, and he wanted to speak
from his heart to his hearers. The more intellectual sermons would have their place by and
by, but he wanted to find out now what each one
of them thought of Jesus Christ. He wanted
to know what those two Benedict brothers
thought of him; and what the two low-browed
men in the back seat thought; and what some
of the pretty giggling girls thought; and what
the elder members of his church, both men and
women, thought. Did they think enough of
Jesus the Christ to enter into the work heart and
soul for his church, bringing all the tithes into
the store-house and proving the Lord of Hosts
for a blessing such as there should not be room
to receive? One might almost have called his
mood exalted as he entered the house of worship and made his way to the little study which
occupied a small space at one side of the pulpit
and opened into the " ladies' parlor."

Deacon Chatterton and Deacon Meakins stood

in this doorway talking and the former stepped up to hand him some church notice.

"By the way, Deacon Chatterton," said the minister, "and you too, Deacon Meakins, you will be glad to learn, I am sure, that there is some mistake about what was said of the Benedicts. I called there this week and find that Miss Benedict is the adopted child of a very dear friend of my mother's I have met her before, and her character is beyond reproach. She is an unusually remarkable Christian, and has been brought up by a woman whose life was one long sermon. I shall rely on you two brethren to correct any absurd report that may have been spread abroad. It is very strange how such a thing could have started. You will find the young woman a great help in church work, I am sure. She was a power among the young people in her former home. She has come among us to stay, she tells me, and will bring her letter at once to this church."

"But—but—the—the—bicycle!" gasped Deacon Meakins anxiously. He wished to have the whole trouble cleared from doubt at once, and he had himself seen the bicycle coming from the freight car, though he would not have told the other deacons so for a good deal.

"I don't understand, Deacon Meakins," said the minister anxiously. He wanted to be alone

for the last minute before the bell should cease
tolling and he thought he had explained fully.
"What had the bicycle to do with it? Certainly she rides, she told me so herself; but very
many young ladies do that now in the city. My
own sister has had a wheel for some time. It is
perfectly respectable."

The bell ceased to toll, and the minister's quiet
moment was gone. The two deacons went to
their seats pondering, one of them relieved in
his righteous soul, the other wondering whether
they had chosen their minister wisely, after all,
if he was going to uphold such things as bicycling for young women. But do him the justice
to remember that he forgot all about it when the
sermon began.

Ruth Benedict dawned on Summerton, and
between her and the new minister the attention
of the Summerton congregation was quite divided.

It would have been a study in human nature
if the thoughts of the different people could
have been pictured that morning. It might
have somewhat discouraged the earnest minister,
and perhaps so disheartened him that he would
have given up at once and missed the blessing,
for there were some souls ready for his message,
and it bore rich fruit in the days that came after.

Ellen Amelia Haskins happened to sit near and

almost behind Ruth Benedict, and her admiring eyes were scarcely taken away from the black velvet hat with its drooping plumes and the sweet oval of the earnest face before her. Once she turned to watch Joseph and David a moment, to try if she could see how they felt, sitting beside such a creature and calling her sister. It was the nearest to a romantic story that had ever come into her life, and she was enjoying it to the full. An intense longing filled her soul to get nearer to this wonderful young woman and know more of her. For a few moments she studied the black velvet hat to see if it was possible to use that dark red velveteen she had intended using for big puffs to her sleeves in any such way. She wondered how the brim took on such a pretty curve and felt sure she could manage it if she only had some of the mysterious stuff they made hat frames from ; but the wonderful feathers were beyond anything she had ever seen in Summerton and she gave up the hat with a half-envious sigh and let herself drift off into enjoyment of the whole lovely figure of the stranger.

Joseph had walked in with haughty mien, straight and protecting, beside his sister. He gave a glance over his shoulder to see if the Brower brothers were there, and when he discovered them sitting with lowering brows sul-

lenly back near the door, he made himself a
little straighter, if that were possible. Only toward the end of the sermon did he listen to
what was going on. Then an illustration caught
him and held his attention to the end; and
when the final amen was pronounced he con-
firmed his first decision that the minister was
"something like it," whatever that meant. Who
shall say that that illustration did not go with
him and help to influence all his future life?
At least he was won to like and listen to the
new minister, and that was a great point gained.

David had set himself to listen at once. He
had liked the minister and he wanted to see now
if he was worth listening to. The former
preacher he had always considered dry. Perhaps too, the fact that he had never known any
other minister in that church since his little
boyhood, made his familiar voice uninteresting.
The very first words this man spoke caught his
attention. "What think ye of Christ?" They
were spoken like a question to him and the
speaker seemed to be looking directly at him.
For some time it did not dawn upon his consciousness that the words were from the Bible.
He almost felt that he must arise in his seat and
give an answer and he began wondering what
his answer would be. Perhaps if the truth must
be frankly told he did not think anything of

Christ. The speaker had caught his hearer.
David had no more time for thought, for he was
carried on the swift wings of the earnest, red-
hot words that came straight from one soul,
charged with an electric current from heaven,
into the soul of another living, dying brother.
When the end came and he stood with the rest
as they sang, some badly, some indifferently, and
a few with their hearts, the words,

> "Behold a stranger at the door !
> He gently knocks, has knocked before,
> Has waited long, is waiting still ;
> You treat no other friend so ill,"

he felt again that strange force bidding him
answer these charges. Was there an unseen
choir present which helped on the village voices,
and bore the song in angelic strains, straight into his soul? Long years afterward something
of this thought came to him, and he did not say
it nay.

"It's just as I thought," said Mrs. Deacon
Chatterton to herself, looking over her spectacles
while the second hymn was being sung; "she's
pretty; that kind always are! Humph!" and
then she felt thankful in a moral kind of exultation that Eliza Barnes was not out at church
to-day; she was saved at least one week of temptation. For some reason Mrs. Chatterton seemed
to consider all things pretty a temptation.

The Brower boys went out from the church feeling uncomfortable, they hardly knew why. The sermon had made them feel so. They were too dull to understand the reason and too wicked to heed what had been spoken to them. Perhaps though, the seed fell not all on stony ground in their hearts. But they said on the way home that they did not like the new minister, and what was more, they never would like him.

The benediction was pronounced and David Benedict was just about to step out into the aisle when the minister placed a detaining hand upon his shoulder.

" One minute, Benedict; I want your sister to teach a class in the Sunday-school and I want you and your brother for my Bible class. Your brother half promised me that he would stay. It won't hinder you to remain, will it? I really need your sister for a teacher very badly."

David gave his consent at once, amazed beyond expression. Joseph had promised to attend Sunday-school! By what power had the minister abstracted that promise, and when had he met Joseph? The millennium must surely be about to dawn. He would not put one hindering stone in the way of either Joseph or his sister. So, although he shrank from going into a class, and tried to get away on pretext of looking after the horses, the minister laughingly

held on to him and he went over to the corner
and sat down with the Bible class, to the amazement of Deacon Chatterton and the gratification
of Deacon Meakins.   And there sat Joseph!
David could not get over it.   The brothers
wisely refrained from looking at one another,
but sat in their places as if they had been accustomed to coming to Sunday-school from time
immemorial.   Truth to tell, Joseph had not intended to stay at all, but some strange power in
that winning smile of the minister forced him
against his will.   Besides, Ruth seemed anxious
to remain.

The minister escorted her down the aisle to
the corner where sat a row of giggling girls, and
placed her in front of the delighted and wholly
devoted Ellen Amelia.   As he went down the
aisle he said in a low tone to his new teacher:
"You are just the one for that class I am sure.
There is one girl who needs you—and probably
more—but I am interested in her.   She is Deacon Haskins' daughter.   You will know her.
She is the one who looks as if she had tried to
and couldn't."

"And am I supposed to help her try to and
can?" asked Ruth, laughing.

"Well, I had not put it that way; I had supposed the proper thing would be to teach her not
to try what she cannot accomplish, but perhaps

it would be better to show her how to attain to
the height of her ambitions."

Then he left her before those girls who were
every one of them ready to adore her at once, if
they ever got quite over being a little afraid of
her. As soon as the first awe of having the
velvet hat in their immediate midst had disappeared somewhat, they began to sing very loud
and look proudly over at the other classes of
girls who had not a new, stylish teacher from
the city. And so is Christ's work mingled with
the wickedness of this world and the petty sins
of the human heart.

CHAPTER XII

" SHE was real solemn part of the time," said
Ellen Amelia as she passed her plate for
some more cabbage. " I wouldn't have thought
she was that kind. She ain't quite like any
girls I ever read of either, for she don't seem
proud one bit, though she does wear such lovely
clothes. She had the cutest little pin on her
collar, a wreath of green leaves with a little
pearl between each one. If I had a pin like that
I'd be just too happy to live. And she had a
beautiful ring on. I saw it when she took off
her glove to write in our class book."

" I'm sure I don't know why you shouldn't be
proud, if you want to, without any pin or ring.
You've just as good a right to as she. Your
father makes more money than hers ever did,
and because he ain't such a fool as to let you
spend it on gewgaws isn't any reason why you
shouldn't be proud of him, if you want to."

It was practical, anxious little Mrs. Haskins
who said this. But Ellen Amelia did not get
her admiration for the romantic from her mother's side of the family. Her mother strongly
disapproved of the " Fireside Companion," on the

160

ground that Ellen Amelia might be better em-
ployed in darning stockings for the younger
Haskinses than in dreaming over its columns.
She never read it herself and therefore had no
moral grounds of objection. But Deacon Haskins was weak and yielding where his daughter
was concerned and quietly subscribed for it in
response to her earnest pleadings.

"Well, I know one thing," went on Ellen
Amelia, with her mouth full of cabbage; "I
mean to cut over my brown basque and fix a
little jacket to it like hers, and make a front out
of that blue and green silk handkerchief Uncle
Timothy sent me from New York. I just know
I could do it."

"No, you are not!" interjected her mother
sharply. "Your brown basque is good enough
as it is, and I won't have you wasting your time
chopping up good things to make an outlandish
copy of a girl you never saw before. If that's the
kind of thing you learn in Sunday-school you
better stay at home."

Probably the young teacher, who was at that
moment kneeling beside her bed and praying
that the words she had spoken to those girls that
morning might not all have been in vain, would
have agreed with the mother could she have listened. But though dress and romance were
uppermost in Ellen Amelia's mind, there was an

undercurrent of something earnest, some longing she had never felt before, which, strange to say, found its outlet in a desire to dress like her new idol. Miss Benedict was lovely. Why could not she be lovely if she could make herself look like that? She had something higher in her soul than Ellen Amelia understood, and Ellen Amelia had resolved to have it too if possible. The only way to get it was to try to be like the girl who possessed it. The only way to be like her was to begin with her dress. Ellen Amelia meant well, and would come out right in the end.

She stood at the window of the front room of her father's house one afternoon of that week digging a pin diligently into the window sash and winking back the tears. She and her mother had just been having a rather angry talk about the brown basque. Ellen Amelia was determined to have the little jacket fronts put on in the way Miss Benedict's had been. She had coaxed and reasoned all in vain. Mrs. Haskins was firm. The brown basque should not be cut up nor its fashion altered in any way. Ellen Amelia hated it. It did not fit her. Its plain darts were too flat and the point at the waist in front stuck out. It was a great trial to her. She had resolved to model herself after this lovely stranger, in short to be such a pattern of loveliness in every respect that her mother should be astonished at her. It need not be thought that Ellen Amelia had not recognized the higher something which Ruth Benedict possessed, for she did and longed to possess it herself ; but how was she to do so if she could not even attain the outward similitude ? The trouble with Ellen Amelia was that she began at the outward instead of the inward to model her likeness. But after all, was she much to blame? She understood better the outward, and who shall say God did not mean the outward adorning sometimes to be the key to the inner one. It is true it might have turned out otherwise had not Ruth's taste in dress been quiet, modest, self-respecting, and lovely. There was nothing of flash or showiness about Ruth Benedict.

Ellen Amelia looked out on the bright autumn world and thought it a dark one. How was she to improve herself and do any of the great things her heroines of the weekly story papers always succeeded in doing in the world, if her mother would persist in throwing hindrances in her path? She sighed discontentedly and wished she could ever have anything she wanted. If only she might have a new dress and make it the way she wanted to! But no, of course her mother would insist on cutting it out in her own way, even if she did have one.

Just then her meditations were interrupted by
the wild gesticulations of her little brother
Amos, who was waving a large paper package
which proved to be an express package, and addressed to her. Ellen Amelia's heart fluttered
and she thought of all the possibilities of princes
in disguise who might have seen her in some
impossible way and fallen in love with her at
first sight, found out who she was in an equally
improbable way, and sent her some rare gift.
Ellen Amelia was always getting up some such
sudden picture of ravishing delight for herself
only to have it dashed in hard practical bits at
her feet by the stern facts of the case. Yet in
spite of repeated disappointments and dashing of
hopes, her buoyant imagination was always
ready for a new possibility of wonder which
should "robe her in gown of the finest texture
and deck her with jewels so fair." Really there
were possibilities of great good or evil in Ellen
Amelia, and if some prince of darkness in disguise had happened to appear about this time in
her path it would have been worse for her. She
was in great danger. But there was a Wiser
than her mother and father watching over her.
Even now some good was coming to her through
a common express package sent by her Uncle
Timothy in New York. He was a policeman
there and well to do. He had no children of his

own, and remembered well how he used to romp with and care for little tow-headed Ellen Amelia when she was but five years old and he a clerk in his brother's hardware store. At long intervals, with no seeming reason like a birthday or Christmas for an excuse, he sent Ellen Amelia something. There had been but two of these gifts before this one. The first had been a gold dollar, and the second the aforementioned blue and green silk handkerchief.

Great excitement prevailed in the Haskins family while the package was being opened, and Ellen Amelia felt her importance. Mother Haskins came with her dish towel over her arm and a teacup she was wiping in her hand. Grandmother Haskins came with a button between her lips and little Tommie Haskins' red flannel "Johnny cloths" she was mending in her hand, while young Amos and Tommie hung over the paper and gloated over each difficult knot in the heavy twine in a transport of delight. If you could not have express packages addressed to yourself, why then surely it was the next best thing to have your sister get one.

The papers fully unwrapped, disclosed to view soft rich folds of dark blue serge material, a good full dress pattern of it. Uncle Timothy certainly had good taste, or else had asked the advice of the dress-goods clerk. Certainly he

could not have selected anything that would
have brought out better the uncertain com-
plexion of Ellen Amelia, who would have liked
to be beautiful, but alas! knew not how to make
the best of what she had.

After the first excitement was over, Ellen
Amelia sat down to enjoy her present by herself. There was a shadow over her joy even so
early. Her mother had said with grim satisfaction, "That'll save buyin' you anythin' new this
winter, thank fortune! We must get at makin'
it as soon's the boys' flannels is out of the way,"
and she had gone back to her labors in the
kitchen, rejoicing truly that her daughter would
have such a beautiful dress, planning the while
to cut it by a pattern which fitted herself, as
Ellen Amelia was growing so large now.

But the daughter took the beautiful goods up
to her room and sat down to think. She had
visions of the dress as it would look if it were
made by her mother,—as her dresses had always
been made,—with her own assistance, of course;
and she also had another vision of the dress as
it would appear if it were modeled after Miss
Benedict's. Oh, if she could but attain to a
city dressmaker! But, of course, that was out
of the question. She had but three dollars and
twenty-five cents of her own, and she did not
feel like asking her father for more for that pur-

pose. Money was not plentiful in the Haskins family. Ellen Amelia sighed again. A dressmaker was out of the question, and even if she were not she would have to be Miss Dunnet, the Summerton dressmaker, from West Winterton, and Ellen Amelia's soul had aspirations beyond Miss Dunnet. She had secretly compared the hang of Georgiana Brummel's skirt with the graceful sweep of Ruth Benedict's last Sunday, and she longed inexpressibly to be enfolded in such long, graceful folds as Miss Benedict was able to compass. Ellen Amelia was a girl of determination, and when she could not do a thing one way she generally managed to do it another. It was perhaps for this reason that she had impressed the minister as one who "tried to and couldn't." Only he did not know. She tried and accomplished, but by so hard and circuitous a route that the result was utterly different from what she had planned. But this time she determined to do a rather daring thing. She would go to Miss Benedict and see if she could borrow a skirt pattern. She had a secret fear that her errand might all be in vain, and that city young ladies did not usually even know that their dresses required a pattern, but she could but fail if she tried. So, making an excuse of some trifling errand, she started out, not without much fear and trembling.

Once on her way, she began to almost repent her hasty action. What would the elegant young city lady think of her, asking for a skirt pattern? Ellen Amelia had walked about a mile and was nearing the border of the Benedict farm, when she determined firmly that she would say nothing whatever about the skirt pattern. Indeed, as she came in sight of the house she began to think maybe it would be better not to go in at all, but to go on up to the Barnes' house and do that errand for her father she had promised to do some time. It would look presuming in her to call on Miss Benedict. To be sure Ruth had kindly invited all her class to come and see her, saying she was lonely and wanted to get acquainted, but Ellen Amelia could scarcely conceive of that being exactly true. How could she be lonely and want common village companionship when she occupied so novel a position, mistress of a grand home, full of beautiful things, and two newly made brothers to worship her—for that Joseph and David thought a great deal of their sister, she had fully decided, during her brief view of their faces on Sunday.

When she reached the gate she paused, half turned to go in, and then quickly looking sidewise at the windows turned and went rapidly on, a few steps. It was a very hard thing, however, to come so near this dream of paradise and not go in. Ellen Amelia looked back again, and saw, oh wonder of wonders, a window thrown up, and a white hand with a dainty handkerchief waving at her, and a voice calling her, "Miss Haskins."

It had really never struck Ellen Amelia in the grown-up sense before, that she was Miss Haskins. It sounded so dignified and far-away. She expected to be Ellen Amelia to the end of her days, unless indeed the wonderful prince came. She had sometimes thought that he might call her "Miss Ellen," or "Miss Alène," or "Miss Amélie," as she variously designated herself after reading some of her favorite serials.

But to be called "Miss Haskins" by another girl, and such a girl, putting her on a level with herself, and speaking the words with such a sweet friendly tone, Ellen Amelia could scarcely believe her ears. She stopped, of course, and obeyed the summons, and was almost overpowered by the splendor and comfort of the room into which she was ushered, which proved to be the library.

Ruth had been praying for this scholar of hers ever since Sunday. She had been asking her Heavenly Father to give her some opportunity of helping her, if it was his will. Therefore she did not feel that it was all chance that she should

look up from her writing desk by her upper
window and see the figure of the girl for whom
she had been praying. There was something
about Ellen Amelia that was unmistakable even
at a distance, if one had once noticed her
carefully. Perhaps it was the "tried-to-and-
couldn't-ness" of her. At least Ruth felt sure
her opportunity was coming, and when, as she
watched, she saw that the girl wanted to come
in and hesitated, she helped on the opportunity
by opening her window and calling to her.

"I am so glad you were passing," began Ruth
when she had seated her bewildered visitor and
insisted on her removing her wraps, for the day
was a cold one. "I was just hoping some one
would come, for I am alone this afternoon."

She was very winning and pleasant and she
seemed to know exactly how to take away the
embarrassment from her visitor. Some fine instinct, or perhaps some higher spiritual guidance,
told her that her guest would be more at her
ease if she could once have opportunity to look
about the room, and wear away her awe of
things, and so Ruth made an excuse to leave her
alone in that wonderful room for full five minutes
on plea of giving a direction to Sally, and when
she came back Ellen Amelia, as she had hoped,
had regained some of her abundant spirit, and
was able to talk. Indeed she even lost her

embarrassment so much as to become quite confidential and to admire her hostess.

"You do have the loveliest life!" said Ellen Amelia with an adoring look in her eyes. "My! I just wish I was you!"

"Oh no, you don't!" said Ruth quickly with something of fun, and something of sadness too, in her tone. "Why, no one's life would exactly suit any one else. And then think." and her voice saddened, "you have a mother and father; and I, though I had two, have been left without either. You wouldn't change places with me for a minute if you would stop to think. You would not give up your father and mother and your grandmother—didn't you tell me you had a grandmother? Just think what it would be to be without them."

"Oh well," said Ellen Amelia uneasily, "of course I wouldn't want them to die; but if I had never known them and could be you it would be lovely. I think it must be awful nice to have things the way you want them without having to ask a soul, and not have your mother always saying 'No' to everything you want. Ma and I just had a time about something. I must say, I think I'm old enough to do as I please."

Ruth's face grew sad and her heart heavy. How was one to talk to a girl who had such unnatural feelings as this one?

"Oh, you don't know what you are saying,
I'm sure, my dear," said Ruth earnestly, placing
her pretty white hand on Ellen Amelia's arm.
"I can't bear to hear you talk like that. If you
were tried once you would feel so differently.
Why, I would give all the world just now to
have my mother, or some one, tell me what to
do. It seems to me I would be willing to do the
most disagreeable thing if only I might have
them to please once more. And you should not
feel so about your mother. A mother is such a
wonderful being, almost like God in some of her
qualities. A mother has to bear so much. Your
mother, I'm sure, does not hinder you from anything that she feels is for your good."

"Oh no, of course not," said Ellen Amelia
with a little of the shrug of her shoulders which
she used at home when she did not like things;
"but her ideas of what is for my good, and
mine, are very different. My mother thinks it
isn't for my good to ever have my own way in
anything. You have your own way all the
time."

"That is where you are utterly mistaken, my
dear," said Ruth, determining to be bright and
not seem to be too severe on the girl the first
time. Indeed, her first feeling on hearing her
guest speak so of her mother to a stranger, had
been one of shocked horror, and she could scarce-

ly forbear a severe rebuke; but further reflection made her feel that probably the mother might be a little hard on her daughter, and if she would help any she must gain the girl's confidence. "Nobody can have his own way in anything in this world without getting into trouble. God is guiding the world, and if we try to take hold and do his work we should get all mixed up. I don't often get my own way and I sometimes have to do things that I don't in the least want to do; but never mind that now. Suppose you tell me the particular thing you want to do, if it is something I may know. I would like to sympathize with you in it at least; or perhaps I can show you it isn't a real trouble after all," and Ruth laughed her happy, contagious laugh.

Ellen Amelia looked down. She suddenly felt shy. She did not like to tell Miss Benedict about her troubles over dress. But the winning voice was saying, "Can't you tell me dear, or is it something I must not know? I don't want to pry into things that are not my affairs, of course."

Ellen Amelia flushed. She did not wish to seem to refuse anything that Miss Benedict asked her, and somehow it was all like a story, her asking her in that frank pleasant way, just like "Ethel" when "Mr. Atholind" asked her if— what was it he asked her in last Saturday night's paper?

"My! but you would make a good character for a book now, you look so pretty sitting in that attitude," said Ellen Amelia suddenly, raising her admiring eyes to Ruth's face.

Ruth was disappointed and showed it in her eyes at once. If Ruth wanted to keep a secret ever, she always had to hide her eyes, for they would tell all they knew in spite of her. Ellen Amelia saw the disappointment and knew it had to do with her. She was repentant at once, and with eyes drooping again she said :

" Yes, I'm going to tell you. It's a thing you can know if you want to ; only I just know you'll laugh at me."

CHAPTER XIII

AFTER repeated assurances from Ruth that she would not laugh, Ellen Amelia burst out with her confidence:

"Well, then, it's my clo'es. I can't have a thing made the way I want it. Just look at that dress!" and she stood up and surveyed the front of a faded novelty-cloth, which had evidently been purchased more for its style than its durability. "You know it doesn't hang right. I don't know what's the matter with it, so I can't fix it. I've got a new dress to-day, a present from my uncle in New York. It's real pretty and I'd like to have it made nice, like some of yours; but ma will have to make it, and she'll make it the way she did my last year's, only with the sleeves a little bigger, I suppose. I want some jackets and front fixings, but she don't know how to make them and she thinks it's a waste of time for me to fuss; and besides, she says I don't know how any more than she does, so I have to have them the way she makes them. I started out here this afternoon to ask you if you had a skirt pattern and would lend it to me, but when I got out here I got scared; besides, I remembered that probably you never had a skirt pattern in the house ; you most likely sent your dresses all to some dressmaker and didn't know how they were made, so I decided to go on.   I wouldn't have come in at all if you hadn't called me.   Now don't you think I'm an awful fool ? "

Ellen Amelia's courage was high pitched and failed her just now, while tears of mortification and embarrassment filled her eyes.   But Ruth soothed her and made her sit down again.

"I'm very glad you came to me, I am indeed. I think I can help you.   Indeed I have plenty of skirt patterns in the house, some very pretty simple ones too, and I do not think I have a single dress that was made by a dressmaker.   I made every one myself.   My mother thought every girl ought to know about that and so she sent me to the finest institution that could be found in the city for learning dressmaking.   You know the schools of domestic science are very fine now.   I made all my own and my mother's dresses for a year or two.   It isn't so hard when you know how.   Suppose you come up here and spend the day on Thursday and bring your new dress along and we'll make it.   I think we can finish it in a day or two if we work fast.   I have done a dress in a day with some one to help. Are you a good seamstress ?   I'm to be alone all

day on Thursday, for my brothers have to drive
over to West Winterton with some sheep. Will
your mother mind? Tell her I know all about
dressmaking, for I went to one of the best
schools. Perhaps she'll be glad to be relieved
of it."

Ellen Amelia's eyes shone and her breath
came quick. Could it be true? This young
woman with the immaculate apparel made all
her wonderful garments herself! And could she
believe her ears? Was she offering to help her?
Would it be possible that a Haskins could ever
look like this city maiden? And a school for
dressmaking! Would the wonders never cease?
She had supposed that dressmaking was some
special gift conferred upon a few maiden ladies
and unfortunate widows, who by patient service
had been granted an ability to make things look
different from anything any one else could do,
and by this earned their living.

She gave her eager and ready consent to spend
Thursday, dress and all, with her new friend, if
she were not imposing too much upon her. She
said she was certain her mother would be pleased,
which I fear was a polite little lie she had
learned from the "Fireside Companion." In her
heart she much feared that her mother would
put her foot down most decidedly upon the proposition, but also in her heart she meant to con-

trive some way to carry out her purpose and
have one dress made as she wanted it; for did not
this dress belong to herself? and surely she ought
to have the right to say how it should be made.

On her return home however, she found to her
surprise that her way had been made plain.
Her mother looked very tired and a shade of
oldness seemed to be upon her face. Ellen
Amelia had never before noticed that her mother
was growing old, and it came to her with something of a shock. She remembered Miss Benedict's words, "You would not give up your
mother." It gave her a strange feeling and she
did up the dishes of her own accord after supper
without waiting to be asked, which was unusual.
She never wanted to leave her reading after supper. The mother seemed to appreciate this unusual mark of daughterliness, for with a gentler
tone than she was accustomed to use she said,
when Ellen Amelia came back to the sitting
room after the kitchen was all in order for the
morning:

"Ellen 'Melia, I'm just afraid you'll have to
give up havin' that new dress made up till after
Thanksgivin', 'tany rate. I've been thinkin'
how I could get it in, and I just can't see my way
clear, not if I go to nurse at Miss Crampton's
them two weeks, and I've give my promise, you
know. I feel sort o' done out to-day, and ef

'twan't fer your grandmother I'm sure I don't
see how I would've got through the work. As
it is, I think I'll go to bed early. I'm sorry
you'll have to wait for your dress, but it can't be
helped. You can console yourself by thinkin'
you wouldn't have hed any at all ef it hadn't
been for your Uncle Timothy."

Now was Ellen Amelia's opportunity.

"Now ma, don't you worry about that dress;
I'm goin' to make it myself. I went to call on
Miss Benedict this afternoon, and she's invited
me to spend the day with her Thursday and
she'll help make it. She's been to a big school
where she learned how to make all her clo'es,
sacks and hats and everything, and she said she
would just like nothin' better'n to show me. I
thought it would be a real relief to you, ma, and
so I told her I'd come if you didn't need me for
anything on Thursday."

Mrs. Haskins did not altogether approve of
the plan, but her pride was somewhat pleased to
have Miss Benedict, with her pretty clothes,
actually willing to help her daughter make a
dress, and the weary mother consented, with
many a sigh and a misgiving. She told Ellen
Amelia she had her doubts about the hang of
the skirt, the set of the waist, and was afraid
there would be too many new-fangled things on
it, but she supposed if Ellen Amelia's heart was

set on it, nothing else would do, and as it was a
present she had a right to spoil it if she pleased.
With which ungracious permission she reflected
with satisfaction that her daughter would have
a dress and she would not have to worry over it.

Thursday morning dawned bright and clear
and found Ellen Amelia on her way to the Benedict farm. Such a gala day had not been before
her since she was a little girl and anticipated for
months beforehand the yearly May-day all-day
picnic. Now she was to have her beloved Miss
Benedict all to herself for a whole day in that
lovely house. To be sure it would have been no
drawback to have had David and Joseph in the
background of the setting for an hour or two at
mealtimes, and it had been no part of the induce-
ment to her coming when Ruth had mentioned
their intended absence. Ellen Amelia had felt
the least bit disappointed. But then one could
not mind about so small a thing when there was
so much in the day besides. She hummed a
tune as she hurried along with her face very
bright. She met the minister hurrying toward
the station and wondered if he was going to
meet "his folks" and wondered what they would
be like and if she would like them. She wished
she could linger to see them, but knew that
every moment was precious to the finishing of
the blue serge, and hastened on.

Ruth had prepared a large sunny room on the second floor as a sewing room, and all her cutting and sewing appliances were arranged ready. The sewing machine was one of the best and would almost sew of itself. Ellen Amelia admired and wondered over it while she was being shown the difference between it and her mother's lumbering old one. The cutting table, the tracing wheel and bright shears, all had a charm that implements of common every-day work did not usually have for this girl. She was fonder of reading than of work. But she sighed and told herself she would love to sew if she could work with such tools. They studied awhile over some fashion plates Ruth had brought out, and Ellen Amelia supposed she was choosing from them the one she would like her dress made after, but in reality she was being advised as to what would become her and suit her material, and was having her eyes opened with regard to a number of points which had heretofore escaped her notice. It would appear that a style suited to a light, thin evening dress for the lazy beauties who lolled on velvet cushions in the weekly story papers, was not suited to heavy wool material intended for church and street wear, nor indeed for sensible, every-day living. Neither did it appear to be in good taste to put much trimming on even handsome material which was to be worn to church or to any other quiet place in the world where one was in earnest. Ellen Amelia learned, without exactly knowing how, that one's dress always expresses one's self, and that if we do not wish to give false impressions of ourselves we must be careful that the dress shall express what we would have our lives show. She pondered over this fact all day and wondered if religion had anything to do with dress, and tried to forgive herself for thinking a thought so irreverent.

Every moment of that morning was an inexpressible delight and excitement to Ellen Amelia. Fortunately the sewing room held no decorations save the simplest, or the mind of the young girl would certainly have been too upset to do much work. But the rapid, trained fingers of the young teacher were making progress all the time, and she had the rare talent of being able to talk pleasantly and without impatience, the while she worked as rapidly as her fingers could fly.

They had as dainty a lunch together as the lofty Sally could prepare. She sniffed a good deal to herself at having to waste her fine arts of cookery on a village girl who would much rather have ham and eggs, she presumed, but she did her mistress' bidding thoroughly, in spite of her sniffing. Ruth had tried to have everything

as dainty as possible and yet not so elaborate
that it could not be easily remembered and
copied if her guest should choose to do so. She
believed most emphatically in the elevating
power of little things. A girl's manners could
not but be made better if she habitually ate at a
dainty table. Also, she tried to have everything
eatable as unlike as possible to that to which she
thought Ellen Amelia was accustomed. And
indeed the girl felt that she was dining on the proverbial nectar and ambrosia. There was a delicate soup of pale pink color, in whose rich,
creamy deliciousness she would never have recognized the familiar tomato. There were tiny,
shell-like cups of rich chocolate, foamed with
whipped cream, and there was some strange,
new delectable custard in little molds, and thin,
sweet wafer crackers. Ellen Amelia's eyes were
bright and her wits were quick. She was rather
afraid of the array of spoons and forks, but she
watched her hostess and tried to appear at her
ease, and really succeeded remarkably well.
Ruth had guessed well that the ceremony and
the strangeness of the dishes would please her
guest more than to have a simple dinner, such
as she had every day at home. Ellen Amelia
was one who liked mystery and newness beyond
anything else in life.

After lunch Ruth left her guest in the parlor for

a few minutes to wander about and look as much as she pleased, and then she came and played and sang a few bright little songs for her and one tender, sweet one, about a mother and a home. She had selected these songs with care and prayer and a view to reaching the different longings she thought she saw in Ellen Amelia's eyes. Then, arm in arm, they went back to their work. Said Ellen Amelia:

"Do you think it is wicked to care awfully for pretty things? I don't suppose you do, because you have so many around you; but I don't quite understand it. You talked in Sunday-school as if you were terribly good."

"No," said Ruth, "I don't think it is at all wicked. On the contrary, I think it is wrong not to have things just as pretty as you can. If it were wicked to have things pretty God would not have made the world beautiful. He might just as well have made the sun go down in gray every night, instead of throwing crimson and gold and purple clouds in the west. Just look at the landscape the next sunset hour and see if it isn't beautiful, and then tell me whether you do not think God likes beautiful things, and loves to have us enjoy them too."

"Well," said Ellen Amelia, "I s'pose that's true about the things he made. But it's wicked to like pretty clo'es, ain't it?"

" Well, no ; I don't think it is. There is a
difference between liking pretty clothes, and being so fond of attracting attention by showy
dressing that one thinks of nothing else. I
think every one ought to be as careful about
having the dress neat and tasteful and becoming
as they are about having their faces washed clean
every day and their hair neatly combed. It
is a duty. Did you ever read ' Ethics of the
Dust' or 'Sesame and Lilies'? No? Well, Mr.
Ruskin says dressing is a virtue. Here, let me
read you a few words while you sew on those
hooks. You'll be interested in that book if you
never read it. Take it home and enjoy all about
the Crystal life and the Crystal sorrows and the
Crystal virtues. I'm sure you will like it if you
read it carefully."

Ruth left the room a moment and while she
was gone her visitor reflected with joy that she
should have a book to take home. She wondered
who this " Sesame " was, and if the Lilies had
to do with another girl, and what the Crystal
things were she had spoken of, if they were anything like that story of the lady of the crystal palace and the sleeping knight she read last year.

Then Ruth came back and read :

" LECTURER. I said their (a girl's) second virtue was dressing.

"MARY. Well! what did you mean by that?

"LECTURER. What do you mean by dressing?

"MARY. Wearing fine clothes.

"LECTURER. Ah! there's the mistake. I mean wearing plain ones.

"MARY. Yes, I daresay! but that's not what girls understand by dressing, you know.

"LECTURER. I can't help that. If they understand by dressing, buying dresses, perhaps they also understand by drawing, buying pictures. But when I hear them say they can draw, I understand that they can make a drawing; and when I hear them say they can dress, I understand that they can make a dress and—what is quite as difficult—wear one.

.   .   .   .

"DORA. Then we are all to learn dressmaking, are we?

"LECTURER. Yes; and always to dress yourselves beautifully; not finely, unless on occasion; but then very finely and beautifully too. Also, you are to dress as many other people as you can; and to teach them how to dress, if they don't know; and to consider every ill-dressed woman or child whom you see anywhere, as a personal disgrace; and to get at them somehow, until everybody is as beautifully dressed as birds. . . . Now you needn't say you can't, for you can and it's what you were meant to do, always; and to dress your houses and your gardens too."

Ruth closed the book and went to work at the blue serge sleeves.

"We shall certainly not get this dress done in a week," she said, laughing, "if I stop to read to you any more, for you don't work while I read." Ellen Amelia laughed and took up another hook, but her mind was on the reading.

"Miss Benedict, do you really mean you think everybody—do you think I could dress well, and —that other thing—how could I dress other people? I don't understand it at all. That book reads something like the Bible, but the Bible says just the other thing. I've had it dinged into my ears ever since I was three, and cried because my apron had a patch of another color right in front. I know it by heart: 'Whose adorning, let it not be of the outward adorning, of the wearing of gold and plaiting the hair.'"

"But, my dear, Mr. Ruskin says nothing opposed to that. He does not say you are to adorn yourself, or wear costly apparel or jewels, nor, in short, to be showy; but simply to make yourself a pleasant object to look upon, so that your presence will soothe others. There is no virtue in an ugly thing. The Bible says, 'He hath made all things beautiful in their season.' Then don't you remember all about Christ's garments? They were not royal, such as an earthly king would have worn, trimmed with ermine and rich gold embroidery, and made of velvets and silks and costly furs. But do you not remember

how the seamless coat he wore was so good and
fine that the soldiers would not divide it but
cast lots for it instead? It has always seemed to
me that Jesus would have worn nothing gay or
fine to attract attention, but I think the wool
was soft and firm and fine, and the color quiet.
He was not rich, nor would he have spent his
money for princely robes if he had been, for
they were not fitting for his work then; but I do
not think it is irreverent to think that Jesus selected what he wore with good taste and good
sense. The highest ideal of dress that is given
in the Bible is the robe of righteousness and
the pure white robe that we shall wear in
heaven. The Bible seems to hold up simplicity
as an ideal of dress and purity. Ellen, may I
ask you a question? I am anxious to know its
answer. Do you belong to Jesus? Are you trying to follow him in everything?"

The question was a quiet one, spoken in a
matter-of-fact tone, and the preceding name
"Ellen" sounded sweet to the girl's ears. She
had been accustomed to hearing the two names
run into one, and, indeed, had been proud of her
double name as something high-sounding, but
this quiet, dignified "Ellen," had a cultured
sound far beyond the high-flown style she had
been cultivating all her life. She liked it, and
was pleased to be called so. It was the first

time Miss Benedict had called her by her first name. But the question itself was embarrassing. She had never been asked this before in her life but once. The old white-haired minister, with his severe countenance, had come up to herself and three other girls as they stood chattering together at the back of the church after service, and said in a kindly, but very grown-up tone, "Little girls, have you entered the ark of safety?" They had been frightened, and had answered "I don't know," and one of them from sheer embarrassment had giggled, because she did not know what else to do, and the old man had sighed and gone on his way, feeling that he had done his duty, and the youthful heart was prone to wickedness. Neither father nor mother had ever said to her, "Daughter, will you give your heart to Jesus now?" They had taught her the words of the Bible and some of the severe side of the meaning, but had not thought anything more necessary, or else had failed in courage to do more.

And now, Ellen Amelia, at sixteen, remembered the scared little group of children huddled together and the old minister towering above them with his question, and giggled and made the same answer, "I don't know."

CHAPTER XIV

THE dress was not finished that day. There was too much talking to be done. Ellen Amelia went home at dusk with her two little books of Ruskin, and a good many new thoughts. She had developed in some measure, be it ever so slightly, during that day, for she saw the sunset. For the first time in her life, really, she saw a sunset and realized that it was one, and was beautiful, and that God made it, and that he made it for her as much as for any one else. The day was cold, and as she started away from Ruth's she could see the great glowing disk of the sun just slipping down behind the long stretch of bare young trees which etched themselves against the sky for a mile or two away upon the horizon at her right. She watched the sun drop and the fire-red glory flame up and over the horizon, and then catching the bits of clouds, turn them from amber to gold, from violet to purple, from rose to the loveliest blush pink, and all set out by the fine lines of the delicate fringe of trees. She saw for the first time the shade of blue on the distant hills, and wondered that colors had existed before for her merely in dress goods and ribbons. She felt uplifted and happier, and then she wondered again how she should answer that last question of Miss Benedict's, for she had promised to bring her an answer the next time she came.

Her mother looked at her curiously and asked for the new dress, and when she found it was not yet completed said: "Humph! Just as I s'posed. You can't expect two young girls to get together and bone right down to work. You've dawdled half your time away, I suppose. I should think two people with two good pairs of hands and nothin' in the wide world to do from early mornin' to dusk at night, could have got one dress done and hung up if they was smart and knew what they was about. What's that you've got? A book? Well, you just tell your Miss Benedic' that I don't thank her for lending you any more books. I'm about crazy now with your everlastin' readin'. For pity sake, don't set down now to read! Here, take off your sack and dish up supper. When is your dress to get done? That's what I should like to know."

The sharp words brought back the disagreeable expression to Ellen Amelia's face, and made her wish to return to the lovely home where the gate of so many new worlds had seemed to open to her that day, and to make her feel that she could almost be willing to try to live an ideal

life even in her own home unchanged. She
laid down the new books with a sigh, and went
to do her mother's bidding. And she is not the
first one who has found life, when one descends
from a mountain, rather tame and spiritless.
Nevertheless is it not a good thing, and a thing
to be desired, to have been upon the mountain?

When the work was out of the way Ellen
Amelia settled herself with great zest to the
reading of her new books, and for a solid half-
hour she applied herself with all her might to
gain an interest in what she was reading. It
was all very wonderful reading, but she seemed
not to understand quite so well as when Miss
Benedict had read it aloud to her, and besides
there was so much to be thought about that one
could not go far at once. It did not hold the
interest of the untrained reader half so well as
did "Cyril Athol's Grief," and in despair she
got out her paper and read over a chapter of
that. There seemed, however, to have come a
staleness over this delightful story since she last
read it two days ago. She put it away in disgust and went to bed, wondering what was
worth while in life anyway, and lay awake a
long time to think over that last serious question. Did she belong to Jesus? She had
always felt a great reverence and awe for him,
but, after serious thinking, she decided that she

did not belong to him, nor love him. She was more afraid of him than anything else. Well, if that was so, whom did she belong to? She shuddered at this thought and tried to turn over and go to sleep, but it would not go away. Altogether Ellen Amelia was glad when morning came and she could get up and do something. Thinking was hard work—unless it was dreaming. She was to go that afternoon again to work on the dress, and she had promised to answer that question definitely after thinking it over. It seemed strange now to her that she had not been able to say at once whether she belonged to Christ or not. Now she dreaded to tell Miss Benedict the real answer.

The dress was farther on its way than when she left it the night before, for the head dressmaker had been working. Ruth met her gayly with chat about the dress, and Ellen Amelia's trepidation concerning the solemn talk she expected to have, had almost been forgotten when Ruth finally came around to the question again as sweetly and naturally as if she had been asking if Ellen Amelia wished her sleeves large or small.

"And what about my question, Ellen? Did you find out that you belong to Jesus or not?"

After a long pause came Ellen Amelia's slow, hesitating, "No."

"Well, then, dear, I have one more question to ask: *Will* you?"

The young girl did not answer.

"You would, Ellen, if you once knew him. You could not help it. You love beautiful things and he is most beautiful of all. If I mistake not you are very fond of romance. You could not find more of it than in his life. You are a loving-hearted girl. Look how easily you have given me your love and confidence, me an utter stranger."

"Oh, but," said Ellen Amelia, her face all eagerness, "you are so good and lovely, and you were so good to me right away. You made me feel as if you loved me."

"Well, but Ellen, he loves you more than any earthly being ever could. He has been waiting for you to give him your love for long years. He has called you many times."

Joseph Benedict was in his room just around a little turn in the hallway. He often came to his room now to lie on that couch and read some of the interesting books his sister had placed there. He had fallen into the habit of the house, of leaving his door open. It was such a cheery house now that they could not any of them bear to cut one corner of it off for a time from the rest by a closed door unless it was necessary. He was weary from extra heavy work they had been doing in the morning. He heard his sister's voice, low and clear, and could hear the words she was speaking. He knew that Haskins girl was in the sewing room with Ruth and that she was doing her some good turn, but he had paid little attention to what was going on. Now he heard his sister's pleading tones and he could but listen for the answers which came so softly that he could not tell whether they were of assent or not. It was strange to him that he should care to have Ellen Amelia Haskins say or do anything, but he really felt quite out of patience with her for not consenting to what his sister put before her. It seemed to him a natural thing that she should do so. As to applying the words to himself just then it never occurred to him. He was interested to have Ruth satisfied, and to have that troubled note dropped from her voice. He went off into meditation of what Ruth was, and all that she had done for them since she came into their home. Pretty soon he heard her voice again as clear as before.

"I couldn't live without Jesus Christ, Ellen," she was saying. "He is my very dearest, most intimate friend. He would be just such a friend to you. You can ask him about everything. You can talk to him about everything, and be sure of his sympathy, and sometimes when I come to the hard places in my life it has seemed to me I could almost hear his voice telling me what to do. I wish you would take him for your friend. It is very easy. I want everybody I love to know him."

Joseph did not hear any more that afternoon. Sally came up for some direction and interrupted the conversation, and when she went down she closed the sewing-room door, so he did not know the result of the talk. He lay there wondering, trying to imagine what the Haskins girl would answer, trying vainly to make an answer that he felt would satisfy Ruth. Once he thought of his sister's last sentence, "I want everybody I love to know him," and wondered vaguely if she ever wanted it for him, and felt sure if she asked him some such question he would at least try to frame such an answer as would keep her from being troubled about him. What the answer might involve otherwise than the mere giving of it he did not stop to ask. It was enough that Ruth wanted it.

Several times that evening he found himself almost on the point of asking Ruth how that talk of hers with that stubborn Haskins girl came out, and then he would remember suddenly what had been the subject of the conversation and would stop and look embarrassed. He saw too a troubled look in Ruth's eyes, and

rightly guessed she was thinking of the young
girl, and was troubled over some unmade decision. Of course Joseph had understood in a
vague way that Ruth was trying to persuade
Ellen Amelia to become a Christian. He had
heard sermons enough to understand the language. But he supposed in a general way that
there must be some special need for this urgency
in the case of Miss Haskins. She must be under
some great temptation or danger and Ruth was
trying, as her Sunday-school teacher, to guard
her against it. He knew nothing whatever of
personal religion himself and cared less, but he
was willing to try to help a young girl, especially if his sister's desire was in that direction.
He would sooner have bitten off his tongue than
speak to Ruth on such a subject; he was not
familiar enough with her for it, but he made up
his mind that if he ever had a chance to shield
that Haskins girl and persuade her to give up
any dangerous amusement, or whatever it was
that Ruth saw she was in peril from, he would
do it.

It was not unlike him then, after such thought,
to follow his impulse the next evening when he
met her returning from his sister's as it was
growing dark, and carrying a large package, to
turn and taking the bundle from her, to walk
back to the village with her. Ellen Amelia was

utterly astonished. Joseph was not the kind of
young man who had shown himself fond of
offering attentions to young girls, and what
little attention he had bestowed had never come
in her direction. Her delight at having so unexpected an escort caused her to be a little silly.
There were so many stories during last year's
serials about young men who had suddenly developed a liking for a lady that it .was impossible not to remember some of them now. She
proceeded to giggle a good deal and make a few
flat remarks about the moon. Perhaps she could
not have chosen a topic more suited to disgust Joseph had his mind been wholly occupied
with what she was saying. But the evening before he and his brother and sister had been reading together a wonderful poem about the moonlight, and they had discussed it at length. His
memory was full of magnificent phrases which
his rapidly awakening intellect was beginning
to appreciate, and the contrast must have been
painful. Perhaps her remarks on the moonlight
may have hastened his purpose in what he had
to say. Certainly a wiser than himself was
guiding his words, for he meditated not on what
he said, and he, who knew not Christ, was bearing a message for him that night.

"Miss Ellen," he began ; he remembered hearing his sister call her that and it pleased him as

being a dignified way to address her. He had
no wish to make a comrade of her except in so
far as it was necessary in order to accomplish
his purpose, which then was to please his sister
and help her gain her point with Ellen Amelia.
"Miss Ellen, my sister is very much troubled
about you. I happened to overhear a few words
of what she said to you yesterday, and I can
see by her face she feels pretty bad that you
won't do as she wants you to." He began to
hesitate for words now. Just what was it he was
going to ask her to do, and how did people ask
such things of others? He tried to remember
some of his sister's overheard phrases, but they
had nearly all escaped. "She told you it wasn't
hard to do," he went on blindly; "and it seems
to me you might be willing to do it." He
stopped. He wanted to tell her that she ought
to be ashamed of herself to make such a girl as
his sister feel badly about anything in the
world ; that she wasn't worth speaking of in the
same day with her, and a few like sentences;
but they did not sound entirely polite and he
was trying to be polite these days to please his
sister. Besides, if he said such things he would
fail of his purpose.

But Ellen Amelia was struck dumb with
amazement. Could this be Joseph Benedict,
talking religion to her? What in the world

had come over him? Then her words came to her.

"Why don't you do it yourself, Joe Benedict, if you think it's so easy? She thinks a heap sight more about your being a Christian than she ever did about me. And she is praying and praying for you, I know, for she told me she had some 'very specials' that she prayed for every little while all day. I knew straight-off you and Dave was them. If I was you with her right there in the house with me all the time, I'd do it. You better not talk to me; you don't know how hard it would be for me, nor how bad I want to do it either."

"Me!" said Joseph, stopping short in the moonlit road and looking down at the girl. "Me!"

The new dress in the crackly paper under Joseph Benedict's arm was forgotten. Ellen Amelia's eyes were full of tears, and Ellen Amelia Haskins was not a girl who easily cried "before folks." Joseph saw the tears and felt sorry for her. There was something pleasant as well as astonishing in the message that had been brought to his soul.

"Why of course, you. I guess if it's for me it's for you too. We've both been taught well enough to know that, haven't we? If you heard what she said yesterday you know that it is for you too. He died for you all alone by yourself, just the same as he died for me all alone by myself. You've got a call to answer for as well as I."

Joseph was honest. He did not feel that he could try to persuade any one to do a thing he was not willing to do himself. It wouldn't be fair. He had always been that way. If he wanted to play a prank with a pin on another boy, he would first try it himself to see if he could bear it; then he would get his fun out of the other boy. Then he felt he had a right to it. He turned to walk on, but he thought of Ruth again, and something too in the miserable little longing face of Ellen Amelia touched him. He looked down at her again.

"I'll tell you what it is, Miss Ellen," he said gravely and slowly, as if he were doing something very hard which he didn't know how to do and yet which he meant to do to the best of his ability, "we'll make a bargain. We won't either of us disappoint her. If you'll do it, I will. I don't know a thing about the business, but I'm willing to learn, if you will. I'll agree to do my best at it."

"All right," said Ellen Amelia after a pause; "I'll do it."

And then they went home.

Joseph, as he walked back to the farm and

looked up to the clear face of the moon, wondered what he had done and how he was going
to keep his promise.   And the Lord was preparing ways all about him for his feet that he knew
not of.

CHAPTER XV

LOUISE CLIFTON stood by the front window of the parsonage, looking out, a discontented curl on her lip. It was plain that she did not like Summerton.

"Mamma, I'm sure I don't see why you ever consented to come here," she said for the fortieth time. "It is the dullest, stupidest old place I ever heard of. You are just burying me. Where shall I have any society I'd like to know? You needn't think I'm going to fall in love with that paragon of a Miss Benedict of Rob's. He is ridiculous. He always was. If we had known he had such an admiration here we needn't have moved heaven and earth and spoiled all our own plans to come to this old hole and make a home for him. If he keeps on like this he will soon have one without our assistance."

"Louise!" said her mother severely. She was a quiet, sad little woman with a white, pensive, refined face. Her daughter Louise had always been too much for her. She had never quite understood her.

"Well, mamma, indeed I can't help it. I wonder what you would have done shut up in

such a place as this at my time of life. You
were one of the belles of New York society.
Why, there won't be a man worth looking at in
this place."

"Louise!" said her mother again in distress.
"You shock me! Are you reduced to the state
that there is nothing worth living for in the
world without a young man? It strikes me that
that is a very bold and immodest way of talking
for a young girl. If your father were here to hear
you say such a thing as that I don't know what
he would do."

"Well now, mamma, I didn't mean anything
so terrible. I only meant that there isn't much
fun in the world without a young man, at least
for a girl like me. You would lift up your
hands in horror at the thought of my going anywhere without an escort. I can't go skating—I
suppose they will condescend to have that much
like the rest of the world in this horrid place.
You know you wouldn't let me go skating alone,
or sledding. As for parties and evening entertain-
ments, it isn't likely there will be any of those,
so you need not worry in that line. But really,
it will be too stupid for anything."

"Daughter, you talk as if you cared for nothing but parties and the like. Have you forgotten your brother? He surely will be all the
escort you will need."

Louise laughed a clear, mocking laugh. "Rob! Fancy Rob, the dignified minister that he has become, going skating with his sister! Why, I presume that paragon of his doesn't believe in skating. I really never heard him say, but I suppose she doesn't from some remarks I've heard him make about her. Mother, you don't know it, but Rob has become as stupid as Summerton. He doesn't believe in doing this, and he thinks that is wicked, until I'm sick of talking to him. I tried to coax him to take me in town next Saturday to the *matinée*, and don't you believe he told me he did not go to *matinées* any more, that he felt there was a great deal of harm done to young people by them and he hoped I would give them up; and he furthermore informed me that if I would like to look into the subject he had several books there I might have to study it up and he would help me. He handed one to me, and it was called ' Plain Talks About the Theatre,' and had 'Ruth Benedict' written in a pretty little hand across the top; so you see I am not so far wrong in thinking he got all his ideas from her."

"Louise, I must insist that you do not speak so disrespectfully of your brother. Remember his holy office, if you have no regard for him. He doubtless borrowed the book you speak of from Miss Benedict; but as to his ideas on the subject

of theatre-going, he changed them long ago,
just about the time of that summer he spent at
the seaside, you remember. I know he told me
at the time, and I thought it was very fitting for
a man who was to be a clergyman to feel as he
felt. I was highly gratified and so was your
father. Of course it was not necessary for you
to be guided by your brother's views so long as
you were living in New York and were in your
own society and your father's home; but remember that you are under your brother's roof
now and a part of his family, and some deference
is due to his views. In his position he could not
well afford to feel otherwise than he does. I
trust that you will not bring your personal
views out for the hearing of other people. It
might hurt your brother seriously."

"Indeed, mamma, I have no idea of being
muzzled. I did not want to come here at all,
and did all I could to prevent it. Rob would
have it, and now he may take the consequences.
I shall not try to make myself agreeable to his
churchful of country boors," and Louise made
her pretty face into a grotesque twist and pirou-
etted away from the window, returning just in
time to look down and meet the gaze of a very
stylish young man who was very evidently a college man visiting his native town on a vacation.
There was something so patronizing in his

air, and his very expression said, "You poor
benighted people, here, see! I honor you with
my benign presence. Be glad that you see me,
for I shall soon be gone from this place again.
I would not stay here if it could be helped, but
as my parents will live here on account of my
father's business interests, I cannot help treading your streets for a little time ; but I despise
you all. You, of course, are proud of me, as
you should be." This was Alonzo Brummel.
He was loud-voiced, self-assertive, long-haired,
walked with the latest English hobble and wore
the latest style in baggy overcoat, patent leather
shoes, with his trousers turned up, and with
stick and tall hat. He stared up at the parsonage window with an undeniably impudent stare,
as much as to say, "Well! I declare! A really
pretty girl in Summerton, and in the parsonage
too! Who in the world can she be?"

And Louise, having much the same feeling
concerning Summerton and its inhabitants and
being fully as astonished to see a well-dressed
young man as he had been to see a pretty girl, I
am afraid stared back for a moment. Then she
dropped her eyes and a pretty flush spread over
her cheek as she turned quickly from the window and began playing the piano furiously that
her mother might not ask the occasion of her
confusion.

However, it was not long before Alonzo Brummel contrived to be introduced to Louise Clifton. He was at home for his Thanksgiving vacation, and by virtue of some petty excuse had managed to have it begin four days earlier than most of the other students, for he was "lazing" through college with as little trouble to himself as possible, and trying to get away with as much money as he could before the time came for him to earn it. His father was a hard-working man, proud of his children and very generous to them, and he looked upon this son as perfection.

The fact that a young man of fashionable appearance had come upon the scene somewhat reconciled Louise Clifton to her present position, at least until after Thanksgiving. She consented to be quite gracious toward Ruth Benedict, and went with her brother to return Ruth's call, which had been made one day when Louise was out with her brother on a long ride.

But when she saw the lovely home and the sweet girl herself, and found that Ruth was, presumably, rich and certainly charming in every way, her impulsive nature turned straight about and fell in love with her at once. She quite tortured her brother with her expressions of affection all the way home and asked him some pointed questions concerning his friendship for Ruth which he did not care at all to answer.

"Mamma, she's lovely!" she said, bursting into the room where her mother sat, on her return from this visit. "I was entirely mistaken. It was all owing to the blue glasses Rob will look at every one through that I thought her such a poke. She has a beautiful home. It is really just a paradise of good taste and artistic ability. I never saw anything so pretty in my life. She and I will be just cronies. And just fancy, mamma, she rides a wheel! I thought she was too straightlaced to live, from what Rob said. She is to ride with me to-morrow, if the weather continues good. I'm just dying to meet those two brothers of hers. They say she has given up a lovely home and lots of friends where she has always lived just to come here and civilize them. I think I will help her. Rob is always at me to do some missionary work, but I don't fancy dirty-faced little girls with sticky fingers always bringing you bunches of dandelions and expecting you to kiss them and get dandelion milk over your new gray kid gloves. I shall never forget the only Sunday I ever tried at the mission in New York, and I don't want to do anything like it again. But this would be perfectly lovely—two young men. Miss Brummel said they were real nice fellows. I could help her I'm sure. I suppose she wants to get them taught manners and be so that they can go

into society. I should enjoy it. They wouldn't
be like little mission-school girls."

"No, they would hardly bring you wilted
dandelions nor expect you to kiss them," said
her brother, who had been listening with increasing disgust and anger to his sister's gushing
words. "Mother, I wish you would try to make
Louise understand that such talk is offensive in
the extreme from a young woman. I fancy there
will be no danger of her undertaking a mission
with either David or Joseph Benedict when she
has once seen them. They will be much more
likely to look upon her as a foolish girl than as
a helper if she talks in as silly a vein as she has
been talking this afternoon." The minister's
nerves had been tried to their utmost by his
sister's flippancy. "And, by the way, mother,"
he went on, "young Brummel is no fit companion for Louise. I don't like his look, and wish
she would keep away from him."

Then the minister settled to his evening paper, and mother and daughter gave one another
a frightened, rather guilty glance, as Louise left
the room. The mother spent a sleepless night
afterward, wondering if she had done wrong to
consent to her daughter's plans, and saying over
and over again to herself, "It is too late to
change anything now, and there will not be any
harm done if he does not know."

The fact about which she was worrying was this : Alonzo Brummel had not been slow in following up his acquaintance with Louise Clifton. He was to be at home not much more than a week, and he meant to have all the fun out of it he could, in that dull town. His sister Georgiana was bribed to assist him, and they had called back and forth several times and planned a walk and a ride. It had also come about that Miss Louise had mentioned her disappointment with regard to the *matinée* to be held in the city about forty miles distant the day before Thanksgiving. Young Brummel had at once taken up with this and planned a party consisting of his sister and himself and Miss Clifton to attend that *matinée*. It fell in exactly with his ideas of a good time. He said the play was a " jolly " one and " no end of fun." Louise, however, having been brought up with strict ideas with regard to chaperones, had insisted that her mother should be one of the party. After much persuasion Mrs. Clifton had consented to accompany them. She did it fearfully and with many compunctions, for she knew her son would object most seriously ; but she insisted that it should be kept strictly a secret, telling Louise to explain to the Brummels that her son's position made him feel that he would rather not have his family attend such places of amusement. She felt herself very lenient toward such things. Then too Louise must have some amusement. Robert could not expect her to give up all her girlhood. So she had arranged to go with Louise to the city, ostensibly to do some shopping, and told her son that they would not return until the late train. Of course the minister had no suspicions, and would not have pried into his mother's affairs if he had.

Meantime the friendship between Ruth Benedict and Louise Clifton was progressing. The minister had said in a low, troubled tone during one of the few talks he had with Ruth alone, "My sister needs your help, Miss Benedict. She is not a Christian. You will understand her, I feel sure, and see just what she needs," and then he had gone on his way, and Ruth had studied the bright pretty young girl and understood.

They took their bicycle ride together. As they passed the Brummel home Alonzo was lounging in the front window smoking and reading. He sat up very straight and bowed to Louise, but stared interestedly at Ruth. He had not seen her before. He decided that her style was ahead of Miss Clifton's and he would try to get acquainted with her at once. She might be more worth while than the minister's sister. She was well enough for fun, but one liked a variety. Of course he had heard of Ruth Bene-

dict, but had paid little attention to the accounts
of her till now.

It was also new to him that Miss Clifton rode
a wheel. He would have one for himself sent
up from the city immediately, as his own was at
college, he not having thought it worth while to
bring it home with him for so short a time. He
would have a ride with Miss Clifton and perhaps
with the other girl as well.

Summerton stared as it rushed to its doors and
windows to behold the minister's sister and the
new Benedict girl flying by. They had supposed that the Benedict girl had had lesson
enough in the spraining of her ankle never to
mount the diabolical machine she called a bicycle again, but here she was sitting up as straight
and smiling and composed as could be. Mother
Haskins, as she looked, sniffed, in spite of the
beautiful new dress which hung upstairs in
Ellen Amelia's closet ; yes and in spite of the
fact that this strange benefactress had evolved
a dainty little hat of blue serge with rolled,
stitched brim, and soft crown, and no expense
except two cheap black wings. It not only
was the most becoming and plainest, neatest hat
Ellen Amelia ever had, besides being exceedingly stylish (which latter point Mother Haskins
did not know), but also saved the expense and
trouble of getting Ellen Amelia something new

for her head, or arguing her into wearing the old last winter's one. Mother Haskins was very much afraid that Ellen Amelia's next ambition would be a bicycle. As for the minister's sister, Mrs. Haskins was scandalized. The minister ought to be told at once, and she would surely make it her business to do so were it not for the darning that must be finished that afternoon. Besides, she dreaded making the first call on the minister's grand little mother. So she retired to her darning, predicting dire trouble for the two innocent riders before the afternoon was over, and was surprised and truly sorry to see them return perhaps two hours later with smiling rosy faces, looking as if they had but just started out.

It was that very evening that Alonzo Brummel, upon pretext of a very rusty acquaintance with Joseph Benedict and some business of questionable importance with David, called at the Benedict farm. He received his introduction to Ruth and before the evening was over endeavored to make her acquaintance more intimately, but found it was not an easy thing to do. Ruth, though she was usually sunny and bright and always on the lookout for winning people for the sake of the good it might do, had a great dislike for a certain class of young men with a bold stare and an ease before strangers which sat

upon their youthful shoulders all too easily.
Alonzo Brummel was one of these. He made
her feel uncomfortable, as if in the presence of
something ugly, she did not exactly know why.
She was not wise enough in the world to understand that the bold stare he gave at a pretty girl
told more than she could read of his knowledge
of the world and its evils. She only knew she
felt uncomfortable and wished to get away from
him. Therefore she declined rather frigidly
when he proposed a bicycle ride in her company,
saying she had other duties at the time he
named, and when he proposed another time she
said firmly that he must excuse her.

David was exceedingly glad of his sister's dis-
cernment. He did not like young Brummel.
Though he had been shut up in this small town
all his life, with only occasional visits to the
neighboring city, still he knew the signs of the
hard young face better than some who have been
among wickedness always. Besides, the city is
not the only place where wickedness lurks in
hidden corners, and a young man with eyes and
a pure heart cannot go through any corner of
the world without seeing the signs of sin.

Alonzo Brummel went home trying to make
up his mind whether it would be worth his
while to pretend to be very religious during the
few days left him of his vacation, in order to

please this rather extraordinary Benedict girl, and finally decided it would be much easier just to have a good time with merry little Louise Clifton. She was much more to his mind after all.

Ruth at that moment on her knees was adding Louise Clifton to her list of those she prayed for most earnestly. As she prayed she remembered the bow between the girl and the young man that afternoon and the few words the gay young girl had said about him, and she added a petition that Louise might be delivered from any danger that might come to her through Alonzo Brummel.

CHAPTER XVI

LOUISE CLIFTON was taking lunch with Ruth Benedict. It had been no part of Ruth's plan to have her brothers come in contact with her new friend any more than necessary, for she did not think that Louise would be a help in influencing them for good. There were girls she could think of who would help wonderfully and whom she felt sure they would like, but Louise was like a dangerous bit of some combustible material. Ruth never knew what she would do next. There was a bright side, and a sweet, lovable side, as well as a gay one, to her character. To Ruth she had shown this principally, though there had been a glimmer now and then of daring; but it remained for David Benedict to bring out a new phase of her disposition.

David and Joseph were to be away all day, as was often the case when they had some business connected with the sale of cattle in some village not far away. Ruth usually arranged to have some one with her on these days to lunch, for she did not wish to bring her outside missionary work in to spoil their home life unless she felt the guests were such as would be pleasant to her brothers. So Louise had been invited for Tuesday. The young men had both started away from the house early, as they had expected to do, David to West Winterton and Joseph in the opposite direction. Louise arrived at the hour appointed and the two girls took a ride together returning home about lunch time, where to her surprise Ruth found her brother David. He had been disappointed in seeing the man with whom he was to transact his business, he having been called away suddenly by the illness of a relative, and thus David came home earlier. Ruth felt a little troubled. She feared lest her brother might not enjoy having this gay, rather frivolous, and certainly very stylish young woman sitting opposite to him at the table. If David should freeze up and be stiff and Louise should take a turn of trying to shock him, Ruth felt that there would be more harm done than any good her endeavors to help Louise might have done. Indeed she had felt rather discouraged about the minister's sister since their morning spent together. Louise, with her impulsive girl-nature had fallen very much in love with Ruth, and gushed a great deal over her, but still she laughed at anything grave she might try to say, and persisted in making herself out to be shockingly wicked, in a bright interesting kind of

way. She would talk of her brother in a mocking strain, laughing at his country church and
making merry over the people. Ruth dreaded
to have David hear her talk so. What would
he think of the minister's religion if it could
touch his own sister no further than to provoke
fun? She flew to her refuge and sent up a petition for help and then remembered that the Lord
was guiding and that no harm could come where
he was and tried not to worry any more about
it. So David was introduced to Louise Clifton
and sat down in the library for a few minutes
talk before lunch, and behold!

Louise shone forth in a new light. Her face
was as full of expression as a kaleidoscope. In
spite of her silly talk about helping those Benedict boys she had meant what she said, and was
truly interested in doing anything to elevate
them. It became doubly interesting also when
she found this one so tall and really handsome.
He could talk so well too, and when he smiled,
that grave face of his and those great deep blue
eyes lit up as if a hidden lamp were suddenly
lighted behind them and shone through his
whole face. He was a new kind of young man
to Louise, and she could not help liking him.
And when Louise Clifton liked any one she
could always win a liking for herself. It was
not deceit, nor theatricals which caused her to

so change her behavior. It was perhaps an instinctive consciousness of what would please the one with whom she was talking, and the natural impulse of kindness. She did not mean to act a part. Perhaps, if the truth might be known, David appealed to the highest and best that there was in her nature and she immediately brought it forth. Certainly no girl could have been sweeter or shyer or more modest than was Louise Clifton. She did not throw herself at the young man and make him take notice of her, neither did she patronize him and try to make talk. She simply and pleasantly asked him questions about Summerton and answered his. She told one or two incidents that had occurred during their ride, and when she looked up and caught his eye her face flushed a pretty shy pink and she looked down again as though she had been making herself too prominent. David thought her truly the brightest, prettiest, sweetest bit of humanity, always barring his sister, he had ever looked upon, and Louise found herself wondering in what way she could possibly help this young man. He seemed to be at ease in talking with a stranger, and not to murder the English language when he spoke. He certainly could not be very wicked, for his mouth had too clean a cut and firm a look for that—though it must be confessed Louise was

hardly as yet a good judge of morality in a man ;
if he wore faultless clothes and could dance and
wait upon her gracefully, it was all she asked as
yet.

Her own moral and intellectual judgment had
hardly been as well developed as her brother's, nor as much so as it would have been had
her father lived.   But there was something new
to her, an independent dignity, in David, and
she was interested.   She would certainly do all
in her power to help him if there was anything
she could do, she told herself ; and meantime
she apparently could not seem other than simple and sweet and childlike in his presence, perhaps because David himself was so simply natural
and frank and in earnest in all he did and said.
After lunch he lingered in the house for nearly
an hour and let Miss Clifton show him about a
laughable little game she had brought over with
her, and Ruth watched her brother in surprise
mingled with a wonder as to what the outcome
was to be of this new acquaintance.   Could it
be possible that these two, whom she had thought
so opposite to one another in everything, were
meant to help each other?   Truly the ways of
God were past finding out, but she would wait
and trust him, for he knew the way he took and
she was walking with him.

Louise liked to provoke that grave face to a

smile. It was something new to watch the play of light that came across David's face, and when he at last got up and said he must go to his work, she turned to Ruth with her old, saucy smile again and said : "Your brother is just as nice in his way as you are in yours. Now let's have that music." And Ruth could never guess from her actions whether her guest regretted her brother's going or not. So much had Louise Clifton's home training been worth. Ruth could but admire her for the frank, pleasant way in which she spoke about her brother, and then dropped the subject. There was nothing of the foolishness in her speech now that there had been concerning Alonzo Brummel. Nevertheless Ruth decided that she would not take the responsibility yet of actually planning to bring these two together again. If the Lord, who was guiding, saw this best he would do it, and he might not want them together again. Ruth could not see the way clear before her, and therefore she did not have to act. It was not long however before her trust was rewarded with being allowed to see something of God's plan and understand a little of the various influences that had been at work.

Louise Clifton leaned back in the car and breathed a sigh of relief. She and her mother

were off to the city for their day of shopping,
and nothing had been discovered by her brother.
She had been almost certain something would
turn up to spoil her pleasure. Young Mr. Brummel and his sister were to come on the noon
train and meet them at an appointed place.
Louise reflected with joy that she was to have
one day of doing as she pleased, and she chattered pleasantly to her mother and tried to
smooth the anxious look from her face. Mrs.
Clifton was not quite sure that she was doing
altogether as her dead husband would have liked
her to do. She did not rouse easily from her
worried little thoughts, and Louise at last began
to study the passengers. There was a man sitting two seats up the aisle across from her with
his face turned to the window. The back of his
head was handsome, and she could not help admiring it as her eyes came back several times to
his broad shoulders and heavy head of hair that
looked like a sealskin coat, she told herself. By
and by he turned his face a little, and then
she saw that it was David Benedict. She was
pleasantly surprised, and wished he would come
and occupy the seat in front of them, and as
they left the car at the city station she tried to
catch his eye and bow, but David was intent on
his own business and apparently did not see
them.

Louise was disappointed that Mr. Benedict had not seen her. He had somehow given her a feeling that he looked up to her as a being far superior to himself, for whom he felt a sort of reverence. This feeling was pleasant to Louise. Other men had admired her and told her so; but none had ever given her the impression that they thought of her as spiritually above them. She had been more a merry companion to others, and was as willing to join in any wild prank as they had been. Mr. Benedict had taken it for granted that a woman who was beautiful, was good and above anything wrong or untruthful or impure. Louise thought she would always like to have him keep this feeling for her. It gave her a respect for herself which she had never felt before, and she felt she would try a little, just a little, to live up to this ideal that she seemed to understand David Benedict had for women. His sister had been so, and of course he saw no reason why she should not prove so also. Louise was pleased.

There was another Summerton traveler that morning in the car. He sat directly behind Mrs. Clifton and her daughter, and he had a set, protruding chin and heavy, uncomfortable eyebrows of grizzled gray. He looked the minister's mother and sister over carefully and severely, shaking his head once and gazing gloom-

ily out of the window. Deacon Chatterton did
not feel particularly pleasant this morning.
Some investments out West were in doubtful
condition, and he was going to town to get a
lawyer to look them up. He did not approve of
a minister having a mother and sister who looked
so gay and fashionable. It showed a spiritual
lack in the minister somewhere.

Meantime at home various things were going
on.

When Ellen Amelia Haskins had entered
church the first Sunday after her new blue serge
was completed, she created more of a sensation
than any stranger that had yet visited Summerton. To have strangers come to church dressed
finely and looking pretty was of course an interesting thing and one to be looked at and remarked upon; but to have one of their own number, who had grown up from babyhood in their
midst, and who had not even been away for a
visit of a few weeks,—nor what was more as-
tounding, even been to the dressmaker, in the
knowledge of any one present,—suddenly appear
before their astonished eyes in gown and bonnet
of faultless style and becomingness undreamed
of, and with her hair arranged in a way unknown to Summerton maidens save as they had
occasionally observed it in their shopping visits
to the city, was a thing not to be gotten over

easily. She seemed to move in a more graceful way, and her whole face took on a really pretty look.

"My land!" whispered Eliza Barnes to Mrs. Deacon Chatterton, with whom she happened to be sitting; "who ever dreamed she could be so pretty!"

"Humph!" said Mrs. Chatterton, as she ob-served the advent of Ellen Amelia with disapproval; "beauty that can be put on and took off ain't much beauty to my mind," and she severely studied the hymn book the remainder of the morning, and rigidly refrained from encouraging Ellen Amelia in her pride by looking once more in the direction of the Haskins pew.

The two young men with lowering brows and thick protruding lips back by the door, who came to church now because there was nothing better to do, looked up with interest. Ellen Amelia had not been an admiration of theirs heretofore, but dressed in this way she seemed to have suddenly grown up and to be worth while. The Brower boys were always looking out for a new girl, and when they had found her she usually regretted it if she allowed their coarse charms to attract her attention. Heretofore Ellen Amelia had never been in danger through them. They preferred pretty girls, and there were plenty of them throughout the

country who were glad of their acquaintance,
for were they not heirs of a great farm and an
estate of dimensions that varied according to the
imagination of the speaker? Ed nudged Bill,
and Bill glowered back at Ed, and nodded and
whispered, " She's great! How'd she do it?"
and after church, when they lingered as was
their wont, by the door and watched the out-
comers, they sauntered along toward her home
by her side, and the poor, silly girl's heart beat
high with wild excitement. She had never had
the like happen to her before. She knew they
were rather wild, to be sure, but they also had the
name of being worldly wise, and they were young
men and well-built, and when they tried to
please, not altogether bad-looking. Remember,
Ellen Amelia's head was full of stories and her
mind was used to idealizing everybody—except
perhaps her own immediate home circle, with
whom she was forced by circumstances to come
in constant contact. Ellen Amelia minced along
between Bill and Ed Brower and cast sidelong
glances to see if the other girls saw her, and
wondered tremblingly what mother would think
if she knew, and whether father would disapprove. And then they almost took her breath
away by a proposition. She was feeling herself
a Cinderella enough already with her new gown
and two princes, but with a ball added her head

was completely turned, and so at her father's
gate she giggled out a sort of promise, as much
of a promise as she dared make, and went in
blindly to sit down and think what kind of a
wild delightful whirl the world had gotten into.
And she forgot completely that she had promised
but three days before to try to love and serve
the Lord Jesus Christ with all her heart and soul
and strength and to make him the first consideration of her life.

When Christians go to sleep then the devil
thinks he may sleep also, or go awhile to other
more important places perhaps; but when some
Christian gets awake and goes to praying, and
one and another and another are stirred by this
one's prayers to kneel, then does the devil hasten
back and send a good force of his emissaries to
the front.   There is no time so easy as a young
Christian's start to turn him in another direction.
If you can spoil everything for him then you
have him with no more trouble.   And so the
devil, seeing that some good live Christian
workers had come to Summerton, and that
things in the sleepy old church were waking up,
and some souls were asking the way to light,
concluded to have a ball.   A ball was an extraordinary thing in Summerton.   People could
not remember when there had been such a thing
before.   It happened that Thanksgiving Day was

the tenth or fiftieth or hundredth anniversary—
it matters little which—of something or other of
mild importance in the town, and what more
fitting than at such a season there should be a
celebration, and what better for a celebration
than a ball? And because it was such a strange,
new thing for Summerton, and because it was
in commemoration of some sacred little event,
people who in general utterly disapproved of
dancing and frowned upon worldly amusements
with more than usual vigor, condoned the offense
of the committee of arrangements, and even
consented to lend their presence for a time. It
was more to them as if they were playing at
having a ball than as if they were to have a real
one. Of course everybody in the town did not
feel in this way, and the whole matter was kept
as quiet as possible so that not until two or
three days before Thanksgiving did the story
leak out and get itself talked about. The invita-
tions had been in the hands of a few, and had
been given quietly, at first to those they were
sure of, and afterward where they had occasioned
much discussion and some bitter words and
bitterer tears on the part of strict parents and
greatly longing children. It is needless to say
that the Brower boys had it in their power to
invite whom they would. And thus poor Ellen
Amelia met her first great temptation.

The ball was to be held in a public hall. It had not even the excuse of being strictly private, but then it was to be only village people, no strangers, and what was the harm ?

Ellen Amelia Haskins, on the first Sabbath afternoon after she had promised to give her life to the Lord Jesus Christ, sat herself down to look over her wardrobe, and see what it was possible to construct out of the accumulations of her few years that would answer for a ball dress, and wished for the hundredth time that her good fairy could waft a wand over her beautiful blue serge and change it into a nile-green silk with real point lace trimming and *Maréchal Neil* roses.

CHAPTER XVII

IT was not until the day before Thanksgiving that the minister heard about it and knew that some of the principal members of his church were involved in the arrangements. He sat in troubled silence after the messenger who brought this unpleasant news had departed, and wondered if he should do anything and what he could do. He half wished his mother were at home that he might consult her, and then remembered that his mother would not understand and would have no help to offer. A faint color stole into his cheek as he realized who was the only helper he felt he could find in true sympathy with his feelings in all his church ; for while there were many good and true members who would frown upon the ball, they would one and all censure the ones who had gotten it up and those who would attend it so severely that there would be no use in asking them to help in any way.

Later in the afternoon he found his way to Ruth Benedict's home and inquired for her. She was in the little music room back of the parlor. Joseph had thrown himself down on the easy couch by the piano after lunch and

begged for a song, and she had given him not
only one but many, bright, funny ones, and gay
and sad; and at last as he lay still she ventured
others in a tenderer tone, some old hymns she
loved, one or two which gave the invitation to
Christ in pleading words, "O prodigal child,
come home, come home."

There were tears in Joseph's eyes under those
closely closed lashes, and he dared not open them
lest the tears would show themselves. He did
not understand the feelings that were moving
him these days, new manliness and courage.
He knew that he had accepted that invitation to
come home, and yet he did not feel that he was
farther than on the threshold of the gateway.
He would have liked to ask Ruth something
about the way, and what he should do with his
new resolutions, but he could not think how to
put it, and the courage was utterly lacking to
speak a word of the matter.

When the knocker sounded through the house
Ruth turned softly, and seeing her brother as
she supposed asleep, she quietly drew the heavy
portière behind the lighter one of beads, and
went to meet the visitor. Joseph lay there, not
asleep, but thinking over his life, and trying to
form some idea of the future out of the chaos
he stood in at present. He heard the minister's
low, troubled tones, and knew that he was ask-

ing advice of his sister, and felt that it was fitting
he should do so. Almost unnoticed the thought
passed through his mind that the minister and
his sister were very much alike in a good many
ways, and ought to enjoy one another's company;
and he was glad that Robert Clifton had come
there to live to make a pleasant friend for Ruth,
as well as for the rest of them. But suddenly
his wandering thoughts stopped, and he listened
intently to what the minister was saying.

"Yes, Miss Benedict, I'm afraid it will reach
a good many of our young people, and hurt them
the more because it seems it is an unusual thing.
You know a new thing always has more influence
than an old one. If they were accustomed to
having dances here we might hope that one
more might not do any especial harm, but some
of the young people who have never tasted the
charms of it before are to have an opportunity
now. I understand that several of our best
families have promised to allow their young
people to attend, and that some have gone so far
as to take a few lessons in dancing in the city in
order that they may appear to advantage on this
occasion. There is one young woman in particular about whom I feel very anxious. She
promised me two weeks ago to think carefully
over the matter of personal religion. I had
hoped she might soon unite with the church.

But now she is to be allowed to attend this ball, and I fear much that it may turn her thoughts in other directions. She is very young and so easily influenced. It is Miss Haskins of whom I speak; and by the way, she is in your Sunday-school class I remember. Perhaps you can do something. I am told that her father cannot say no to any request of hers—he is rather weak in a good many ways I should judge—and that her mother, though strict in such matters usually, has for once been overruled and the girl is to go. Just the mere fact of her going might not be so bad, perhaps, if she were not to be escorted by a low-lived scoundrel who is not fit to be in decent society. Those Brower boys are really much beneath her in every way. I cannot understand what her father can be about to allow it. The poor girl is too young to understand how danger-ous they are."

The minister and Ruth said a good deal more and made some plans for future work, and pos-sible help for some of the young ball-goers, but Joseph heard no more. He was making some plans of his own. Then as the minister took his departure he thanked the earnest hostess gravely and told her, his face illumined with a kind of spiritual light, that he always had occa-sion to thank God for her words whenever he met her. And then their eyes met and these

words which he had intended should sound so
commonplace took on an added meaning, because
his eyes could not keep it secret that they meant
a great deal to him, and Ruth's eyes went down
and her cheeks flushed a little as she tried to
take them in the commonplace way in which he
had spoken, and then after he had gone she
went to her room to think it all over, and make
up her mind why it was that she seemed to feel
so happy over what Mr. Clifton had said more
than over ordinary praise. But she remembered
her brother Joseph soon, and going softly to the
closed *portière* to see if he had awakened, found
him gone. Joseph was in his room making a
toilet for his first call upon a young lady. When
he made up his mind a thing had to be done he
did it right away.

Louise Clifton's plans had progressed very
well. She found all the things at the stores
that she had come in search of, and her mother
had consented to her buying several things she
had set her heart upon. Mr. and Miss Brummel
had met them at the appointed hour, and gone
with them to the appointed high-class restaurant
where they had indulged themselves in all the
indigestibles that Summerton did not produce.
They were now on their way to the opera house.
Georgiana and Mrs. Clifton were ahead. Alonzo

Brummel and Louise lingered behind chatting and stopping to look at a fine display of orchids in a florist's window.   Mrs. Clifton walked rather rapidly.   She felt uncomfortable about this part of the journey, and she wanted to have it over as soon as possible.   Georgiana wished she would not go quite so fast, and suggested once or twice that the others were far behind, but Mrs. Clifton said she wanted to get there and sit down, she was tired.   So they had stood for several minutes waiting in the entrance way when Louise and her escort finally came up the many stone steps.

It was nearly time for the early train to Summerton, and David Benedict was hurrying along the street.   He noticed young Brummel's peculiar jaunty hat ahead of him, and as he rapidly drew nearer he recognized Louise Clifton walking with him.   It gave him an unpleasant sensation as it always did when he saw something pure and white in close proximity to something filthy, but he thought nothing of it except to wonder mildly how they happened both to be here; but then he was here himself, and it was no great wonder if they had happened to meet upon the street in a city so near their homes. However, just as he was passing them they turned across his path and mounted the stone steps. He bowed and looked up quickly to see where it was they were going, and then with a shade

of something like disappointment crossing his
face his eyes met Louise's smiling face, and she
felt almost imperceptibly that she was in danger
of falling from the high eminence where he had
seemed to place her in his esteem. She bowed
and smiled and the color mounted into her cheek
and David was gone. But though she laughed
and talked freely she felt uncomfortable, and
could not forget the look in David's eyes.

Young Brummel had seen her bow, and from
force of habit had lifted his hand to his hat, and
then, looking to see who was the recipient of her
favor, he gave a coarse, familiar nod, and laughed,
asking her how she came to be so intimate with
that clodhopper. Louise's face grew suddenly
pink with indignation. She never could bear
to see injustice done, and she knew in her heart
that David was far superior in every way—unless it might be in the cut of his clothes, which
indeed were not bad—to the young man who
was making fun of him. With a touch of the
hauteur she could sometimes employ to advantage, she told him icily that Mr. Benedict
was the brother of her dearest friend, the loveliest girl in the world. And then young Brummel thought it wise to change the subject. But
somehow Louise's pleasure in the afternoon's
performance was clouded. She criticised the
scenery and the dresses, and did not like the

soprano's voice, and curled her lip over some of
the jokes which Alonzo thought exceedingly
funny and laughed uncontrollably over. She
wondered how he could enjoy it. Indeed the
play itself seemed vapid and uninteresting. She
did not know that she was defiantly trying to
look at it all through David Benedict's eyes, and
prove to herself that if he were here he could not
possibly see anything out of the way in it, while
she saw a great deal that did not please even
herself, now that her eyes were somewhat opened.

Then she began wondering how it was that
David had any ideas about theatre-going at all,
living as he did in the country where there were
no theatres. Why should he have opinions on
the subject? It was absurd. Surely Ruth could
not have had reason or opportunity to speak to
him on the subject. She must have been mistaken in thinking she saw disapproval in his
eyes, and what right had he to disapprove of her
actions, anyway? But indignation with him did
not suit her mood. She was anxious to help
him in some way. She truly wanted to be a
missionary, and had an indistinct idea that while
she was not a Christian herself, nor had any personal interest in the matter, she supposed it was
a very good thing for a young man, and if she
could help him to procure some religion of the
right sort to help him well through the world

and keep him from being wild—which term in her mind had a very dim and misty meaning— she would like to do so. It was certainly annoying to be blocked in her influence at the outset by some notion of his concerning theatre-going. It was also provoking when one had once tasted the joy of being an angel of light to a young man to suddenly see him discover a flaw in his angel. Altogether Louise was cross and a little unreasonable, and when on the journey home, Alonzo Brummel contrived it so that his sister and Mrs. Clifton should sit together and he should be with Louise again, she was very quiet and unresponsive. He had been getting ready all the afternoon and making this opportunity to tell her of the Summerton ball, and ask if she would not like to go just for fun, and "to laugh at the rest," for he had taken it for granted that she felt as superior to the village as he did.

However, when Alonzo Brummel broached the subject of the ball Louise was all attention. It sounded even more like what she was wont to call a "lark" than this trip to the city. Of course her brother would object, but what of that? He might as well learn soon as late that he could not control her movements and that she was not going to walk in a straitlaced fashion just because he was a minister and she had been forced to come and live with him. She felt a

little uncertain about her mother's consent however, for Mrs. Clifton had shown decided signs
of wavering concerning this city trip, and it
would be better not to endanger the ball by
mentioning it to her so soon after the other
escapade. Better let her have time to recover
from her worry and see that no harm came from it.
Besides, Mr. Brummel suggested that she should
spend the evening at their house and they would
all go from there. He represented that his sister would be going. Poor Georgiana served her
brother many a turn that she never knew of during this short vacation. He forgot perhaps to
state that Georgiana could not tread a measure
to music to save her life, and that his mother
was so bitterly opposed to the grand affair getting up at the hall that Georgiana would no
more be allowed to enter its precincts than she
would to take a walk down the broad road to
destruction. Mrs. Brummel had a few stanch
principles which she had inherited with the
"Lives of the Martyrs," and from which she in
nowise allowed herself or her daughter to depart.
She supposed that her son reverenced them also,
and he took care that she should not find out
otherwise.

And so Louise Clifton arranged to spend the
evening with the Brummels, and did not notice
that Georgiana looked rather surprised when,

as they parted, she said : "Well, I shall see you
to-morrow evening," and Alonzo had difficulty
during the remainder of their walk home to in-
vent a suitable reason for her having said this
which should not interfere with his plans.

And while these plans were going on, those
who had been set to watch the walls of Zion
were continuing in prayer, and planning for
warfare with the evil one. Ruth in her own
quiet chamber was trying to remember once again
that the work was God's and not hers, and that he
could make right come from even what seemed
all wrong. She turned over plan after plan.
Should she try, for instance, to have a little impromptu Thanksgiving party of her own?
—have her Sabbath-school class and any others
who were in peculiar danger from the next
evening's entertainment, and invite the minister
and have a delightful time that would outshine
the other's attraction? No, there were objec-
tions to that. It was too late. The young people who were going had all gotten ready by this
time and could not be detained now by a quiet
evening of popcorn and conundrums. Besides,
she could not hope to prolong such an entertainment late enough to save them all from going
to the hall afterward, for that entertainment was
likely to last till the small hours of the morning. She saw ideas in this thought for future

use, but none that would do to carry out now, for the simple reason that none of her guests who needed it would be willing to come to anything she might offer them that night. But Summerton wanted entertaining, it was plain, and if the good of life would not give it them then they were ready to take it from the evil.

David was wondering in his heart why he was so certain that his sister Ruth would not go to that ball nor have anything to do with it. His first intimation of it had been some days before. He had heard the Brower boys talking in the grocery, and he thought he heard his sister's name mentioned, but when he came in sight of them there was no more said. He ground his teeth to think that his sister might be mentioned by such lips as theirs and was thankful that breath of theirs need never reach her ears.

The minister was praying and lingering in prayer for his church. He was young and these were his first people, and he fairly agonized over them, as a mother will with her first child, whenever they were in danger or doing wrong. It hurt his sensitive nature to have them grieve their Saviour. His high-strung temperament was constantly feeling the slights put upon his Master and theirs. Would they never come to Christ and live for him? Must Satan ever have the mastery? He would not give up the work though he could not see his way clear before him ; but he felt sorely discouraged now at the outset. It was the old weary problem so often quoted from Lowell:

Truth forever on the scaffold, Wrong forever on the throne,—
Yet that scaffold sways the future, and behind the dim unknown
Standeth God within the shadow, keeping watch above his own.

CHAPTER XVIII

JOSEPH BENEDICT stood before the Haskins door and knocked as an evening caller knocks. He had never stood there in such capacity before. He had never gone to call upon a young woman before, but all the strangeness of his position was overcome by the solemn errand which he felt he had to perform. He had taken vows upon himself with this girl that they would both try to live a Christian life. Without any instruction in the matter, Joseph understood that a public ball was no place in which to keep such a contract. It is a strange fact that the untutored, un-Christian mind almost always puts down theatre-going, dancing, card-playing, and the like as things unfit for a follower of Jesus. You will find this is especially the case among young men who have been brought up in the country and are familiar with only the crudest kinds of these amusements. Whether they would be refined into thinking differently by coming into constant contact with worldly Christians is a question. But these are by no means all found in the cities. It is true that sometimes such persons, when they become

244

Christians themselves, will be found indulging
in and condoning such amusements ; but usually
before they come to Christ they will criticise
them in one who professes Christianity. Such
people as Joseph will often have higher ideals
for Christians than they have for themselves.

"Is Miss Ellen in?" he asked of the young-
est Haskins, who opened the door and his own
mouth at the same time and at about the same
width. The boy seemed not to understand, and
the question had to be asked again. Then the
boy retreated, leaving the door wide open and
revealing the Haskins sitting room with the family just gathering after supper. "Ma!" called
the boy, "ma, come 'ere!"

"Who is it, and what does he want?" answered a woman's voice.

"It's Joe Ben'dict! He said 'Mi'zellen'!"
said the boy incoherently.

Mother Haskins went curiously to the door to
see what might be the matter.

"Is Miss Ellen in?" asked Joseph with a
bow, as he had seen the minister do when he
came to call on his sister.

"Miss Ellen?" repeated the mother dazedly ;
"oh, you mean Ellenmelya. Yes. She's here.
Did you want to see her?" Mother Haskins
did not quite like the idea of so many young
men coming around her daughter all at once.

She was suspicious, but she supposed he had some message from his sister, and as he did not seem disposed to subject it first to her judgment, she went in search of her daughter.

Ellen Amelia came, looking tired and surprised. She had been working hard all day on a ball dress which was not nile-green silk, but which nevertheless did credit both in fashion and taste to her few recent lessons in dressmaking. She had caught the style from one of Ruth's papers, which she wished with all her heart she dared borrow; but something uneasy in her heart told her it was wiser not to let her teacher know of her intention to go to that ball, and so she had plodded on by herself, and had been disappointed even to tears many times, but had still persevered.

She invited Joseph into the grim and silent parlor, which was as stiff and unwholesome as the Benedict parlor had been before the advent of Ruth, and Joseph looked about and pitied the girl from the depths of his heart because she had no lovely home like his. It was his way to go straight to business, and so without waiting to be seated he began.

"Miss Ellen," he said with the manner an older brother might have used, "I heard you were about on the point of breaking your promise, or leastways of putting yourself in the way of breaking it, and I came around to see about it. You know there's two of us in it, and I take it that it is the duty of each to see that the other does his part."

"What in the world are you gettin' at, Joe Benedict?" asked Ellen Amelia sharply, a troubled feeling beginning to steal over her as she remembered how little thought she had given to the solemn promise made so short a time ago.

"Are you going to that ball in the town hall?"

"Well, what if I am?" said Ellen, her cheeks getting red and her eyes defying him. "I don't see what that's got to do with what you were talking about. What's the harm? All the church folks are going. Why don't you go yourself?"

"I don't go because I don't want to," answered Joseph honestly; "but if I did, I wouldn't after that promise I made. I don't count that as one of the ways to keep such a promise. I don't pretend to know much about this new kind of living we've agreed to try and do, you've had more teaching on the subject than I; but if I know anything, I know that hall to-morrow night won't be a fit place for any young girl, let alone a Christian, and I wish you wouldn't."

There was a little change in Joseph's voice

now, a note of anxiety lest he might fail, the
smallest trifle of a pleading inflection. It touched
the girl's pride and her coquetry at once. She
was pleased and would see how far he would go,
and how much he cared. Not that she meant
to give up the ball now, with that pink tarletan
dress almost done on her bed upstairs, and that
dollar and a quarter paid to the city dancing-
master to teach her a few forbidden steps.

"But I can't help it now, it's too late. I've
promised, Joe, and besides it'll be heaps of fun."

"Then it's true you're goin' with one of those
fellows? I didn't believe that. Ellen Amelia
Haskins, don't you know better than to trust
yourself for one hour with either of those fellows? If you knew half what I know about
them you'd never let them speak to you again."

"Now, Joe Benedict, I never thought you'd go
to slandering other fellows just out of jealousy";
it certainly was very silly and conceited and unwise and really unpardonable in Ellen Amelia
to so forget herself, but she did say it. She
spent many hours of repentance over those few
words afterward and remembered them through
her life with shame, but she said them, and Joseph stood towering above her, wrath and disgust
and pity mingled in his face. He felt that the
girl needed a thorough lesson. He wished it
was not his duty to give it, for that moment he

felt a contempt rising in his heart for the poor
silly girl. He jealous! But she saw what she
had said, and shame began to rise in her face at
sight of his. Then pity came for her and he
suppressed his anger by a mighty effort.

"Now, look here, Miss Ellen," he said, his
voice kind but firm; "you know you didn't
mean to say that. You know that I never asked
you to go to that ball, and wouldn't have, and
that if I had wanted your company there were
other ways to get it than talking about the man
you were going with. That all goes without saying. You wouldn't have said that if you hadn't
been put out. I suppose you want to go, and
you'll be disappointed about it, and all that, but
it really can't be helped. It isn't a proper place
for any good woman to go. I wouldn't let my
sister go there, no, nor go near those two men
either, and isn't it my duty to do all I can to
take care of my sister's friend? You know I
don't care, except for her sake and for the sake
of the promise we both made. If you meant
anything by that you must give up this ball.
Can't you believe me when I tell you it isn't
a fit place for you?"

Something in his masterful tone touched
Ellen Amelia. Something shamed, and something frightened her too. She could not trust
her womanhood in a place of which a man

spoke in this way. She had innate refinement
enough in her nature for that. It may have
been something the same feeling that came to
Louise Clifton when she found that she was in
danger of falling from her spiritual supremacy
over David Benedict. Ellen Amelia said nothing
and the tears came to her eyes. For a few minutes words were impossible. She choked and
tried to gain control over herself. All thought
of the pink dress had vanished now. She felt
as if God had sent her a condemning message
and she could but yield before it.

"What shall I do? I promised," she said
helplessly, looking up at Joseph, who still stood
quietly watching her, hardly knowing what to
say now that her tears had come and his errand
had been told.

"Tell them you can't go. Write a note. Put
it in the post office."

"But," said Ellen Amelia, the blood rolling
in rich waves over her temples and forehead,
"they don't take ' no ' easy. I did tell them first I
couldn't, 'cause I knew ma wouldn't like it, and I
didn't think it was any use tryin' to get pa to
say so, he a deacon in the church ; but they said,
Oh yes, I could, they would come for me and
get me off somehow. And now I've promised,
they'll be mad. And Bill, he was comin' for
me ; he'll come anyhow. I just know he will ;

he's awful set in his way and he said he'd chosen me for his partner to-morrow night, and you see he won't have any other. If he should come after me I don't know what I'd do. I'm afraid I'll have to go anyhow, now. I couldn't do anything. He wouldn't understand if I'd tell him all day why I couldn't go."

Joseph set his lips firmly and stopped to consider a moment. As he had come in he made up his mind that Bill Brower should be frustrated in some way. How? He looked down at the melting flakes on his sleeve and on the tops of his boots. It had begun to snow quite hard before he came in. Ah! There was an idea. If it kept on all night there would be sleighing. He looked up with quick decision.

"I will come for you. I will come to take you sleigh-riding. We will go up to our house. You are to take dinner with my sister. Will you be ready? I will come early; it will be dark at six oclock, and even if they were lingering about they could not know."

Half an hour later Ellen Amelia stood in her own little room and looked in the seven-by-nine looking-glass watching the color roll over her face and neck as she thought again of the words she had spoken, taunting this young man and telling him he was jealous of another's having her company. Then she grew redder as she re-

membered his words which had come with the
immediate frankness which utter indifference
toward her would prompt, "You know I don't
care except for my sister's sake."

She tried to flash her eyes in indignation at
herself for having submitted to his talk after
that, and called herself a fool for giving up a
pleasant companion who admired her, and a
whole evening full of untold delights, to go
with this man who had said he cared nothing
about her, to take a sleigh ride which neither
cared to take, and like as not be a burden at a
Thanksgiving dinner where she was not planned
for nor wanted. But only tears would come instead of flashes, and she turned out her light, and
hung away the pink tarletan without noticing
how she crushed it, and cried herself to sleep
without trying to pray. Poor miserable child!
Had God forsaken her at the outset of her
trying to walk with him? How tenderly did
the watching Father look down upon his child
that night! He saw just how he was to lead her
feet to pleasant paths and beside still waters by
and by.

Downstairs Ellen Amelia had been obliged to
answer numerous questions as best she could, and
she had tried to keep her own counsel, but had
failed. What her mother and grandmother could
not divine they could draw out of any one. Be-

fore the note was written declining to go to the
town ball in company with Bill Brower, Mrs.
Haskins senior and junior were in possession of
such of the facts as they thought were worth
while. They did not count Joseph in the case
except so far as the sleigh-ride was concerned,
though Mrs. Haskins addressed the deacon after
their daughter had retired, as follows :

"Deacon Haskins, I think it's time your
daughter was attended to. She ought to be
sent away to school or somethin', unless you
want her carried right off before your face and
eyes. Since that Benedic' girl has come and
rigged her up in those new-fangled things,
here's been three young men to see her, and she
ain't more'n a babe yet in her understandin' of
things. If she can't be made to understand
housework, or care for it, maybe she could learn
a little more and get ready to teach somethin',
for the land knows, if she should be left to keep
herself now she'd have to starve ! And I'll miss
my guess if she wouldn't do it gladly in company
with them story papers of hers. I will say in
justice to that Benedic' girl, that she has done
one good thing in gettin' Ellen 'Melia to give
up that ball, but I shouldn't be surprised to hear
that there's somethin' a good deal worse gettin'
up to match it, or she'd never have give it up.
It seems to me it's a pretty state of things, any-

way, when a chit of a girl can come in town
and get my daughter to do a thing with a few
words, that I've failed in with hours and hours
of lectures."

Deacon Haskins was not the man to reply that
if she had lectured less she might have accomplished more. He only replied that "Perhaps it
might be a good plan to send the gearl to schule
awhile longer," and then he turned over his paper
and was absorbed in its columns.

Joseph strode home through the fast-thick-
ening snowflakes wondering why on earth he had
done all this and brought so much extra trouble
on himself, and what he should do now, with a
sleigh-ride and a dinner party on his own untrained
hands. Could it be possible that he was trying
to do something in this way for his new Master,
or was it merely to get ahead of Bill Brower?
He decided that it was a little of both. Then
he went to his sister.

It was rather hard explaining, but he managed to do it. He tried to make it out that he
had done it all for Ruth, and explained carefully
that he heard her and the minister talking about
it the day before as he was dozing on the sofa.
According to his account the whole thing had
been a most commonplace happening. He had
"seen" Ellen Amelia and the subject of the ball
had "come up," and he had "found she was

going," and had told her it was not going to be a fit place for girls to go to and she had better come to their house, Ruth wanted her.

Ruth's eyes brightened and her heart grew glad. This brother was joining with her in her plans to help others, and also he was showing his confidence in her by inviting a dinner party for her before he told her. She was pleased beyond expression. Entering heartily into the plan she wrote a graceful note to Ellen Amelia saying that she was so glad she could come, that they wanted to have a pleasant little frolic on Thanksgiving evening. This she dispatched the next morning by the willing Joseph, together with a little note to the minister in which she asked his presence at her impromptu dinner and desired that he should tell her if there were any others whom he would like her to invite. David to her surprise quite entered into the affair, offering several helpful suggestions. She had feared he might wish to withdraw from the party altogether, but instead he seemed to be planning things on a much larger scale than she had thought of. When Ruth wondered what she should do for extra help in the kitchen, so that Sally might be able to attend to the waiting at the table, it was David who thought of a woman, went to see if she would come, and promised to take her back before nine o'clock to put her little children to bed. So though the party was hastily gotten up, things were in fine trim for the evening before the high-noon had come. And then Ruth had time to go to her room and pray with trembling and with hope for the success of her evening. For there were others to come besides Ellen Amelia, suggested by the minister and Joseph, who suddenly developed into an excellent enemy to the town-hall ball.

Could Ruth have known as she knelt for those few moments by her bed in prayer before she went to finish her other arrangements, that her brother Joseph was just then standing soberly by the couch in his room, looking out at the window, thinking that some higher power than theirs must be asked to help their plans, and wondering how people prayed, and finally kneeling solemnly down and closing his eyes—how would her heart have throbbed with joy! No words came. His thoughts took no expression. Common words that he had heard other people pray in meeting did not fit his thought, besides he felt awkward and afraid of blundering in such a grave matter. But he knelt there for several minutes in reverent waiting, and then arose and went to carry out a commission of his sister's. And that was Joseph Benedict's first real prayer; and it was not for himself.

CHAPTER XIX

IT was near six o'clock. The last tardy member of the decorating committee had left the hall and the janitor had thankfully locked the door and hurried home to his supper, feeling glad that the affair would be over before many more hours, and his responsibility and attendance would cease. He had scarce ever had such arduous labor connected with his duties, except the time when those city people had taken possession and tried to raise some money to found a Home for Aged and Decrepit Canines, by a fancy bazar and amateur theatricals, and had made three dollars and seventy-five cents over expenses, which they had given to the janitor for his five days of extra labor, and then having had their fun, departed for more fertile pastures, leaving the Summerton cats and dogs to live and die unblessed and uncared-for.

The members of the committee of arrangements were eating hasty suppers, and scolding their husbands for forgetting to send certain last things to the hall. Some few had even begun to dress, or were exhibiting hastily constructed dresses to admiring grandmothers, who were to remain at home with the small children, and who must get their pleasure in some way.

Ellen Amelia, not having to eat any supper, stood before her small looking-glass arrayed in coarse pink tarletan. She had bought it in the village drygoods store, and it cost very little because it had been on hand for several years, Summerton not being given to pink tarletan except by the eighth of a yard to dress an occasional doll, or make popcorn bags for the Christmas tree. Mrs. Haskins had set her lips firmly when she discovered what had been bought, but the money had been Ellen Amelia's own, saved for a long time, and it was spent, so what was the use in scolding? She only said, "I'd like to know what earthly use you'll ever make of that thing afterward! It ain't strong enough for mosquito bars," and shut Ellen Amelia's bedroom door hard and went downstairs, and the daughter had sighed and thought how very hard it was to be like other people with such a mother. It is true she had her doubts about the propriety of wearing it to a dinner at the Benedicts', but they were largely overbalanced by her desire to wear the gown now that she had sacrificed her money and her time to get it ready. Besides, a dinner, according to her literary experience, was a grand affair, at which Miss Benedict would probably be arrayed in "black

velvet, with a necklace of large solitaire dia-
monds encircling her lily white throat, whose
whiteness far outshone the gems in brilliancy."
She wondered if Ruth would have her brothers
adopt full evening dress. She was not quite
sure what that was, but she was full of anxiety
to see it.

The dress certainly was pretty and becoming;
although, had she but known it, she would have
looked better in blue. But her cheeks were red
with excitement and her eyes shone like two
stars. She was not going to the ball, but she
was going to something, and with a young man,
and that was a great deal, even if he had told
her he cared nothing for her except for his sister's sake. The pink dress had large puffed
sleeves to the elbow, below which her plump
arms were bare. She looked regretfully at them
with a sort of apologetic feeling because she
had no gorgeous bracelets to deck them with.
She had cut the neck as *décolleté* as she dared,
her father being a deacon and her mother a little
behind the times as to fashion, and being frightened with the rather undressed effect, had shirred
a full ruffle of soft, very old muslin in to help
piece out the way to her throat. The muslin
had been a dainty little fancy apron that had
been a treasure and delight in days gone by, but
she had ruthlessly cut it up without a sigh for

this grand occasion. An old summer hat contained three very pink, very crushed roses and some buds. These she renovated and placed on her left shoulder where they drooped as gracefully among the cheap pink and white ruches as if they had been real flowers amid costly silk and chiffon. She surveyed the effect awhile and longed for a necklace of pearls or something of that sort, even if it were but a gold chain ; but gold chains were not plentiful in the Haskins family, and she finally contented herself with a rusty bit of black velvet ribbon tied about her throat, which added much to the effect and really helped to bring out the color in her cheeks. Altogether she made a pretty picture as she came down the stairs into the dining room where the young Haskinses were gathered, prepared to get what comfort they could from the remains of the dinner's turkey. Tommy stopped chewing, with one end of the wishbone in his mouth, and Amos dropped his under jaw in mild amaze. Deacon Haskins looked and saw before him his young wife as she was years ago in a pretty pink calico, and wondered, and was delighted that his daughter could look so like an angel, and the heart of the New York grandmother throbbed with pleased exultation that a grandchild of hers should appear in such good style. But practical Mother Haskins,

who had yet good common sense among her virtues, stood in the kitchen door with the coffee
pot and spoke out in indignation :

"Ellen Amelia Haskins, you little fool ! Are
you actually thinkin' of wearin' that tawdry rag
to Farmer Benedict's house to supper? Now
you can turn right round and go back upstairs
and dress yourself decent. Bare neck an' arms
in the middle o' winter, and you a deacon's
daughter too. Pa, why don't you speak up an'
tell her she's a disgrace to her bringin'-up. This
is some more o' them trashy papers ! Now I
shall clean them out o' this house. Deacon, I
hope you see now what you've done by humorin'
her in them story-readin' notions."

But Ellen Amelia, with a graceful sweep of
the gown, long practised before her nine-inch
mirror in imitation of that given by the Countess
Luclarion, swept out of the door into the hall
leading to the front room, only saying impres-
sively and in tones that should not reach the
ears of the waiting young man, "Certainly, ma,
I shall wear it. Did you s'pose I paid my
money out and made it for nothin' ? "

Then did Ellen Amelia appear before Joseph
Benedict, and in the smoky light made by the
kerosene lamp which Amos had hastily brought
when he opened the door for Joseph, she looked
like some delicate pink angel floating before

him. He did not know that the tarletan was
coarse and cheap, nor the velvet ribbon rusty
and creased, nor the flowers soiled and crumpled.
He only saw the artistic whole, with all the defects hidden by the kindly shadows of the room.
He looked and dropped his eyes, for it seemed
that it was some beautiful vision which almost
ought not to be looked upon by common, disin-
terested eyes. Neither was he used to *décolleté*
dressing and he felt a little startled by it. He
had an innate instinct that made him drop his
eyes from the plump round neck. But there was
no denying that Ellen Amelia had been suddenly
transformed into a beautiful being, the like of
which he had never seen before. At last he
gained his senses and his voice. He spoke
gravely. It seemed that he could not be otherwise with this girl. She was to him like the
visible presence of his promise to God. She
was the paper on which his promise was written
and must be guarded and reverenced, not for the
paper's sake but for the promise it held. Ellen
Amelia felt this, and although she did not understand it, she resented it. She wanted to be
reverenced for her own sake and not for the
promise, however sacredly she might regard the
promise.

" You are very beautiful," he said, slowly
brushing his hand across his eyes as if to clear

them from the blinding vision; "but isn't that rather thin?" and he reached out a rough finger and awkwardly felt of the material in the enormous puff that surrounded her arm. "You'll catch an awful cold such a night as this. It isn't safe. I'll just sit down and wait while you go get a good warm flannel dress on," and he suited the word to the deed and sat down.

Poor Ellen Amelia! Her humiliation was complete. She turned without a word and fairly flew through the hall and dining room and up the stairs and threw herself upon her bed and cried. It was some twenty minutes later that she appeared in the front room arrayed in her dark blue serge, with her coat and hat and a thick veil over her face. She had washed the tear stains away as much as possible, and she trusted to the cold air and snowflakes to do the rest. As for Mother Haskins, there never was a more surprised mother in her life. She had no more expected that Ellen Amelia would go upstairs and change her dress than she had expected the gray cat to change his fur for white. What had happened to the girl?

That ride was a peculiar one. Ellen Amelia scarcely spoke a word from the time she was carefully tucked into the sleigh until she was handed out on the doorstep at the Benedict home. There was something in her silence which em-

barrassed Joseph, and made him endeavor to get
up a conversation. However, he was not encour-
aged much and he soon gave it up.

Early in the evening young Brummel called
at the parsonage for Miss Clifton. He had a
horse and cutter and asked her if she would mind
taking a short turn in the snow before going to
the hall. It was not until they had taken quite
a ride and were turned toward the village once
more that Mr. Brummel casually mentioned that
his sister was suffering from a severe headache
and would not be able to go with them that
evening, and, "How about it?" Should he stop
at the hall at once? It was later than he supposed, and fully time to go if they meant to
have any fun before the rather early hour when
Louise's mother would expect her to return.
Louise consented to go at once to the hall,
though she felt just the least bit uncomfortable
about going without even Georgiana as *chaperon*.
At the door he left her, pointing out the dressing room and telling her he would return in just
a moment, as soon as he could find a man to take
the horse to a neighboring stable.

David Benedict had slipped away from the
table as soon as dinner was over. He had promised Mrs. Stevens to get her home as soon as
possible after the dinner was out of the way, and
David never neglected a promise. He went and

harnessed the horses to the sleigh, the same one
in which Joseph and Ellen Haskins had taken
their silent ride, and in a few minutes Mrs.
Stevens was flying through the snow to her
children with a basket of good things under the
seat for their delectation.

David deposited Mrs. Stevens and her basket
at her own door, and then, bethinking himself
that possibly the post office might be open thus
late in the evening, even though it was a holiday, and there might be a letter for Ruth, he
drove over to the stores. The town hall was
the next door but one to the post office, and as
David hitched his horses he naturally looked
over toward the hall and wondered who would go
there. He saw another cutter standing before
the door and a lady being helped out. As the
lady parted from the gentleman at the door the
full light of the entrance-way fell on her face and
he saw it for just an instant before she passed in.
It was Louise Clifton. One glance at the retreat-
ing form in the cutter and he felt certain that
her escort was Alonzo Brummel. Hot indignation burned in David's veins. Here was this
girl's brother at his home, doing his best to save
some of the young people from going to the hall,
and here was his sister entering as if it were a
matter of course. But no thought that it was
her fault crossed his mind. She did not know

of course, where she was going.　It was all the fault of young Brummel.　He was capable of any sort of misrepresentation, David believed, if he was at all like what he had been in their old days in the village school.　With a sudden impulse that was unusual for him, for he was a cool-headed man, David flung the reins into the sleigh and strode across the intervening space between himself and the open hall door.　Louise had disappeared within.　The two Brower boys were lounging in the doorway, evidently just preparing to go in.　He heard their coarse laugh and more.　He heard a sentence about the lady who had just passed in, that sent his blood racing at fever heat to his brain.　Then these men were exulting over the thought that the minister's sister was to be a guest with themselves this evening, and were even boasting of the number of times they would put their vile arms about her, and take her pure white fingers in their polluted ones.　David could scarcely keep his hands off them as they entered the door with him.　He set his teeth hard and clenched his fists unconsciously.　One thing he meant to do.　Louise must be rescued from this open door to the pit even if he had to carry her away by main force.　He would not have it rest upon his soul that a pure girl should be allowed to suffer the touch of hands like those that had just gone in, and he knew

many others who were in all probability in the
hall now, who were no better. If he did anything, it must be done at once before Alonzo
Brummel returned. With desperate haste he
turned to the door labeled, "Ladies' dressing
room," and knocked.

"Is Miss Clifton here?" he asked of the
frightened girl with a curling-iron in her hand
and several hairpins in her mouth who opened
the door a very small crack. "Please tell her
some one is waiting for her at the door, and wishes
her to make haste. It is very important."

David did not stop to think what he should
say. He spoke with authority, and his face
looked white and drawn. He turned and went
outside. He did not wish to meet her in the
glare of the light before every one. He did not
yet know what he should say to her.

The girl with the curling iron conveyed her
message and added by way of explanation as
Louise turned with a scornful surprise toward
the messenger, "I suppose it is the minister
waiting outside perhaps. I guess something's
happened. He looked awful scared when he
give me the word." This was spoken in a
cheerful tone and intended to excite interest, but
it struck terror to Louise's heart. What had
happened? Her mother? Her brother? Was
some one sick or was Robert merely angry? No,

Robert had gone out to dinner, she did not know where. He could not have found out possibly, so soon, for not a soul knew yet except herself and Mr. Brummel that she had come here. It must be sudden illness, or the house on fire, or something dreadful—a telegram from New York perhaps. A hundred awful possibilities rushed through Louise's excited brain as she struggled with her wraps and hurried out to the steps.

She wondered a little and was still more frightened when she found it was David Benedict who was waiting for her.

"What is it?" she asked excitedly. "Oh, what is the matter, and where is my brother? or Mr. Brummel?"

"Come this way and I'll tell you," said David gravely, hurrying her across the snowy pavement to his own cutter, putting her in with haste, and tucking the robes scientifically about her. She saw that he was hurrying with all his might and she kept quite still, her heart throbbing painfully, until he jumped in beside her and started the horses off at a furious rate. He felt that he must get her far away from the vicinity of those two vile creatures who had dared to speak of her in the way he had heard, as fast as he possibly could.

"Now tell me quick," she pleaded, laying her hand earnestly on his arm, "what is it? My mother—is she sick? Don't be afraid to tell me the worst at once. I can bear it. I can bear anything but suspense!" Poor child, she thought she could bear anything, and yet when she found out what was the matter she could not bear it at all.

David looked at her in surprise. "Don't be frightened," he said almost tenderly. "It is not your mother. There is nothing to be frightened at now. You are safe. I will take care of you."

"What is it then? What do you mean? I was not in any danger was I? How could I be?"

And then David Benedict perceived that he was not going to have an easy task to explain to the kidnapped young woman his strange and summary action.

CHAPTER XX

" I DO not understand," said Louise. " What possible peril could I be in, and how did you come to find it out?"

" Did you know what kind of a place you were going into just now?" asked David.

" Certainly," answered she with some asperity ; "I was in the town hall, was I not? I understood that was the name of the place. I was going to a ball, just to see what it was like. I wish you would tell me at once what is the matter. I do not in the least understand." Her tone was quite determined. She was prepared to give her rescuer a hearing, but it must be no trivial matter for which he had thus meddled with her affairs. He saw that he must explain fully, and that he had but one chance to save himself in her eyes. That chance was to tell her the truth—the whole truth. He never stopped, however, to think how she might regard him. His only care was for her. She must not be allowed to go back to that place even if he was obliged to resort to using force, or in other words, his advantage of the sleigh and two good horses over her. He would take her to her brother and let him manage the affair if she would not be persuaded. David set his lips, for his task was made the harder by the sudden dull disappointment that settled upon him when he found that the young woman did not regard a public ball with any degree of shrinking at all.

" Miss Clifton, did you know when you went to that place that you would be expected to dance, and to dance with every one present? Did you know that some of the dancing and the dancers would be unpleasantly familiar, and that some of the men with whom you would be thrown would not be fit companions for you? "

Louise's cheeks fairly blazed.

"Do you mean to say that you have undertaken to manage me?" she asked indignantly. "I do not understand what all this means. I knew, of course, what sort of an entertainment I was going to attend and, of course, I expected to have a little fun in dancing. As for the young men, I think I could take care of myself, and I am bound by no village laws to dance with all of them. Indeed, I suppose there are very few with whom I should have cared to do so. If that is what you have made all this fuss about, please turn about this moment and take me back. Mr. Brummel will think it unpardonable in me to have gone off in this unexplained fashion. I thought at least that some one was dead by the way you acted. Did my brother send you after me? I demand to know that! He has no right whatever to keep me from any entertainment I wish to attend. I cannot help it that he has silly notions. I am not a minister, if he is. I insist upon being taken back at once, Mr. Benedict." She lifted her head imperiously, but David only answered quietly:

"That I decline to do, Miss Clifton."

"What do you mean?" asked Louise, her voice fairly shaking with her anger.

"I mean to protect you," said her driver again quietly.

"From what, pray? I shall need to claim protection from you if you keep on like this."

"From yourself," said David, "and from the devil," he added fiercely under his breath.

"From myself! What do you mean? I can attend to myself. And you need not insult me by swearing in my presence."

"Yes, from yourself," answered the quiet voice again. "I must protect you so that you will do nothing that you would regret if you knew all about it. And I was not swearing. I meant those other words. If the devil was ever anywhere you would have found him in that hall to-night."

"Again I demand to know what all this mystery is about. You have hinted darkly at awful

things. Now if there is anything awful you
must tell me."

"I will try," said David his voice almost
pained in its tensity. "Though I'm afraid you
will wish you had taken my word for it. If you
will let me I will take you to my sister and she
will explain."

But Louise was high-wrought by this time.
She had a strong suspicion that some notions of
either Ruth Benedict or her own brother had
been at the bottom of all this and she was in no
mood to wish to see Ruth.

"I demand to know, and to know at once!
If there was anything the matter you can certainly tell me. Had some one threatened to kill
me?" with an ill-concealed smile.

David took a firm hold on the reins and
turned his eyes full upon her, and even in the
starlight she felt the steady, calm gaze. There
was a quieting effect in his tone which seemed
almost masterful and he said clearly and with
no hesitation now: "Then I will tell you, Miss
Clifton, as well as I can. In the first place I do
not know what dancing is in the city, but I have
an idea that it is very different here. For instance, you would not have been allowed to
choose your partners sometimes, but would have
been forced, in a wild, frolicsome way, to dance
with whoever chose to seize you about the waist.

Your attempt at a refusal would only have put them—these young gentlemen—on their mettle and rendered it certain that you would be subjected to further liberties. If a girl does not wish to dance with any particular person then that particular person is supposed to attempt to make her dance with him, if not by fair means then by foul ones; and you might, you probably would, have found yourself whirling about in the arms of young men, whom if you knew, you would not speak to, to say nothing of touching, and utterly unable to leave the place or even get your footing till you had been carried twice or thrice around the room. I have been to these places; you have not. I am not a Christian, I am sorry to say. I hope I am a gentleman. At any rate I was so disgusted that I never go myself any more, and I could not bear to think of my sister or any one for whom I cared being found there. Have I said enough, Miss Clifton?"

"I was not aware that you were a crank as well as the rest," broke in the girl in an icy tone. "I think this has gone far enough. If you do not take me back at once I shall scream for help when we pass the next house."

"Ah," said David with a heavy sigh, "I see I have not said enough. Wait one moment, Miss Clifton, let me tell you the rest; I had hoped not to have had to say this, but you force me to do so." In his unconscious absorption he stopped the horses and looked her full in the face again.

"You said you could take care of yourself. The two young men who are the vilest of all that would have been there to-night, and who would have appeared to the best advantage because they have money and dress well, were standing by the door as you went in. I happened to be within hearing at the moment. *They were betting which would have the privilege of holding you in his arms the greater number of times to-night;* and wait; they were exulting over the thought of—they spoke of—they said —heaven help me! I cannot repeat to you the words they spoke! You would never look me in the face again. But believe me, on my honor as a gentleman, it was such a thing that only the fear of dragging your name in the filth prevented me from knocking them down then and there. Though they are young their lives are vile, their words are vile, their very thought is vile; and these would have been your partners in the dance by this time." David suddenly ceased, shut his lips hard, picked up the reins, and struck the horses a cut that sent them flying. He felt a dreadful fear that in his excitement he had forgotten himself and gone too far, saying things that were unpardonable if said to a young lady, yet somehow he did not care, either. He had risked a great deal, but it was to win, and he had won.

Louise sat suddenly stunned. She too had a dim idea that David was saying something which was improper to hear, and that she ought to stop him, but had she not brought it upon herself? and could it be true, this awful thing he was saying? She shuddered to think what the coarse mouths might have been saying, or rather she could not dream what it was, but some instinct told her that it was bad enough and made her loathe herself for giving them any chance to speak of her at all. As David went on, his earnest, manly tones, and the way in which he bravely spoke out, although his voice quivered with feeling, those words not usually spoken so plainly by a young man to a young woman, and which were evidently so hard for him to speak, gave her a new respect for him. There was something grand after all in his telling her this, though she was so ashamed of herself for making him do it that she could scarcely hold up her head. There suddenly came over her a wonderful change. She was frightened meekness itself. The tears had come to her eyes, a strange thing for Louise Clifton, for crying was a thing as utterly alien to her nature as frowning to a rose. They sat in silence for some minutes and then David as they skimmed along slowly reined in the horses until they came down to a more moderate pace. At last Louise gained voice to ask meekly in a choked tone :

"Where are we going?"

David stopped the horses as suddenly as before and answered with a deference which was quite a contrast to his manner a few moments before :

"Wherever you say, Miss Clifton. Will you go to my sister?"

"Oh, I guess so," answered the poor girl. She felt utterly crushed by the terrible thing which had been told her. She had been one of those girls who had always said in answer to any argument against promiscuous dancing, "Nonsense! Men are not all so bad as they make them out, nor girls either. I would never dance with a man who was as bad as that. Don't you think I'd like to hear of any man daring to talk in that way about me?" and her eyes would flash and she would hold her head high, and walk indignantly away; while her satisfied, ignorant little mother would look pleased, and smile and murmur, "No one would ever dare breathe an evil word in connection with my daughter. To the pure all things are pure," and the matter would be dropped.

Louise remembered several occasions when a
maiden aunt had undertaken to make her mother
believe that dancing schools were terrible places,
and the mother had indignantly repudiated the
idea and sent her daughter from the room, saying
that her aunt's talks and the selections she read
from her various tracts were more contaminating
for a young girl's purity than if she danced all
her life through.

Now these things came back to her. It was
true then that men talked about girls. Oh, it
was awful to think that another man, and surely
a good one, had heard them. Here Louise
turned and stole a look at the outline of the face
near her, clear-cut against the cold starry sky.
There were purity, tenderness, and pity in his
face. She could see that he wished with all his
heart to atone in some way for the severity he
had been obliged to use. But he kept a kindly
silence for the most part, only once or twice saying a word about the snow, and once calling her
attention to the view as they came in full sight
of a lovely bit of landscape, the new moon
hanging, starred about, above a little tree-fringed
hill, a tiny dark house below with a speck of
light in the window, and dark, bare poplars lifting their brown arms piteously against the lu-
minous sky.

As they neared the Benedict house Louise

roused suddenly from her painful thoughts. She saw the many lights and knew there must be guests.

"Oh, who is there?" she asked suddenly, putting out her hand to the reins to stop him, and quickly he obeyed her wish and stopped in the gateway. "Have you strangers?" she asked.

"No, only a few friends from the village," he answered reassuringly. "Your brother is there. They will be glad to see you. I shall say nothing to them."

"Oh, no, I can't go in," said Louise shrinking back, "not if my brother is there. I would not have him know for anything. I went to Brummels' to spend the evening with Georgiana. He will think it strange and ask me questions. I cannot tell him now. Take me home, please. Or no! Mother does not know. Oh, what shall I do?" She covered her face with her hands and cried outright. David sat only a moment regarding her, and then suddenly taking up the reins he turned the cutter about and gave a word to his horses which made them fairly fly over the frozen snow. Louise looked up pretty soon and saw that they were not going home, and she did not know the direction.

"We are just taking a sleigh-ride," answered David cheerily. "Are you warm enough?" and he tucked the robes carefully about her again. "It is a beautiful night and perhaps this will be as pleasant a way as any for you to pass your time. At what hour does your mother expect you to return? You can go home then and simply say you have had a ride. If I had a mother I think I would tell her all about this, but I don't suppose I am competent to advise, and I'll fix it all right for you so that you can do as you please."

Louise looked timidly up at him. He was very kind to her. Somehow she seemed to have grown very young and ignorant all at once and felt that he was some one to look up to. He seemed so strong and good and kind.

"It would frighten my mother terribly," she said after a few minutes of thought. "She doesn't know the world much. My father shielded her from all knowledge of such things. She would think I had done some dreadful thing and could never be trusted again, and I am sure I don't know that I can."

"You must not feel in that way," said David earnestly. "You will be all the more careful now. You were taken care of. Some strange power that I did not understand made me go to the post office against my better judgment to-night, for I knew there was scarcely a possibility of there being anything in the office on a holiday evening." Then a sudden flash illumined his

face and he said solemnly and reverently and
wonderingly, " Maybe it was God. Miss Clifton,
do you know God? Are you what they call a
Christian ? "

Louise sat in wonder. The question, the very
question that she had sat in her room two days
before and pondered whether she could ask of
him. For she had actually considered whether
she might not try a little real missionary work
by finding out if religion was what he was supposed to need to make him a success in the
world. It may seem strange that one who did
not belong to Christ would care to try to bring
another, but it is nevertheless true that some do.
They see that religion is a good thing—or would
be for another—and while they get along in the
world very well themselves without it, they have
kind-heartedness enough to make a little effort
to help some one else get it. Louise decided
that it would be a very novel and a very interesting thing to do, besides being a thing which
would surprise and please her mother and brother
and Ruth, and perhaps make them treat her
with a little more respect.

And now she found her heathen actually asking the very question of his would-be missionary
which she had half planned to ask of him if the
opportunity ever offered.

Altogether it was a strange ride and a strange

talk those two had out under the starlight that
Thanksgiving evening, but there will never come
an anniversary of that day when they will cease
to be thankful for the ride and the talk and the
decisions that resulted therefrom.

Louise found herself set down at her brother's
door at ten o'clock a crushed and meek little being whose main desire was to get to her room
and cry, and whose heart was burdened with the
thought of the searching questions which had
been asked her by one who did not know Christ
himself yet, but was seeking to find him.

When Alonzo Brummel returned from attend-
ing to his horse and after making himself pre-
sentable in the gentlemen's dressing room went
to the appointed spot to meet his young lady, and
found her not, he concluded that she had grown
tired of waiting and had probably gone into the
main hall with some of the girls, as it was a
very informal affair. He made his way slowly
through the hall speaking in his patronizing way
to this pretty girl and that whom he had known
in his younger and less pompous days. He was
puzzled as to what could have become of Louise.
Just then Eliza Barnes, the girl of the hair curler
in the dressing room, who had opened the door
for David, accosted him.

"Hello! there's Lonnie Brummel, girls. Wait

a minute; I want to speak to him. Say, Lon,
Miss Clifton's gone. I thought you might be
lookin' fer her. I guess 'twas her brother come
after her in a mighty big hurry, and she looked
scared enough. Dave Benedict brought the
word in for her to come right out. I s'pose the
minister didn't want to come into the hall. He
hustled her into a sleigh and drove off quick
and slick. I peeped through the curtains and
seen 'em myself."

Alonzo Brummel uttered a word under his
breath that he would scarcely have liked to
speak before the minister's sister; but finding
that he was hopelessly left to his own resources
he set about finding the prettiest and silliest
girls in the room and having as good a time as
possible, going home somewhat later than he
had planned to take Miss Clifton away, it must
be confessed, and letting himself quietly into his
father's house by a way known to his younger
days when his mother kept a more strict watch
over his bedroom door than could have been
desired. He received, however, the next morning, a stiff, violet-scented note informing him
that Miss Clifton begged his pardon for having
left him so abruptly the evening before, and
desired to explain that she had been called for
in great haste and had not had time to leave
any word for him. It was so altogether cutting

and summary in its tone that Alonzo Brummel
decided to spend the remainder of his vacation
with a friend in New York, and he departed that
day for a more genial atmosphere. He did not
just care to be at home when his mother should
discover where he had been spending his time
the evening before.

When David reached home at last he found
that the guests were preparing to take their
departure. Indeed, Joseph had been much worried to know how he was to get Ellen Amelia
home without the horses and the cutter.

When the last one had gone and David had
helped to put Miss Haskins into the cutter and
watched them drive away, he turned back and
stood by his sister Ruth, his face deeply serious.

"Ruth," said he, and she knew by his tone
that he had something to tell her which meant
more to him than anything he had ever said to
her before. "Ruth, you pray, I know. I want
you to pray for a—for some one who needs help
very much, some one who doesn't know how to
pray."

Ruth looked up quickly, her face lighting
with glad surprise.

"O David," said she, "do you love Jesus?
And is it yourself you mean? I will gladly, but
why don't you pray too?"

"No, I don't think I know Jesus yet," he an-

swered simply, as a little child might; "but I
want to. I mean to," he added with emphasis,
"and I'd like you to pray for me too, if you will.
But this other one is a woman, and she hasn't
anything to stay her life on. I shall try to pray
for her myself, but I wanted you to help. You
know how better than I. She needs it very much.
And Ruth, you thought it was queer, I suppose,
that I stayed away so long to-night; but I want
you to know I had to. No, I didn't go to that
ball," he said as he caught a shade of anxiety
across her face. "I was afraid you'd think I did,
but I'm not that kind. I had to keep some one
else away. If God ever sent any one anywhere
he certainly sent me downtown this evening."

He took his sister's hand and stooped and
kissed her on the forehead, and then went upstairs to his room.

And as Ruth went to her room to pray as she
had promised, she carried a worry in her heart.
What village girl had gotten a hold upon David?
Was there some one then who would be a drag
upon him? Had his heart already been entan-
gled? She had grown to love her brother David
very deeply. She sighed and wondered and
wished, and then she prayed, and as she prayed
the weight passed away from her heart and she
rejoiced; for was not David seeking for Jesus?
And a voice had whispered behind her:

Fearest sometimes that thy Father
　　Hath forgot?
When the clouds around thee gather,
　　Doubt him not !
Always hath the daylight broken—
Always hath he comfort spoken—
Better hath he been for years,
　　Than thy fears.

CHAPTER XXI

ELLEN AMELIA had been very quiet during the entire evening spent at the Benedict Thanksgiving party. She did not seem to recover from the successive humiliations which had brought her here in quiet and accustomed clothing. Her usually gay and voluble tongue was so still that the other girls asked her if she was sick, and Ruth looked at her in a troubled way many times fearing that Ellen was disappointed because she had not gone to the ball instead of coming to her.

Joseph too watched her in a kind of maze. He had not been at church the Sunday preceding and therefore the effect of the new dark blue dress was particularly bewildering. He was hardly sure he knew Ellen Amelia. She certainly did not look like the same girl he had known all his life and gone to school with, and, it must be confessed, at whose follies he had laughed many times.

What had she done? He was not well enough versed in the art of dress to lay it all to that. The pink tarletan had dazzled him, but the whole question of apparel appeared in a new light when

he had noted the marked change in Ellen Amelia
wrought, as he had presently to acknowledge to
himself, by the donning of a new gown and, most
mysterious of all, one not at all extraordinary
either in fashion or in material. He could not
understand why one dress rather than another
should make a person's appearance so different.
He did not know that there was all the difference
in the world between a dress that fitted the form
and one that did not. Neither did he reckon on
graceful folds and lines that curved just right, nor
—and perhaps this made the most difference of
all—upon the soft waves of hair about her face
and the low coil behind, which just fitted her
face, in place of the hard unbecoming knot and
tight frizzes which she had hitherto supposed to
be the height of fashion. Ruth had somehow
managed to get in a lesson in hair-dressing with
all the rest, and the result was a much more
pleasing Ellen Amelia. Joseph looked at her as
she sat in the big chair in the corner and thought
she was not unpleasing. Indeed, on second
thought he was not sure that she was not pretty.
If she was not so awfully silly he did not know
but she would be interesting, but as it was he
did not understand how Ruth could waste her
time on her. He wondered for the hundredth
time why Ruth did it, and then the thought came
and softened his expression, "She does it for

Christ's sake," and he thought perhaps he would like to help her, or some one, for that reason.

The minister had interrupted his thoughts just then, sitting down beside him and gradually drawing him out with stories of his own life. He asked Joseph about his school days and drew from him the wish that he could have kept on with his studies. "Father always meant I should," he said suddenly with an impulse of confidence in the man who seemed to be so interested in him. "And my brother was anxious for it too. He had two years at the academy in the city, you know. But we both agreed that I ought not to do it till the farm was clear of the mortgage, and now that it's out of the way I've grown too old." He heaved a little sigh of regret, like the winding sheet to his desire, and seemed to lay the subject away. Not so the minister:

"Not a bit of it. One is never too old to learn. Why, man, you have so much to learn, and if you don't do it here you'll have to waste a great many years of eternity learning it. Learn what you can now." There followed a quick succession of questions on the part of the minister and answers by Joseph.

"Well," said the minister straightening up at last, an eager light in his eyes, "there is no reason why you shouldn't catch up soon if you want to, and go on to college. I had no idea the schools

in Summerton carried one so far. Now, if you
would really like to go on with your studies I
should be delighted to help you. You know I'm
not long from college and I love to teach. You'll
have plenty of time these long winter evenings,
and if you make good use of them who knows
but you might be ready to enter college by next
fall? I'm not saying you could, you know, for I
haven't examined you yet; but you might.
Stranger things have happened. Will you do it?"

"Do you mean," said Joseph his eyes burning
with excitement and his hands clenched in his
earnestness, "do you really mean you think I
could make something of myself in the world?"

"I certainly do," answered the minister.

Joseph was so occupied with the wonderful
new thoughts that the minister had awakened in
him and the stirring of old ambitions, that he
scarcely noticed Ellen Amelia till they were half-
way home. Then she aroused from her silence
and made a remark.

"I wish I could get away from Summerton,
and learn something and be somebody!"

It was said half fiercely, and not in the least
as if she expected an answer, but more as if she
were thinking aloud. But there was a note in
her words which appealed to Joseph. He had
had these very same feelings before Ruth had
come to them to make home something worth

while, and even now his sister's sweetness and
brightness made him long to do something to
make himself more on a plane with her intellec-
tually. Now this evening a way had been opened,
a hope that after all he might possibly be something more than he was, and in his exultation he
felt a sympathy for this girl beside him who
had the same desires and no hope of their ful-
fillment, for of course Ellen Amelia had no possibility before her but to live and die in Summerton.
He tried to arouse himself from his own pleasant
thoughts and say something to comfort her, even
as the minister had brought hope to him, but
what could he say? He could not promise to
help her, for she had been through the same
schools in which he had been graduated. She
was as far advanced as he. "Couldn't you get
some book to read?" he offered lamely as an al-
ternative in place of going away.

"Where would I get books, and how would I
know what to read? I've read all my life, and
it only seems to make me more unhappy. Ma
don't like me to read, anyway. Sometimes I
think I'll just give up and never touch a
book again, if that's what she wants, and go into
the kitchen and never do another thing but bake
and scrub and wash dishes the rest of my life.
I don't see how I'm a-going to keep that promise
I made to you, anyway. There isn't any chance

at home. I s'pose, to be good, one ought to be willing to do all sorts of ugly things and not care, and not ever want anything else; but I can't help wanting other things. I'd like to do something big and grand. I s'pose I ain't fit; but I'd be willing to go through most anything to make me fit, if there was a chance for anything better than just what all the Summerton girls live for."

"I s'pose," said Joseph, speaking slowly, as if he were treading on unfamiliar ground and must choose his words carefully, " that if you do the best you can, God will see to the rest. The Bible talks like that, and most all sermons say so, and it seems as if the Christians professed to believe that, though to be sure there don't many of them act as though they remembered it. But look here, Miss Ellen, let us be different from that sort of Christians. If the thing's worth doing at all, let us do it as well as it can be done by us. It seems to me, it isn't fair to God not to do our best. Then, if he's anything, he's to be trusted to bring it out straight, somehow. I s'pose if he wants you to do some grand work in the world, he could fix it out so you could manage to do it; but if I was you, I'd do first the little things at home he's given you. I tried to find a place last night I used to hear father read at prayers sometimes when I was a little chap, about being faithful in little things and then you'd get to be a ruler over a good deal more, perhaps, sometime. Anyhow, if I was you I'd try it."

"I will," said Ellen Amelia, with her usual prompt decision. " I'll begin to-morrow morning and darn every stocking in mother's basket before I touch my paper that comes in the morning mail."

They were at her father's door by this time, and as Joseph helped her out and turned his horses homeward once more, he felt a sense of exultation that the little work he had tried to do for Ellen Amelia had not been wholly without effect. There was a new kind of joy in doing this sort of thing, which is given to souls who labor to help others, and which made him long to do more for his new Master. He mused over what the girl had said as he put the horses up and wondered what kind of a paper she took, and thought he would ask her sometime. She might be more advanced than he knew. He had never dreamed that she took a paper all herself. But he decided that in all probability it was a fashion paper.

With much excitement and eagerness he went on the appointed evening to meet the minister and take his first lesson in Latin. He had not told Ruth nor David yet. He wished to see

whether he could really do anything at it first.
He was charmed with the lesson. And indeed
he might well have been had he possessed a mind
even less eager for knowledge than his really
was, for Robert Clifton was a teacher of no mean
ability. He had considered seriously at one time
whether he would not let his passion for teaching have the mastery over his life, but the Lord
had called in the direction of the ministry, and
he had obeyed. Ruth would have been astonished to know that a little word of hers, spoken
unwittingly at a time when he was unsettled
about the matter in that summer of their meeting long ago, had sent the final conviction to his
heart that his Master wished him to work as a
minister.

The hour of the lesson was long drawn out,
and neither teacher nor pupil was willing to
stop when the clock struck a warning hour.
Mrs. Clifton wondered what in the world Robert
could be doing with that young man in the study
so long, and wished that—if it was true, as he
said, that the fellow was worth anything at all—
he would have thoughtfulness enough to bring
him downstairs to talk a little while to his sister.
Louise was very restless and unhappy. She
tried to read and to play and to embroider, and
finally, after sitting for a few moments in every
chair in the room, had retired. Mrs. Clifton

sighed and wondered how long she was going to be able to keep Louise in this little town, and half wished Robert would get married, that she might take Louise where she would not feel hampered by her brother's profession.

But the young man was allowed to depart finally without having even been brought into the parlor, and Mrs. Clifton retired, with her curiosity unsatisfied.

As Joseph walked homeward that night, his busy thoughts went far ahead of the present, and he pictured to himself many things he would do in the world with the knowledge he should acquire. Summerton was asleep, for the hour was late. As he passed Deacon Haskins' house, a sudden thought struck him. He stopped short and looked up at the house. "Maybe I might," he soliloquized aloud. "If I thought He wanted me to I would." He walked on after that, looking up at the clear starlit sky and letting his soul reach out behind that "dim unknown." He had read Lowell's great poem not many days before, and admired it, and certain lines of it came to him now. He wondered if God was really there behind the dim unknown, standing within the shadow, keeping watch above his own. He wished, as many another has wished, that he could see him once, and be sure—sure beyond the possibility of a doubt—that God did

care for little things that people did and said.
And there came to him through the still midnight a conviction that God did care.

It was the very next evening that Joseph
Benedict presented himself at Deacon Haskins'
door and asked for the daughter of the house.
Her mother called her, and herself gave her the
sitting-room lamp to carry into the parlor; but
when an hour had passed and there seemed to
be no sign of the visitor taking his leave, she
thought it high time to do something. She
cautiously opened the parlor door, and to her
horror saw Joseph and Ellen Amelia bending
their heads together over a book. They did not
see her, nor apparently hear her, as she opened
the door, and went on with earnest talk about
some jargon she did not in the least understand.
She stood contemplating them for a moment,
and then as softly shut the door and turned away.
She sat down at her sewing again, but there was
a compressed look about her mouth, as if she
knew something and had surmised a good deal
more, though she said nothing. When Joseph
went away, which he did in a few minutes, for
he was in a hurry to get back to his own study,
Ellen Amelia lingered in the chilly haircloth
parlor, and her mother, going in search of her,
found her poring over a paper, upon which were
carefully written rows of words.

"Ellen 'Melya, what on earth has possession of you? I should like to know what that Benedic' girl has on hand now? I do wish you'd come out here and finish up that job of mending you begun. I've got to have them things right away."

The daughter came and sewed quietly for the remainder of the evening, only answering abstractedly, "It's Latin, mother. I'm studying Latin." But from time to time as she sewed she glanced at the paper in her lap and her lips moved constantly. Mrs. Haskins looked at her eldest child with trouble in her eyes.

"I'm just that troubled about her I can't sleep," she remarked to her mother the next day. "She goes around mumbling all the time, '*A mo, a mass, a mat.*' I'm sure I don't know what high-flown notion 'll take her next. If she wanted to study she could have done it some other way than getting a young know-nothin' of a fellow to teach what he don't know himself. I don't know but I'd rather she'd have even gone to that ball with the Brower boy. He at least looks decent. And after she got her dress made and all!"

But Ellen Amelia was engrossed in Latin and saw nothing else that went on, though she did honestly try to do her best in everything that came to her hand. This Latin was something that came nearly up to the measure of her heart's desire. Joseph had promised to give her every lesson he took himself, and while she knew very well that he was not doing it on her account at all, but only for the sake of doing his best to keep his part of the promise, she meekly accepted the help she got and began to look up to and admire her teacher with a kind of awe mingled with deep respect.

Things went on at this rate for about six or eight weeks, and at last Mother Haskins got the deacon sufficiently aroused to the danger of his daughter's present amusements to send her to West Winterton to the academy. Ellen Amelia was perhaps a little disappointed to give up her Latin lessons, but she was told that Latin was taught there and that by real teachers, and was bidden look upon the added advantages of the other studies she would have. So she stifled the wish she felt to have things to go on as they were, and managed to feel a degree of the gratitude that would have been hers a half-year before, and took her departure, leaving Joseph free to use all his time in study. He felt relieved at first to find that the task he had set himself was no longer required of him, but after a few days he began to miss the pleasure he had had in imparting knowledge to this eager learner, and to think it might even be an advantage to him to teach some one else, for in teaching he learned so much himself, and so he looked about for another pupil. Ellen Amelia came home every Friday now and saw Joseph across the church every Sunday, and once he bowed and asked her how she was getting on in her studies. She remembered that bow with pleasure, for there seemed to be a touch of the courteous respect in it which he gave to his own sister.

The communion occurred soon after she had begun to attend the West Winterton Academy, and Ellen Amelia, David and Joseph Benedict, were among those who, having publicly professed their faith in the Lord Jesus, were welcomed to membership. This first accession to the church since the coming of the new pastor created a stir of astonishment in the community. It was long since there had been any one to unite with their church save an occasional person by letter from the city. The young people had almost without exception remained outside the church. Now to see them coming in so willingly, nay eagerly, made their elders ask, "What is it?" There had been no special services as yet, only the earnest preaching of the conscientious young pastor. They did not know of the quiet, heart-to-heart talks he had taken time for, with this one and that. They only saw the results. Men who had heretofore stayed at home on Sunday

now were uniting with God's church. David
Benedict was generally supposed to be somewhat
indifferent, if not slightly infidel in his tenden-
cies ; but yet he had been the first to offer himself, even before the meeting at which the invitation had been given, and his brother had not
been far behind. The deacons shook their heads
and said they did not know about taking in people in such a wholesale way, to be put out perhaps in a year or two, or else be a dead weight
to the church ; and Deacon Chatterton allowed
that in his opinion the examination ought to be
a very rigid one. He certainly did his part to
make it as much of an ordeal as possible. Poor
Ellen Amelia Haskins felt that there were no
more trials left in life for her worth mentioning
when she came out of that lecture room. She
trembled from head to foot and her face was almost as white as her handkerchief. Mrs. Chatterton never quite understood how it was that all
her prophecies concerning the harm that Benedict girl would do in Summerton and in her own
home never came to anything. She looked with
doubt on the three young people as they stood
together in the front of the church. She would
not believe that there would not come retribu-
tion of some sort upon them all, just for what,
she did not state even to herself.

Ruth was very happy. She had longed and

prayed that her brothers might find Jesus and yet she had hardly hoped that they would come so soon. After that Thanksgiving night when David had asked her to pray for some one, she had been able to talk with him about being a Christian. They had had many long talks together and David had ended by becoming a simple-hearted, earnest Christian, giving himself to God as a little child might do, and having the glad heart-rejoicing just as a child rejoices over his sins forgiven. He was so happy he went about singing and whistling all the time. There seemed to be a bond warm and deep between the brother and sister now which never could be broken. They had begun at once to pray for Joseph, claiming the promise "If two of you shall agree on earth as touching anything that they shall ask, it shall be done for them," never knowing that their prayer was already answered and that Joseph was trying every day to walk in the straight and narrow way. David and Ruth had been sitting together in the twilight of the Sunday afternoon talking about their brother. They were worried about him lately. He spent a great many evenings away from the house and never explained where he went. He seemed much absorbed in something too. Ruth wondered if it could be one of the village girls. She was always a little troubled about those village girls. Just as they were saying that they must tell Joseph about their intention to unite with the church next Sabbath, he entered the room and, sitting down beside Ruth, began in his straightforward way to say what he had come to tell them.

"I wanted you to know beforehand," he said, "that I am going to unite with the church. I've been thinking about it a long time and I'm going to do it now."

Before he had finished speaking, David had grasped him by the hand and there was a pleasant surprise for Joseph to find that his elder brother was already a Christian. "Before they call, I will answer ; and while they are yet speaking, I will hear," repeated Ruth solemnly.

And that night there was a family altar set up in the Benedict home, and from it went up prayers of thanksgiving and praise. There must have been joy around the throne of God and among the angels in heaven and among the saved ones there, for the father and mother surely were permitted to look down to earth and know that their two boys would meet them by and by, and that it was through the agency of their dear daughter.

CHAPTER XXII

ELLEN AMELIA HASKINS was certainly changing greatly. Her mother noticed that she was quieter and more willing to help when she came home Friday nights. She really began to have hope that her daughter would settle down and be like other girls. She still read books to be sure, but they were solid-looking study books. There came no more illustrated story papers into the house. They had ceased suddenly, shortly after Ellen Amelia began the study of Latin. Mrs. Haskins supposed that the deacon had " braced up " at last, and heeded her many injunctions to stop the paper; but the truth was that Joseph Benedict had asked her what paper it was she took that she had mentioned to him the other night, and she had triumphantly displayed the latest arrival to him, whereupon his decided face took on a decided frown, and he tore the paper in half and told her it was not fit for her to read. Ellen Amelia was dismayed, but by this time Latin and her teacher had such a hold upon her that she did not say him nay, and after a good cry by herself, and a good deal of faltering resolution, she wrote a letter and stopped her paper nine weeks before its subscription ran out. And when in due course of time her father had asked her if it wasn't about time she needed to fix up that paper business for another year, and secretly handed out the money with a confidential nod, she surprised him by saying that she wouldn't take the paper any more, but if he would just as soon she would take the money for a study book she needed very much.

Her father and mother had been much surprised and pleased when she united with the church, though her mother's expression of it to her was that she was "sure Ellen Amelia hadn't acted much like a Christian durin' the past year, but she hoped they'd see a change now." And Ellen had made up her mind that not only they but God should see a change in her. And they did, although it did not come all at once. She was still Ellen Amelia. She still showed much silliness. It was not to be expected that her habits of thought could change all at once. But God and his workers were molding her for her place in the world, and although she did not see it, wonderful things were in preparation for her.

Out of the Thanksgiving party had grown a permanent source of culture and growth, not only to Ellen Amelia, but to many other of the young girls in Summerton, beginning with Ruth

Benedict's Sunday-school class. Something had been said about Ellen Amelia's new dress, and it had been admired openly by the other girls. Ruth answered brightly, "Yes, isn't it pretty? And she made it herself too." The girls exclaimed over this, and would have been almost inclined to doubt it had any other than Miss Benedict made the statement. But Ellen Amelia with her native honesty came to the front at once:

"Yes; I made it myself after I was taught. Girls, you don't know what a teacher we've got. She can do anything. She showed me how to cut and fit this dress, and helped sew it. I think it would be a good deal honester myself to say she made it and I helped a little, but she insists that I did it."

The other girls admired more, and wistfully wished they could have something as nice, and before the evening was over Miss Benedict had an eager class in dressmaking, all ready to begin work whenever she should set the day. Ruth sighed when she went to her room that night, to think how much more eager they were to learn dressmaking than they had been to take up some extra Bible study she had suggested. She wondered if maybe she was doing right to go on and get them interested in things of the world? Might it not take their thoughts from higher things? These things were important, of course, but were they worth while if they took the entire attention? She pondered long over the question, but at last decided that it was worth while, and that she felt she might be able to make the class profitable in other ways, as well as to teach the girls how to make pretty dresses well and economically.

And so the class began in a large upper room which Ruth had decided should be used for any Christian work the Lord sent to her. It had been used as an attic, and had never been entirely finished off, for the rafters and beams were uncovered. But the ceiling was high, and the windows large and many. Ruth saw possibilities for a gymnasium and many other things as well as dressmaking classes. David, her helper now in all good schemes, and more than that, a believer in her schemes—for it is a great thing to have one person who believes in you, when you have a plan to carry out—made several long, strong tables, rough but serviceable, and one bright Saturday morning the girls, including Ellen Amelia, gathered there with scissors and thimble and cloth and thread, prepared to do as they were bidden. The first lesson proved a success. The girls were wild over their work, and would have been delighted to meet oftener. They were given a certain amount of sewing

each to have finished before the next lesson.
While they sewed they talked, and the talk ran
on various themes, all suggested by the girls,
but guided by Ruth.

"Miss Ruth," said Effie Haines, a pretty but-
terfly sort of girl who hummed from one thing
to another, like a bee among the flowers, and
who was very fond of brightness and fun,
"Miss Ruth, you didn't go to the ball the other
night, and you didn't want any of us to go ; we
know that, but would you please tell us just all
the reasons why? I know some people say
dancing is wicked, but I never knew why. Do
you think it is?"

"Not in the least," answered Ruth smiling, at
which every girl in the room stopped sewing,
and opened her eyes wide in amazement.

"You don't!" ejaculated Ellen Amelia.
"Why, I thought—Joe sa——" then she stopped
unnoticed, but the red blood stole up in her
cheeks, and she said no more.

"Why, no ; of course not," answered Ruth
innocently. "What possible harm could there
be in getting up on the floor and hopping
around?"

They all laughed uneasily, feeling certain
that there was a catch somewhere.

"They danced in the Bible, you know," said
Ruth, "and danced unto the Lord. There were

a great many times when dancing was used as
praise to God in the old days. It's a pity it
wasn't used more nowadays that way." Ruth
went quietly on with her sewing, as if she had
said the most commonplace thing.

The girls could not see whither she was leading them and Effie Haines protested. "But,
Miss Ruth, that isn't real dancing; they just
danced around with timbrels all alone."

"Well, we use a piano. What's the difference? A piano isn't wicked, is it?"

The girls laughed embarrassedly now. Ruth
saw that they did not know what to answer her.

"Dear girls," she said, "you asked me an
honest question and I answered it honestly. I
do think that dancing as it is carried on to-day
is wrong, and not only wrong, but exceedingly
dangerous. I do not believe that dancing just
of itself is wicked, and by that I mean whirling
around to music just from pure joy in life. But
I know that you meant more than that by your
question. You meant to ask me whether I
would dance myself, and whether I would advise you to dance, and I say no to that, most decidedly. The dangers that lurk in dancing are
so great that it seems to me one is only safe to
let it entirely alone in every form. You see
dancing nowadays isn't merely hopping about
alone as Effie has said. It means hopping

around with some one else, and that some one
else is sometimes a man. Now tell me honestly
girls, would you, any of you, allow a man under
any other circumstances, unless you were engaged or married to him of course, to take such
liberties with you as are allowed in dancing?"
The girls looked down at their work and their
cheeks grew a shade redder. All of them had
not had such careful teaching as had their
teacher, but they knew what she meant, and if
some few of them had occasionally allowed a
young man to hold their hands in the dark on
their way home from meeting, and to kiss them
at the gate just for fun occasionally, they were
ashamed of it now, and hoped Miss Ruth would
never find it out, and resolved never to allow
such a liberty again.

And then Ruth entered into a serious talk
which would have done credit to a wiser head
than her own. She told them solemnly what a
wonderful, awful power was this gift of God,
this influence of woman over man, and man
over woman. She reminded them that when
they came to give their earthly lives into the
keeping of some man who was all the world to
them, they would want to bring hands unsoiled
by the touch of other men, and lips unkissed by
any other half-love or play love. The girls sat
back and neglected their work while they

watched her earnest face and drank in her words.
They had never heard such talk before and it
appealed to the best that was in their natures.

Ellen Amelia, watching her, made up her
mind that here was a higher ideal of manhood
and womanhood than any which she had ever
found in the columns of her weekly story paper.

"My goodness!" said Effie Haines thoughtfully as she wended her way home with the rest
of the girls.   " It must be an awful lot of trouble
to live with all those ideas ; but they're lovely
though, aren't they, girls?   Isn't she good!
My! I wish I was like her."

That was the first talk they had. Thereafter
it became a regular thing after the special lesson
in cutting or fitting had been given for the day,
to ask questions. Sometimes the questions were
written, and the themes discussed were as various
as the characters of the girls. The mysteries of
love, the sacredness of marriage, were themes
which interested these girls, who discovered
that they truly wanted to find out the right
about everything. Not that Ruth laid down
her way of thinking as law to them. She only
talked over things and suggested reasons to
them. Sometimes she read a selection from
some good writer bearing on their topic. Sometimes she was ready with clippings from the
newspapers and quotations from the encyclopæ-

dia to prove certain facts which they had never
heard of before. She was teaching these girls
to think, and to reason out right and wrong for
themselves, and above all she had the Bible to
refer to constantly. Sometimes the girls had
dainty cards given them containing a single
verse which answered a question they had asked
at the last Saturday class. The class grew larger
and the members were quite regular. When
Ruth found that they all loved dancing so, and
that the mere motion to music was pleasure to
them, she suggested some gymnastics, and at a
certain hour the various gowns and other garments upon which they had been working were
laid aside and they all stood up in the great
attic room and went through some most delightful exercises which were utterly new to them.
Ruth was an adept in all sorts of gymnastics,
and made the little work she gave them intensely
interesting as well as profitable physically to
them. This last feature of the class took like
wildfire in Summerton. The girls told their
friends of course, and every girl in town was
crazy to join. Ruth was flooded with petitions
from interested mothers and eager girls, and at
last a class was formed in the town hall, and a
piano and an accompanist hired. "I can do
some good and gain some influence by it perhaps, and certainly I can give them something

delightful which may take the place of dancing," she said to herself, and she went to her
class feeling that her Master had called her to
it.

Deacon Chatterton shook his head of course
and declared it was all wrong and just as bad as
dancing—frivolous, wicked to waste time in
such useless ways—and no good would come
of it.

But many and many a time Ruth had opportunity before or after her class, when she was
helping some girl in a particularly difficult turn
with the Indian clubs, or the dumb-bells, to get
in a little word about her longing to have the
girl give herself to Jesus, and many a one first
found Jesus Christ in the old town hall, sitting
in a darkening corner late in the afternoon after
the rest of the class had gone, and talking in
low tones with the earnest-faced little teacher.

The dressmaking-class was confined, however,
to Ruth's own Sunday-school class, and the earnest talks over the sewing were long to be remembered by all of them. There came a day
too when Ruth ventured a new plan. Just before they were folding their work to go home
she said:

"Girls, I wish you would kneel down with
me here and let us have a little prayer meeting
together. I know I am asking something un-

usual, but I would like it so much. You know
I've been praying for you all ever since I took
the class, and isn't it about time you helped
me? Some of you don't belong to Jesus. I do
want you to know him right away. Can't we
just kneel down here together and will you try
to think God is here and you could see him if
you looked up, and then will you each ask of
him what you most want? I don't want to force
any of you to pray, of course, if you are not
willing, and I don't want any of you to do it
just because I ask. If you have nothing in
your heart to say, then never mind ; but I think
you all could say, 'Dear Jesus, I want to be
saved,' or 'Dear Lord, show me the way to thee.'
Ellen, dear, will you pray first and will the
others follow right around the room, please?"
And then as quietly as if she had been asking
them to cut a skirt lining this peculiar girl
knelt down and waited.

Her tone had been so every-day and matter-
of-course that not one of them had thought to
demur. Indeed they were too frightened to do
so, had she given them a chance. They knelt
quickly to get away from their own embarrassment.

Poor Ellen Amelia Haskins knelt, her heart
beating faster than she had ever known it to do
before, and wondered what she should say. There

was an element of the dramatic and noble which
would have struck her in this strange scene if
she had not been a part of it, but as it was there
suddenly came to her a sense of her utter inad-
equateness to fill the position required of her.
And yet she was a professed Christian. She
knelt and waited, and Ruth's words came to
her: "Try to think God is here and you could
see him if you looked up." Then she was
ashamed that she had no words for the great
God, and she choked and the tears came, and at
last in desperation she stumbled out the words,
"O God, forgive me!" There were pauses, and
then the others, all but two, asked something—
some humble, frightened petition. And after
Ruth had prayed a few words which seemed to
bring the realization of Christ's presence plainly
to their minds they rose with tears on their
cheeks.

"I think that was the first time I ever really
prayed," whispered Effie Haines as she took
her leave, pressing her tear-wet face on Ruth's
shoulder; "I am glad I did it. Maybe I'll try
again."

And that was not the last little prayer meeting that ended a day of dressmaking at the Benedict farm, for that was where Ellen Haskins
learned to pray.

But Louise Clifton had gone to New York on

a visit shortly after Thanksgiving, to get rid of her troublesome thoughts, and indulge some of her worldly longings, and she was not a part of all this. It seemed a pity to David, looking on, that the one for whom he was praying with strong, deep desire, earnest purpose, and firm belief, should have been allowed to go away just now when she might have been drawn into this tide of helpfulness that was sweeping through the village. He thought a good deal about it sometimes, and when he came to pray he was troubled to find a questioning note of the wisdom of God's planning in this particular case, and then he pulled himself up short and said: "See here, David Benedict, are you running this, or is God? Don't you suppose God knew and loved this bright, sweet girl before ever you knew there was such a being, and before ever you found out what danger there was surrounding her? Now you just let things alone and God will manage. If you do your part God will surely do his."

But always he prayed night and morning that God's angels would surround her and guard her feet from temptation. And his prayer was answered. Louise had sought to do this and that thing to amuse and distract her, and was constantly foiled in her attempts. There was something strange about it. Accident or weather or the sudden illness of a friend would keep her away from places she most desired to attend. When she did succeed in going, troublesome thoughts would seize upon her and destroy all pleasure in what she heard or saw. She began to feel like a child and to wish for her mother. Her nerves seemed all unstrung. In truth she was not well, and constantly her mind would go back with shame to that uncomfortable night when David Benedict had been obliged to kidnap her and carry her off like a little child to save her from a terrible danger into which she had foolishly thrown herself in her ignorance.

Once at a concert she saw Alonzo Brummel in the distance, and he came over to her and tried to appear upon very intimate terms with her, but she fairly froze him with her coolness, until her friend Fannie Gleason, whom she was visiting, said:

"What is the matter with the poor little man, Lou dear? You were very hard on him. I quite liked him. He was real bright and handsome, and was elegantly dressed. Who is he?"

And that night Louise Clifton wrote to her mother that she would like to come home at once.

CHAPTER XXIII

THERE was a large religious gathering in
session for two days in the city near Summerton, and thither Robert Clifton and David
Benedict had gone. They had arranged to spend
the night that they might attend the evening
and early morning meetings, which were important. It was the first gathering of the kind
David had ever attended and it was a treat indeed to him. Joseph would have liked to go too,
but they could not both be away and he declared
that it was more important for David to attend,
as it had to do with Sunday-school work, and
David, having just taken a class, was eager to
learn all he could about it. Ruth rejoiced in
the thought that her brother had gone to a Sunday-school convention in company with the
minister. Her brothers were a great source of
happiness to her in these days.

The second day of the meetings was drawing
to a close. The afternoon session was over and
the minister was preparing to take the train
home that he might be in time for a special
meeting, while David was to stay for the evening closing session to hear an especially fine

speaker whom Robert Clifton was anxious that
he should not miss. They were walking slowly
up the steps to the hotel when one of the messenger boys of the house stepped up to the minister and asked, " Ain't you Mr. Robert Clifton?
Well, here's a telegram been waitin' fer you an
hour. I went down to the church, but couldn't
find no trace of you."

The minister tore the yellow envelope open
hastily, a shade of anxious anticipation on his
face, and as he read, the expression changed to
one of annoyance and perplexity.

"I'm sure I don't know what I'm to do," he
said, looking up at David in a troubled way.
" My mother has telegraphed me to take the
midnight train for New York and bring my
sister home. I cannot possibly go unless it is
a question of life and death. She does not say
Louise is ill, merely that she wants to come
home. I can't leave that temperance meeting
at home this evening, after being so prominent
in getting it up and after promising to speak.
And there is Judge Tanner's funeral to-morrow
morning, which will last all day, as they are to
bury away over at East Ivy Hill. And it is getting toward Sunday. I could not possibly go
until Monday. I don't understand mother's
sending me this special word just now. She
must have forgotten the funeral."

In his heart the minister knew that to his mother the funeral would make no difference. She deemed that his duty toward her and his sister was far above any duty he had to the church or to any outsider, dead or alive. He had tried many times to explain such things to her, but she had cried and told him that his father had not so looked upon duty, and that he would be ashamed of his son if he could know how utterly bereft of a care-taker she and her daughter were. But he did not so far forget himself as to mention these things to David Benedict.

David had listened courteously and when the trouble was made known he instantly said :

" Could not I be of assistance to you ? I will gladly go to New York if you will trust me with the care of your sister. I could not well take the meeting and the funeral or I would be as willing to do that."

The cloud lifted from Robert Clifton's face at once.

" The very thing," he said in a relieved tone. " Wouldn't you mind a bit ? I'd gladly pay your fare twice over to get rid of the journey, and just now especially."

" I should enjoy it immensely. You needn't think of paying my fare. I have thought for some time of taking a trip to New York and there is no reason why I cannot as well take it

now as at any time, if you will tell my sister
what has become of me and ask Joseph to attend
to one or two matters for me. Do you think
your sister will object?"

"Certainly not," answered the minister decidedly. "Why should she? I know of no
one with whom I would sooner trust her."

Robert Clifton had but a few minutes in which
to make his train, so they had not much time to
talk. He wrote a hasty telegram to his sister,
"Be ready to start home to-morrow," signing his
own name, and giving careful directions to
David how to find the house where his sister was
visiting, he hastened away to his sermons and
his meeting and funeral, feeling relieved beyond
measure that he need not stop all his work just
at this his busy season, to take the long trip to
New York.

David Benedict, the evening meetings of the
convention over, sat him down in the railroad
station to await the train to New York. He
was exultantly happy. He had not yet stopped
to examine himself to see why he was so deeply
glad. There was time enough for that. To
his sister Ruth he had sent a single message,
"Please pray that I may be led of the Lord,"
and Ruth, as she read it a few hours later,
smiled to herself, and was glad that her brother
was so changed as to make this a natural mes-

sage for him to send her, and yet it sounded
very like the David he had been during the past
few weeks. Then she read it again, and remembered the first night he had ever asked her to
pray for some one, and thought a moment and
said aloud, "I wonder if it can be she."

David was interested in all that went on about
him. He watched an elegant young man who
came in with immaculate overcoat, umbrella,
and dress-suit case. He observed the accustomed air with which he bought his ticket, and
the matter-of-fact way in which he asked a few
pertinent questions concerning his train. There
was something about the young man that David
liked. He looked down at himself and was dissatisfied for the first time with his own Summerton ready-made clothes. Not that they were not
fine and good, but there was a finish about the
city young man that pleased David. He felt
that he would move with more ease if he were
dressed in that way. He began to reflect that it
might be a good plan for him to look after a
few minor details of dress himself if he was to
escort a young woman on a journey. She must
not be made to be ashamed of him. He wondered if there were little things about traveling
which he ought to know in order to make the
journey a pleasant one for her. He would watch
this young man and see. And presently, as if

to help him, there entered a young woman with an elderly gentleman, who seemed to be the sister of the young man and who was apparently going in company with him. David made up his mind that he would let nothing escape him, and see if he could profit by their conduct for the homeward trip. Accordingly, when the train was called he followed them out and attempted to enter the same car, but a uniformed porter forbade him saying, " Sleeper ticket, sir. This is the sleeper for New York." Ah! David had forgotten that. He was willing enough to sit up all night if need be, for the journey was a pleasant novelty to him; but if he would keep near these two he must do as they did, so he hastened back to the station and managed to secure the last berth left. Luckily it proved to be in the same car with the two, and he watched the numerous little attentions of this young man for his sister with increasing interest, noting carefully the orders to the porter and the mysteries of electric bells. He would know all he needed to know without having the humiliation of asking the young woman he was to escort.

David did not sleep that night. It was too novel a position for him to care to sleep much, but he rested and thought. Alone in the darkness of his berth there came to him a realization of the wondrous care of God. He thought of the train and how it was plunging along in darkness, and how he lay there as quietly and safely as in his own home. God was caring for him. He rejoiced that he knew the wonderful God. He was a Christian who really and truly "rejoiced in the Lord." Life seemed to be opening before him so rich and full.

Then he began to examine himself. What was this other feeling, a sort of elation, which seemed to belong especially to this journey? It was something very sweet and beautiful. He had not stopped before to ask himself what it was. Was it?—yes, it surely was because of the fact that he was going after Louise Clifton, and that it was to be his precious task to bring her safely home, and that now she was to remain at home and would be among them again. Was that a wrong feeling for him to have? No, he could not feel that it was. She was one of God's creations. Had he not been praying for her with his whole soul for weeks and months? He could not tell why he had felt the burden of her salvation so strongly upon him, but it had been there, and he had fully obeyed all commands it had laid upon him, and fairly poured out his soul before the throne for her. It had been given him to realize her danger and her need so fully that night of their Thanksgiving ride, that he had felt God must and would answer and show her the light. He had not doubted but that the answer would come. She was so sweet and bright and beautiful. His own feeling about her he had never questioned. His anxiety had been for her, and so he had prayed. Now it suddenly came to him, " I love her," and he rejoiced in that love as he would rejoice in any other great gift. He felt at the first that his love did not necessarily include the return of it by her, neither did it include his possession of even her friendship; but he and she were in the world and he could love her, and he was glad that he could. It was a new joy he had not thought of before with relation to himself, and it was all the more pure and holy in that it was as yet utterly unconnected with any thought of the future or of possession. He guarded this newly discovered treasure in his heart as sacred. He would not even think about it too much lest it should be tarnished by constant handling. A beautiful hope began to come to him. Perhaps, oh, perhaps, the Master would accept his humble service and let him be the messenger through whom the message of life and salvation should be brought to her soul. And all that night long David Benedict, the new-made follower of the blessed Jesus, lay in his berth and prayed, and in the morning he arose peaceful and refreshed notwithstanding his vigil.

Meantime the minister had been passing through less calm seas. His train was late for one thing. A freight wreck ahead of them had kept them almost an hour on a side track. When they finally reached Summerton he had but forty-five minutes in which to go home, eat some supper, dress, and prepare to present himself at the town hall temperance mass-meeting.

His trouble began as he took his latchkey from the parsonage door. His mother appeared on the upper stair-landing in as much consternation as her small body could express.

"Robert! My dear boy! What has happened? Didn't you get my telegram? Where is your sister?"

The minister was tired and worried. He had been trying all the way up from the station to remember whether he had left his notes for that evening's address on his study table. If he had he feared much for their present existence, for one of the things which he could not persuade his over-scrupulous mother to do was to let his desk, with its multitudinous papers, alone. She would clear it off every time he went out, explaining carefully, "No one has touched it, Robert, but myself, and of course I would not throw away anything of value," and she could not be made to understand that the scraps of scribbled paper were sometimes of more value

than all else the minister had on his table. He
was too loyal and courteous a son to scold after
such occurrences, and merely made his request
that it should not be touched again, but always
with the same result. He was growing now so
that he carefully put under lock and key all
papers before he went out; but he had a strong
suspicion that he had not gone back to the study
to do so before he left for the convention, on account of a sudden call to the parlor to see a man
just before train time. It was this worry which
perhaps made his tone seem a little annoyed and
sharp to his mother. He had forgotten completely about Louise and the telegram until
his mother brought it to his mind, and now
for the first time it dawned upon his inner
consciousness that in all probability she would
not think he had done the best he might have
done in sending David Benedict in his place.

"Yes, I received your telegram, mother; but
you surely knew I could not go to New York
this week. You were well aware that I had
to speak at a meeting in the town hall this
evening, and that I had a funeral to-morrow
morning which would keep me all day, and that
Sunday is almost here with its two sermons
which are scarcely touched as yet."

There were times when Mrs. Clifton could
grow exceedingly indignant, and at such times

she waxed quite eloquent. This was such an
occasion. She had worked herself into a fretful
state over Louise's letter lest the girl were sick,
which might perhaps excuse her seeming unrea-
sonableness.

"Robert, you cannot mean that you ignored
it! You do not intend to tell me that you
count any duty in the world above that you hold
to your mother and sister? I should not have
telegraphed you if there had not been a sufficient
reason. There is something the matter with
Louise, and she needs to come home to her
mother at once. Certainly, I remembered the
temperance meeting to-night, but I also remembered that it was only a temperance meeting.
There won't be half a dozen people out, and
Deacon Chatterton can talk well enough for
them. As for the funeral, the minister of the
other church could go. The living are of more
account than the dead, always. And your sermons don't need to be fussed over so long. You
can get up and talk well enough for these people
for once. You always put a great deal more
work on your sermons than they appreciate,
anyway. I insist, I command, as your mother,
Robert, that you leave to-night to bring your
sister home."

Mrs. Clifton's cheeks were red and her eyes
were bright. There were signs of recent tears

on her face which her son did not see. She had been worrying about her daughter and crying for her departed husband all day long.

"Mother, you forget yourself. I shall have to remind you that you do not know all about my duties or you would not speak so. It would be utterly impossible for me to go to-night unless it were a matter of life and death. But you need not get so excited. I have sent for Louise. What does she say is the reason for her sudden desire to come home?"

Mrs. Clifton ignored the question.

"Sent for her!" she fairly screamed. "Do you expect Louise to travel alone? Oh, if your father could see you now and know!" and she ended with a groan.

Her son put his hand upon her shoulder and tried to quiet her.

"No, mother dear; listen. I have sent a suitable escort for her. Do not worry like this. Please order some supper, for I have but a few moments before I must be at the hall."

Mrs. Clifton straightened up.

"Whom have you sent for your sister? I wish to know at once."

"Mother, I have sent a suitable, safe person."

"Tell me at once who the person is. When you get so far as to turn your family duties over to the hands of strangers I wish to be consulted."

"Mother, I have sent a person whom I would trust with the most precious possession I have in the world. I have sent David Benedict. He offered to go when he saw my perplexity." The minister stopped. Somehow he felt as he had when he had done a naughty thing as a little boy and stood before his mother to account for his conduct. This sending of a young man for his sister seemed suddenly to appear before him as a heinous offense.

Mrs. Clifton's consternation silenced her for a moment. "David Benedict, indeed! Well, thank fortune, she is well enough trained to refuse to come with him! The impertinence of his suggesting such a thing! Well, it appears that I shall have to go after my child myself." Whereupon she swept into her room and closed the door to dissolve in tears of bewilderment and grief, while her puzzled, worried son recovered from his shock and rummaged wildly through his papers for some suitable notes—his intended address being gone beyond recovery—and finally rushed supperless and addressless to the meeting to search his mind in vain for any trace of what he had so carefully prepared. He wondered vaguely in the meantime why it had been so dreadful to send a good Christian young man to escort his sister home. There was just one little ray of comfort in the whole troubled evening, and

that was that he had promised to let Ruth Benedict know what had become of her brother, and
he knew that her smile or some word of hers
would pour oil into his wounds and make him
glad. He had known this certainly for some
time now, and it gave him deep joy. But he
felt very uncertain whether she even quite ap-
proved of him yet. He dared not hope it. Once
he found a little scrap of a poem which seemed
as if it were written to give him help. He cut
it out and pasted it in the fly leaf of his mem-
oranda book :

God's plans for thee are graciously unfolding,
   And leaf by leaf they blossom perfectly,
As yon fair rose, from its soft enfolding,
   In marvelous beauty opens fragrantly.
Oh, wait in patience for thy dear Lord's coming,
   For sure deliverance he'll bring to thee ;
Then, how thou shalt rejoice at the fair dawning
   Of that sweet morn which ends thy long captivity.

CHAPTER XXIV

IT was rather early in the morning for New York high life when David Benedict presented himself at the house where Louise Clifton was staying and asked to see her at once. He had done a good deal of sightseeing. He had purchased a dress-suit case like the one he had seen on the way, for it had struck him as a very useful article. He had stowed it with various gifts for Ruth and Joseph and a few articles for himself, which it had occurred to him would be good things to have, and which he had not hitherto considered necessaries. The young man on the train had made a difference in David Benedict's ideas of cultured life and refinement. He had left his old overcoat at a coffee and mission house, where he had stepped in for a few minutes to join in the singing and rejoice in the number of reformed men who were testifying to the power of Jesus to save, and he had bought a new one, the counterpart as nearly as he could find it, of the one his admiration of the night before had worn. The new overcoat had necessitated a new hat also, and he had added gloves. Altogether, had he but known it, he looked a great deal better than the young man he had so admired, for David was a handsome man, with a rugged, unconscious, homely beauty that had much sterling character behind it.

Louise, and Fannie Gleason were attired in becoming wrappers, sipping chocolate and eating delicately toasted bread. Each had a book beside her, and they were having a delightfully late breakfast in their room, having just arisen, and not having anything particular in view for the morning's occupation. Louise's long golden hair was hanging down her back over her rich creamy cashmere wrapper. She liked occasionally to be lazy and pretend that she was a damsel of an Oriental court, who lolled and lived in defiance of the stern laws of work-a-day life. Besides, she meant to try a new way of arranging her hair soon, and she wished to take plenty of time to it.

The servant brought her a telegram which proved to be from her brother. Louise tossed it on the table, and felt a little disappointed now that she knew she was actually to return to the stupid little town. She had not thought her mother would be so summary. She had hoped she would come on and make a visit or go somewhere else with her. Besides, there was a delightful invitation for next week, which had arrived just after she mailed her last letter to her

mother. She did not want to go home nearly
so much as she had done two days before. She
told Fannie about it, and they talked it over and
decided to keep Robert over the next week if
possible. Fannie was only too eager for an interesting young man to add to their pleasant
circle. He needed a change and rest. All young
ministers were worked to death; that was a matter of course. Louise was not so certain that
she could keep him; but she decided she would
at least let him return alone if he would not
wait a few days, and then, while they were talking, the servant came again announcing a young
man who did not give his name, but had said,
"Please tell Miss Clifton I have come for
her."

"It's Robert, of course," said Louise, getting
up annoyed, "and he will be in a hurry, of
course, and here I am in this rig. I can't go in
this way, and my hair all down too. He'll just
have to wait till I'm dressed. I shall not have an
easy task, Fannie, I assure you, for Rob is awfully
set in his way and as devoted to his seven-by-
nine church as a mother to her child. I wish I
was ready, for by the time I get down he will
be so worked up over having to wait that I
sha'n't have nearly so easy a task."

"What do you wait to dress for? Go along,
now, and I'll fix it all up. Maggie, tell the

gentleman to go to the morning sitting room
and his sister will come at once. There, go
along. There isn't a soul about now. Mamma
went to her executive meeting half an hour ago,
and nobody will see you but the servants. You
look as sweet as a picture. My! I only wish I
had such hair."

The morning sitting room was on the second
floor, and was furnished all in soft, dull yellows
and browns with luxurious couches and deep
easy-chairs and pillows. David was ushered into
it, and not many minutes later he heard a soft
step on carpeted stairs, and Louise stood in the
doorway, coming to meet him with a smile
of welcome on her face intended for her brother.
She paused in the center of the room, taken
aback by the presence of a stranger. She
stood just where a patch of morning sunshine
caught her hair and made a glory of it, and the
soft tones of golden brown and yellow in the
draperies of a door and couch behind her made
a fitting background for the creamy folds of her
morning gown, which was all soft and white,
with a touch of lace, filmy and rich, at throat
and wrists, and a clasp of gold filigree at her
waist. Louise dearly loved the artistic in her
toilets, and it was perhaps for this reason that
she had fallen so quickly in love with Ruth, for
she felt they had an artistic bond in common.

David had risen when he heard her step, and now he stood spellbound gazing upon her. He had never seen any one so lovely. She looked like some bright celestial spirit as she stood there with her halo of golden hair. He could not speak, he could only gaze, and his earnest, truth-telling face must have almost frightened the girl with its intensity of admiration if she had not been bewildered by his unexpected appearance. She stood dazed a moment, fully realizing her position and her costume, and unable to collect her faculties sufficiently to know what to do. But the quietness and deep reverence of David's gaze suddenly brought her to herself, and she turned and fled. Had he been almost any other young man of her acquaintance, Louise would have blushed and laughed, and though she would have been embarrassed, she would have quickly twisted up the flowing hair which gave her so much trouble and sat down with a comical explanation; but being David, she fled. She did not know why she felt so about this young man, but she did. She flew up the stairs to her room, only pausing to give a passing servant a stiff message for the waiting gentleman in the morning room that she would be down by and by, and then locking her door she made a more leisurely and careful toilet than even she was accustomed to do. The young man might wait now as long as he chose. When next he saw her she would be as dignified and distant as it was possible for apparel to make her. She even meditated putting on a hat, but decided that that would be absurd. Her cheeks grew redder and redder as she progressed with her toilet. She was beginning to grow indignant with David for having gotten her into such a ridiculous plight. She would not be reasonable and see that it was all her own fault. She was thankful that Fannie had gone into her mother's room and was not there to witness her excitement.

And David, his vision vanished, stood staring at the spot where she had stood, almost blinded with the sight. When the servant entered the room with the message, he bowed quietly and sat down; but when he was alone he looked again at the place where she had stood, and said in a reverent tone and with an almost holy light upon his face, "I love her," and then putting up his hand as if to cover his eyes, he added in an audible voice, as if he were registering a vow, "But it shall not make any difference."

Then he sat back and leaned his head against the soft upholstery and looked like a man who had been privileged above many. There was a rapt look upon his face. You would have believed it if you had been told that he was praying. And the time did not seem long to him before Louise returned. He understood it all. He did not need her dignified explanation and apology. He greeted her with a gentle, deferential tone, and he forestalled all she had to say by apologizing for causing her any trouble. Then he told her simply that he had come for her, and asked when she could be ready.

"But where is my brother?" asked the astonished young woman. "He was to come for me."

"He could not come, Miss Clifton; there was a meeting and a funeral, and he feared you would not like to wait until next week, so he sent me. I am sorry you are not to have a more desirable companion, but I will do my best."

"Well, I'm sorry if you have been to any trouble," began Louise, determining at once not to go home in David Benedict's company under the present circumstances. "But I had decided not to return until next week or the week after. I shall write my mother so at once. I hope you did not make a special trip on my account. I supposed you were here on business. My brother will doubtless be able to come for me soon, or— I could go alone. It is not a difficult journey." Louise realized that she was being almost rude by the way she was talking to her visitor, but she stumbled ahead blindly, making it worse with every sentence.

With just a shadow on his quiet face and a
note of something different in his voice, did
David express the sudden pain she gave him by
her words, as he said, "Have you then not forgiven me yet?"   Then his tone changed to the
old masterful one, and Louise was at once
reminded of her compulsory sleigh-ride on
Thanksgiving night.   "Miss Clifton, I have no
right, of course, to insist; but I have been
charged to bring you home, and I wish you
would come.   Indeed, I think it would be better.
Your mother is expecting you and I should not
like to return without you."

In spite of herself Louise had to give in, for
she was ashamed of herself.   She talked haughtily
a few moments more, but she knew in her heart
from that first masterful sentence he had spoken
that she would consent to go.

Fannie, in her room again, was growing impa-
tient to know the result of the conference.   She
had made a hasty toilet after Louise left and sat
waiting for her return.

"You don't mean to say you're really going,
and going to-day!   Why, Lou!   You can't possibly get ready; the train leaves in two hours.
And who is he?   Is he a special friend of the
family?   Maggie says he's awfully handsome.
Is he fond of you?   My, I envy you!   You'll
have a grand time on the way—a whole young

man to yourself for so many hours! I predict
all sorts of interesting episodes. He must be
awfully nice or your mother would never let you
go alone with him. She is so particular about
chaperons and such things. Do take me down,
Lou, and introduce me, quick. I won't be left
out altogether."

So Fannie rattled on, while Louise opened
bureau drawers and without seeming to care or
know what she did, unceremoniously dumped
their contents into her trunk. Having made up
her mind to go, Louise seemed to be in a fever
of impatience to get ready lest they might miss
the train. And all the time she kept wondering
to herself why it was she did as David told her.

Fannie was taken down and introduced, and
came back to help her friend with the last little
preparations, going into raptures over David.

"Why Lou, he's just magnificent! I think
you are the slyest girl I ever saw; you never
once mentioned his name all the time you were
here. Oh, I know there's a good deal more to
this than you will admit. Wasn't he at home
when you left? I can't think what made you
come away. Had you been quarreling? I just
believe you had; and I'll tell you, Louie dear, it
doesn't do to quarrel with men that have such
firm chins, for they always get the better of one.
Tell me the truth, Lou, did you get clear into the

room so that he saw you with your hair down before you discovered it wasn't your brother? Oh,
I just know you did by your face; and I would
have given anything to have seen his face when
he first looked at you. You were a perfect angel
in that white and gold gown."

Louise was very much annoyed by this talk.
It seemed as if all sorts of sacred things were
being tumbled about and torn open by Fannie's
curious tongue. She got away from her at last,
though she had to spend a very tiresome hour
with her while David went away for his lunch
and to order a carriage. He had watched that
morning as the young man of the sleeper ordered
a carriage and put his sister in and then sat down
beside her. David made up his mind that he
would do likewise with the lady of his care.

Fannie went with them to the station and
chattered with David all the way, and he was
grave and pleasant and respectful. He was
wondering what Louise found in her to like.
But she was Louise's friend and he treated her
accordingly.

It was a relief when at last the train moved
out from the station. David had secured two
chairs in the parlor car. As there was no sleeper
on the day train he discovered that the chair car
took its place. He seated Louise and waited upon
her in all the ways he had seen that other young

man use, and then he set himself for an hour to
be as agreeable as it was in him to be. He had
read much and could talk well. He was not all
gravity, as Louise discovered. He could make
witty remarks and tell bright stories; and while
he knew nothing at all about the "small talk"
which was common parlance with most of her
young men acquaintances, he succeeded in making her forget herself and her unusual position.
Then he bought one or two of the latest and best
magazines, and with a delicacy born of innate
refinement decided that he would not bore her
with too much of his company, so murmuring
some excuse of hunting up the porter and giving
orders for supper at the best point he went away.
He really seated himself in the common car for
an hour and closed his eyes and prayed.

When he returned to the parlor car he found
that the young lady had finished looking at the
papers and was gazing out of the window looking
tired and somewhat cross. She looked up as he
sat down beside her, and asked:

"Mr. Benedict, do you smoke?"

She asked the question as if she wanted to
find out for a definite purpose, not as if she ob-
jected to it particularly. David looked at her in
astonishment, and then a sudden light broke over
his face and he smiled.

"No, I do not smoke. You thought that was

why I went away for so long? It was not. I
wanted to give you a rest from my company.
Do you like smoking?"

"You need not do that again, Mr. Benedict; I
would rather have you stay here. I am ashamed
for the way in which I treated you about coming
home to-day. I was—well, I——" Louise found
she could not quite explain what had been the
matter without saying more than she cared to,
so she stopped in confusion.

"I understand," said David; "never mind
that; and thank you for saying you would
rather I would stay."

He was looking at her so earnestly now that
it confused her, and struggling to find a topic
for conversation she seized his last unanswered
question.

"No, Mr. Benedict, I don't really like smoking; but I don't know any reason why I should
object. Nearly all my friends do smoke, except
my brother; but—I was a little surprised that
you should, you seem so—so—well, so different——"

"Thank you. I'm glad I don't seem like a
smoker; but I must be honest and tell you I used
to smoke until I found my sister, and she made
me see how disagreeable a thing it is. I'm sorry
I ever smoked. I never will again. But, Miss
Clifton, I want to presume very much on what

you said a moment ago. You said you would
rather I would stay here, and I am going to ask
you to be kind enough to let me tell you what I
have wanted to say to you for a long time. It
may seem unfair to you that I should take this
time, when you are so situated that you cannot
get away from me if you would; but I think
you will bear with me. It is very important. I
don't think I can promise to stop, even if you
ask me, till I have told you all I wish. Will
you bear with me?"

Louise looked up with frightened eyes. She
had seen David's grave, steady gaze at her during
the few hours they had been together that day,
and it had made her heart throb with wonder
and a strange new kind of joy she did not understand, but she dreaded anything that he might
say. It was so new she did not want to have it
brought out and looked at till she had time to
think and understand herself. Instinctively she
knew that his look had been of something deeper
than friendship. Was he going to speak of it
now? She could not utter a syllable, and her
silence seemed to give him the permission he
asked. Yes, it was a story of love he had to
tell—of wonderful love—but not of his own.
Louise, as she listened—and she could not but
listen, because the words came from a heart which
had communed much with God, and knew ex-

actly what it was speaking about—felt that she
was a little child being shown Jesus for the first
time. So simply, so gently did David put the
whole matter of being a Christian before her,
that she felt as if it would be the most natural
thing in the world to give herself entirely to
Christ right away that minute, and not stop to
think how it would affect this or that question.
David had thought about this talk for weeks and
even months. He had not even fixed it in his
mind that he was to have the opportunity for it;
but still he felt that sometime the chance might
come, and he kept asking himself just what
would reach him if he were a young girl like
this one. He had thought about it so much and
prayed about it so much that when the Master
gave the opportunity he was ready for the work,
and the Spirit gave the words. He spoke,
Louise afterward many a time thought, as if he
were inspired for the time. If his words were
written here, which they cannot be, because
there is no record of them except in Louise's
heart, they might not be understood. It was
partly the earnestness and fire with which he
spoke, the high, exalted look on his face, the
firm conviction of his listener that he knew and
had proved what he said to be true, the great
longing in his whole expression, his own great
love for Jesus—that won her first to listen, then

to long, and then to love this Saviour whom he would fain bring to her knowledge.

It was growing dark. The train rushed along through the blurr of indistinguishable objects. Their chairs were turned together toward the darkened window, and they did not notice that the porter coming through had lighted all the lamps. For a full hour David had leaned forward eagerly and talked in low impassioned tones, of reason, pleading, explanation. Louise had answered very little. Her face was turned away toward the window and her eyes were drooping to hide the tears which gathered fast. To her it was as if the Saviour in very presence stood there between them pleading for her soul, and she was longing to give her heart to him but could not do it, and the ache of resistance was very great. At last David seemed to have said all that he had to say. His purpose was almost accomplished. He placed his hand reverently on one of her little trembling, cold, gloved hands and said in tones that almost pierced her with the longing they expressed,

" Won't you, oh, won't you come to him now ? "

They sat for a full minute thus. David hardly dared breathe, and Louise could not speak or get control of her voice. An undiscerning observer on the other side of the car curiously wondered what kind of a quarrel that handsome bride and groom were having which kept them busy so long, and then retired behind his paper, concluding it was not worth while to watch, and never knew that a decision was being made which would affect two worlds. And then Louise turned her head toward David with a quick motion, and looking him straight in his earnest, longing eyes, with her own brimming over with tears, answered him tremblingly:

"Yes, I will. Show me how, please."

The rest of that evening's ride flew swiftly by for the two. The supper which the porter presently served to them seemed nectar and ambrosia, and might have been chips for all they knew about it. Louise said little, but she felt much. It may be because she had so joyful a leader in her first steps in the new life that she felt so very happy. Her heart seemed lighter than the air. She felt that everything was new, and Jesus had been made to her a reality. That was the secret of it all. He loved her and she loved him. She looked up with a new reverence at the young man who had shown her the way, and whose face was shining with the joy of an angel and a man together. Henceforth he would to her stand out from and above all other men on the earth. He was more like Jesus Christ than any one she had ever seen, and Jesus Christ he had made to become her ideal.

CHAPTER XXV

I T was late that evening when Louise Clifton finally arrived in Summerton. Her anxious brother had paced the platform for an hour trying to escape his mother's reproaches. He was afraid that his sister would come and afraid that she would not come. He was not sure which would be the worse, for his mother was in a terrible state about the impropriety of her traveling so far in company with a young man. However, he was relieved to see her. As she kissed her brother, she wondered shyly if he would care for the decision she had made this evening, and she drew a sigh of almost dismay a few moments later when she realized that David, who had been such a strong tower of help to her, was to leave her now, and she would have to walk alone. No, not alone either, for Jesus would be with her; but that thought was so new that she did not always remember it at first.

She wondered what David would do, in her place, a few minutes later when she saw her mother. Mrs. Clifton met her daughter with open arms and tears.

"You poor, dear child! To think you had to come with that man! It was dreadful! I could not help it. I suppose you did not dare to stay there when Robert had sent him. I was so sorry for you."

"Why, mamma dear, what do you mean?" said Louise, her happy face puzzled for a moment. "Mr. Benedict was very kind and good. I could not have had a more considerate traveling companion; he did everything that a mortal could do to make it pleasant for me. And, mamma dear, I've something I want to tell you, something I think you will be glad about. I have given my heart to Christ, and I'm going to try to be a Christian. I haven't been the kind of daughter I ought to have been in lots of ways, and I wanted to tell you the first thing, that I'm going to try to be different now."

But the mother looked at her with dismay. She did not understand such talk.

"My darling child!" she exclaimed; "don't talk in that way, I beg of you. You have always been a dear, good daughter, and as for being a Christian, of course you are. You have been well brought up and taught to believe. You have never known anything else. Come now, my dear, and get to your room. You are utterly tired out. You will not feel so melancholy in the morning."

In vain did Louise urge that she was not in the least melancholy. She was very happy. The mother only looked the more frightened, and smiled and tried to get her to rest, and at last with a sinking heart she gave up the attempt and let her mother go. David had been so heartfelt in his joy over her salvation that she had unconsciously felt that her own loved ones would be also. It rather chilled her to have her mother take it in this way. Was the new life going to begin so hard at once?

The mother, poor bewildered soul, went to her long-suffering son for comfort.

"Robert," she said in excited tones, when she had closed his study door, "Louise is ill. She is not herself. She is talking religion, and you know how utterly foreign to her nature anything sad or melancholy is. I am afraid she is going to die or have a fit of sickness or something. I have heard of people talking in this way before dying. I knew something terrible would come of all this—putting meetings before your own family. Oh, if you or I had only gone for her instead of letting her be brought in this way!"

"What do you mean, mother?" demanded the thoroughly aroused and much-berated young minister. His nerves were quivering with the strain of the past two days. But the mother turned away, and he walked out of the study and went at once in alarm to his sister's door.

"Louie, may I come in?" he called anxiously. "Mother says you are sick. What is it? Tell me all about it. Didn't David take good care of you?"

She opened the door, laughing and crying all at once, and burying her face in his coat had a good cry, which was what she needed after the excitement of the day and the nerve tension she had been under for weeks. In a minute, when she could get control of herself, she told him shyly and sweetly how David had helped her, and how she had given herself to Jesus. "And mother doesn't understand me," she added wistfully.

"But I do," said her brother, a ring in his voice she had never heard him use for her before. And he stooped and kissed her in such a way that she felt comforted.

Coming back to his mother in the study later the minister said in joyful voice: "Mother, you are mistaken about Louie. She is not going to die; she has only just begun to live."

During these days Ellen Amelia Haskins had been steadily improving in mind and spirit. She was much under Ruth's influence, which could not be other than a blessing to her. Some things were happening too which helped to change the current of her life and give her a purpose. The minister's wife in West Winterton had a sister, a missionary, and it chanced this winter that she came home on a visit and spent a week with her sister. The minister availed himself of this opportunity to hold a missionary meeting, and as it came on a week night when Ellen was in West Winterton, and was held in the academy hall, she attended the meeting. Then a new influence reached her. She listened spellbound to the woman's story of the trials, the joys, the triumphs, of the missionary's life, and her soul was filled with longing to go. She recognized that here was something great in life that she could do which would please her Master, and she formed a settled purpose in her heart that she would do all she could toward getting ready, and then if the Lord willed it she would go. "I'll just get as far ready as I can," she said to herself, "and then he can do as he pleases about sending me." She said it with a humble, willing spirit and she set her energies to learn all she could in every way she could. Her mother began to be proud of her and to take heart of hope and predict a marriage with a thrifty farmer, and ask her if she didn't intend to try to secure a school to teach in a good district for the next winter, but Ellen said she didn't know and worked steadily on.

And then something wonderful happened to her. The Lord was opening her way step by step. It was almost time for the summer vacation when the word came that Uncle Timothy had died very suddenly, and that he had left to Ellen Amelia the sum of three thousand dollars to do with as she pleased.

"If I was you I'd just quit school at once," said her mother, a pleased, proud look on her face; "you'll not have any need for any more schoolin' now; you won't have to teach, and anybody'll be glad to get you, now you're well off. It makes a difference, in spite of all they say, and you can be more independent when you marry, if you have money of your own (Mrs. Haskins had been possessed of eight hundred dollars when she married the deacon, which she had willingly and humbly put into his business to help him along, but she often used the remembrance of her dowry as a rod with which to rule her husband). I wouldn't stay on at the 'cademy another day 'f I was you. You don't need to care whether you pass or not now."

But Ellen Amelia closed her lips which were becoming refined with gentleness and following her Saviour and went to pray about the matter. Having laid the subject before her all-wise Leader she went quietly to her father and put her plan before him.

The deacon sat on the back porch whittling and waiting for his dinner. He put down his knife and the front legs of his chair and listened carefully to his daughter's story, a film of mist gathering over his eyes as she talked. He answered her slowly at last and with a choke in his voice.

"Wal, Ellen, you couldn't do anythin' that would be a greater honor to yer ancestors 'n to be a missionary. I mus' say I am pleased to have a child of mine willin' to make such sacrifizes. I mightily hate to lose my little girl, but if yer heart's set on goin' I sha'n't say the word that'll stop you. Go ahead to your college or whatever you like. The money's yours an' it might be worse spent. I'll help you all I can," and then he sat and chewed the end of his stick and remembered how Ellen Amelia had looked when she was two years old in a pink calico pinafore and her face all bread and molasses.

But when Mother Haskins heard of the proposed plan, her first practical objection was: "Wal, I should like to know what you need of more schoolin' ef you're goin' to bury yourself out in some outlandish place in the-land-knows-where, with little naked heathens. I guess, if you've got enough knowledge to teach here in this Christian land, you've got enough to teach sinners that don't know their a-b-c's."

Mother Haskins, it must be explained, was disappointed. Missionaries were well enough, she felt, for a cousin once or twice removed, but she had looked to see her daughter marry a rich farmer and settle down where she might superintend the new home and manage Ellen Amelia's children. However, she found that her talk was of no avail as she could not immediately produce the rich, thrifty farmer to help her out, and so she settled down to console herself with what glory reflected upon her for having brought up a daughter who was to go to college with the life of a missionary as a halo in the future. And she found it not empty of honor, but rather one upon which she reflected with increasing satisfaction.

One afternoon in the sewing circle she remarked with pardonable pride and a pin in her mouth :

" Yes, it will be hard to give her up, but then it's a great blessing to have one's children turn to the ways of righteousness ; and they do say that 'out there' (which term applied to some far-away mission field and represented her daughter's future home veiled in the mist of somewhere or nowhere to her mother) they don't have sech hard times, with plenty of servants to do everythin' for one and not a livin' thing to do but preach the gospil. No, I don't suppose she'll have much trouble learnin' the langwidge ;

she's so up on her Latin an' Greek that these uncivilized langwidges can't be much mor'n a-b-c's to her."

Mrs. Deacon Chatterton, on the other side of the room, felt that Deacon Haskins' wife was getting too puffed up and needed her pride taken down, and so she remarked with one of her characteristic "Humphs!" that she would "just like to see Ellen'melia when she got real seasick on the ocean, and if she wouldn't be ready to cry for Summerton and her ma then she'd miss her guess;" and then she shut her lips firmly, feeling that she had done her duty, and experienced a pang of something like envy for the woman who had a daughter who was to go as a missionary; for Mrs. Chatterton really loved the Lord and was zealous for his work, and enjoyed what glory reflected upon her as being a member of a church whence should go out a messenger who should help to bring in the Kingdom.

But Ellen Amelia went about her work from day to day with a growing expression of sweetness and content. The way in which the Lord was leading her was so wonderful to her that she had been awed into perfect trust.

'Tis so sweet to trust in Jesus,
  Just to take him at his word,
Just to rest upon his promise,
  Just to know, "Thus saith the Lord."

She had heard those words sung in that missionary meeting in West Winterton and had asked for the book that she might copy and learn them. There was another hymn that went over and over in her mind and she hummed it at her work in these days. It was this:

> I would not have the restless will
>   That hurries to and fro,
> Seeking for some great thing to do,
>   Or secret thing to know :
> I would be treated as a child,
>   And guided where I go.
> I ask Thee for the daily strength,
>   To none that ask denied,
> A mind to blend with outward life,
>   While keeping at thy side ;
> Content to fill a little space,
>   If thou be glorified.

She was learning to make these words truly her own and as she sang them she sometimes thought of the time when Joseph Benedict had told her that if she would try to be faithful in the little things there might be a chance some day that she would rule over many. She wondered if he ever thought about her and her Christian life and if he knew how she thanked him in her heart for the words he had spoken before he knew the Lord, and of the promise he had made her give. She resolved that if, in the future years, the Lord ever opened the way for her to go to a foreign land and teach others the way to Christ, she would, before she went, if there was any opportunity, tell him how much he had done for her, and thank him for it all, under God. She felt that it would be a fitting time when she was leaving her home perhaps forever.

Then in the fall Ellen went away to college. Ruth had a hand in planning where she should go, and helped her with her outfit and sent messages to some of the teachers and pupils who were friends of her own, to be kind to this friend whom she loved, and finally took a short trip just to see her safely established and be sure that she would be happy and under the right influences. Then began a new life for Ellen Haskins, and for a time she drifted out of Summerton life entirely and began to be looked upon by the Sunday-school children as a wonderful being with an unworldly spirit, who was willing to give up everything that life held good to go and preach dry sermons to wicked people who were a great deal more interesting to them unsaved and uncultured.

Joseph Benedict had gone away too, and for him the minister and David had prayed and rejoiced and labored much. Robert Clifton had made sure that he was in just the best college that could be found and himself made many arrangements which opened the way for Joseph's broader, better life, and Joseph went with a heart full of high ambitions and holy thoughts to see what the world contained for him. And lo, and behold! the first thing that he came across which fascinated him was the student's volunteer missionary movement, which he joined forthwith, and there were two from the Summerton church, albeit Summerton did not know it yet.

Just at this time Summerton was occupied with the lovely ways of the minister's sister and the marked attention which was openly paid her by David Benedict. Summerton of course could not keep still about that, it was not to be expected; but the strangest part of it all was that neither David nor Louise seemed to care to try to hide it, as a good many others would have done.

Mrs. Clifton had not understood her daughter's new character at all at first; she was so sweet and willing to do what was asked of her, and seemed to have lost all her old dissatisfaction with life. Her mother worried and even cried about her, but gradually her worry changed to a new alarm and she made plans to take her daughter away at once. What was all this that was come upon her? A young farmer, a common, ordinary man with no polish and no manners to speak of, nothing in fact—and who

knew how much or how little money behind it?
—was constantly with her cherished daughter
and that daughter smiled upon him and watched
and obeyed his least wish as if it were law, and
seemed living in a maze of happiness. Mrs.
Clifton became peremptory at once. She de-
creed that Louise should never see him again,
that he should not enter the house and ordered
Robert to prohibit him the grounds. She also
told her daughter to prepare at once to leave
with her for New York on a trip whose time
limit should not be set at present. Louise in
dismay went to her brother, and together they
tried to dissuade their mother from her purpose,
for David had already told the minister how his
sister had become the love of his life. But it
was all to no purpose. Louise tried to be sub-
missive, but she could not keep the tears from
coming, and she suddenly discovered to herself
what a world of desolation it would be to her
without David.

And then, just as they thought there was
nothing else they could do to persuade their
mother to remain quietly in Summerton during
the winter with her son and daughter, there
stepped in a new influence, and it was no other
than David. Robert had thought of Ruth and
had talked with his sister about asking her to
try her persuasive powers on their mother, but

neither would have thought of asking David.
Indeed they would have considered his appearance as disastrous to their wishes beyond anything that could have been done. Louise called
upon Ruth and mentioned that she was feeling
sad that her mother wished her to go away and
could not be persuaded to give it up, and that
this was to be a farewell call for the winter perhaps instead of a pleasant hour of converse about
their various plans of work. Wise Ruth guessed
at some things which Louise did not tell, and,
troubled over the sorrow this would bring her
brother, went to her Heavenly Father with it,
and then told David.

Then David went out into the starlight and
walked to the parsonage and ringing the bell
asked to see Mrs. Clifton. She came down, and
stranger than all the rest, she was gracious and
was conquered. In truth, no one could see
David without liking him—I had almost said
loving him. Mrs. Clifton was struck by his unusual appearance and character. He told her so
frankly that he loved her daughter, and he asked
her blessing on his suit so engagingly that she
surprised even herself by giving it. Somehow it
was given to David in a remarkable way to
win hearts, and he won Mrs. Clifton's at once.
So courteously did he treat her, so tenderly did
he calm her fears about certain little foibles of

her own, that fifteen minutes later she went back
to her room and Louise, who was sorrowfully
packing handkerchiefs by the open trunk, and
with a smile on her face and a real motherly
tear of mingled joy and sorrow said: "Louie,
dear, you may stop packing and go downstairs.
Somebody wants to see you in the parlor; and I
guess you may as well tell Morton on the way
to come and help me put these things away. I
suppose I may as well give up this trip now, for
I should have to take it alone if I went."

CHAPTER XXVI

THERE was to be a great missionary meeting in Summerton. It was a sort of missionary conference. West Winterton, North Springville, and several surrounding towns were to attend in full force. There was an all-day conference and an evening mass-meeting. Robert Clifton had planned the whole thing, but perhaps the first suggestion came from Ruth Benedict. Of course Ruth and Louise and David had had a good deal to do with the getting of it all up. Summerton church was a bower of beauty. The pulpit was a mass of evergreen and glossy leaves and feathery white blossoms. Every window held a bank of green. There were festoons of lovely ground pine hung from the center of the ceiling and draped to every corner and niche available. Nothing lovelier could have been imagined. Louise Clifton was an adept in decoration. Ruth had drilled and trained some little children in missionary exercises and recitations and singing. Summerton was to be astonished for once over what her children could do. But above all that there was to be a double surprise for the people. The two

young volunteer missionaries were to be present
and to speak.

It is wonderful what a change two years will
make in two people. Ellen Haskins had not
been at home since she left for college nearly
two years before. It had happened that during
her first college winter she had heard a great
deal about a summer school where there was instruction for Christian workers and especially
for young missionaries. Her heart longed to go,
and her father gave his permission since if she
chose to use some of her money in this way he
was well satisfied. Her mother pursed up her lips
and thought her daughter might as well come
home and help with the canning and get a little
of the winter sewing out of the way; but it was
made easy for Ellen to go and everything seemed
to point in that direction, and so she went. The
summer had rushed by all too soon, and with her
mind full of wonderful new thoughts and her
note book and Bible filled with themes for future
study this eager student went back to her college
duties. But now they were to come home for
an event which was to come off soon, and so
Mother Haskins was to have her desire at last,
and her pride would not be obliged to live entirely upon the first threadbare glory of her
daughter's stated intention for distinction.

And they came. Not even Mrs. Haskins

knew that Ellen was to speak. Ruth had written her and had persuaded her to put her eager earnestness into words for her home people to hear. Ruth had received from Ellen many long letters full of eager enthusiasm for missions. She felt certain that Ellen could speak about this theme so dear to her heart, and Ellen, after prayer and consideration, had consented.

But not even Ruth had counted on the changes that two years away from home and the contact with the college girls and books and all the world she had met since she had left them would make in her. She knew that Ellen's letters had changed, that they were better expressed and better written, and that there was in them an earnest tone which meant much for the future work of the girl.

By some mistake or delay of trains Ellen did not arrive until an hour or two before the hour for the meeting. Indeed they began to fear that she would not reach them at all that night and their surprise would not come off after all. But she came just in time to make a hasty toilet and go to the church. There was, of course, no opportunity to see her or note any changes. Robert Clifton had been dubious about allowing her to speak at this important meeting before they had tested her in a smaller one, but Ruth

had thought it a good thing and so he had
yielded, for in truth he had come to feel that
Ruth was generally right. However, she began
to feel just the least bit nervous for the girl herself, as the time drew near and she had had no
opportunity to talk with her. She could only
sit and pray for her while the music of the grand
missionary hymn rolled down the aisles. There
was a great crowd out that night. All Summerton knew that "Joe Benedic'" was home
from college and they wanted a good chance to
watch him. They also knew that some strangers were to speak. The church people were
out in full force. The "Brower boys," who still
retained that name together with their former
reputation, were there. They had not been to
church much of late. They had interests in
other directions, but the prospect of a lot of
strangers from out of town was alluring. They
lounged into the back seats and eyed the speakers
as they came upon the platform. There were
four or five men with the minister, a young
woman with some music in her hand who was
to sing, and another woman, tall and almost
stately in her carriage and with an unmistakable
"style" in her plain, perfectly-fitting, and becoming gown.

"I say, she's a stunner!" ejaculated Bill
Brower, pursing up his lips in a disgusting

pucker to squirt some tobacco juice in just the right spot under the dress of the lady who sat in front of him. " I wonder who she is ! "

" Well, I'll be eaten alive if that ain't Joe Benedic'," said his brother in answer as he sat and stared in open-mouthed wonder.

Joseph was greatly changed as well as Ellen. It was quite astonishing to hear him introduced as a "student volunteer," to be told what that mystical title meant, and then to look at Joe Benedict, whom they had known since he was in long clothes and as a barefoot boy, and see him a handsome, graceful, well-dressed young man and hear him talk the smooth easy English of the minister. What was he saying? Deacon Meakins took out his red cotton handkerchief and blew his nose very loud after the first few sentences. Was this really his friend, Mr. Benedict's boy, talking? Why, he was so enthusiastic that the old deacon almost felt he would like to go to a foreign field himself. The hard lines around Mrs. Chatterton's mouth relaxed and even Deacon Chatterton himself nodded his approval in a series of jerky, severe bobbings of his head.

Joseph had early decided to study for the ministry and had not been long in finding out that the foreign field was where his heart would fain carry him. He had been in many meetings ever since he first entered college and he had made a point to hear all the missionaries and good speakers on the subject that came in his way, so he had plenty of experience and knowledge to speak from. He told the audience some of those interesting facts concerning the amount of money spent for luxuries, necessities, drink, and tobacco in this country, and then showed them how little they gave to missions. He had a rod with lengths of colored ribbons representing these different facts. When he came to the black one —close beside the little white one indicating the money expended in missions—representing the amount of money spent for liquor in this country and flung the end far out into the audience, Bill and Ed Brower looked in amaze, and Bill said, " I'll be gormed." Just exactly what that epithet meant nobody ever knew, but Bill always used it when he was particularly overcome and wished to be reverent. He hardly ever swore during his remarks in the church. This word was used to take its place when swearing was inappropriate.

When Joseph sat down Ruth wished with all her heart that his speech had been put last, as she felt sure it would make a good impression which would bear fruit if left in the minds of the hearers. She had assisted in preparing the programme for this meeting, and had urged that

Ellen be put at the end, for something had told her that Ellen would be impressive and helpful as well. Now she began to fear that she had overestimated the girl and that she might fail and spoil the whole. She half wished that Ellen would, even at this late hour, whisper to the minister that she could not speak, Joseph had done so well. Ruth was proud indeed of her brother.

Joseph sat down and bowed his head a moment, as it was his custom, to ask the Master's blessing when he had finished a message. The young woman with the music was singing now:

> Hark! the voice of Jesus calling,
> Who will go and work to-day?

It was strange indeed that Joseph Benedict had not been told that Ellen Haskins was to address the meeting that night. No one had thought to mention the matter to him. He had been much with David during the few hours he had been at home, and David never dreamed it would be of any particular interest to him, nor would it except as it would arouse a kind curiosity. As Joseph began to listen to the singing and raised his eyes to the singer, he became aware of an annoyingly loud whisper. It was just behind him, one of the West Winterton ministers and a stranger whispering together,

and Joseph could not but hear what they were
saying inasmuch as they were mentioning his
name and did not seem to try to speak quietly.

"You say the young woman who is to speak
next is the wife of this Mr. Benedict who has
just spoken? She is a remarkably fine-looking
woman. If she can speak as well as she looks
she will make a splendid helper for a man in a
foreign field."

"No," said the West Winterton minister, who
had a loud wheezy whisper, "I only said they
both came from Summerton and from this
church. No, she is a single lady. She attended
our academy some time since."

"Oh, indeed," said the stranger, who was an
elderly gentleman and seemed to know a good
deal about missionary matters. "Well, it is a
pity. They won't succeed near so well. They'd
better make up their minds to marry. It is a
great deal better. I'm told the Board is advis-
ing it in all cases. They can do more good."

And then the singing ceased and Joseph looked
up, indignation in his heart, to see who was the
young woman whose fate was being so summarily
disposed of at the direction of a Board.

Robert Clifton was introducing the tall young
woman. Joseph had only noticed her casually
as they had been coming in. He did not in the
least know who she was. What did the minister

mean? He was saying she was one of their own number, and—Miss Haskins! What Miss Haskins? Not Ellen Amelia, surely! Why, she was—she did not look like that! And what a voice! So rich and full and strong, and not the least bit self-conscious. She was in earnest too. She meant every word she said. She was ready to throw every bit of her magnificent energy and talent into the work. Joseph sat up straight and listened, and wondered, and his heart throbbed over the stories she had to tell. Where had she found all this information? What she had to say was new and original. It almost seemed as if she must have been at work in Africa or China or some of the other places she talked about, so familiar was she with their needs.

Joseph was not the only one who listened to Ellen's words in wonder and surprise and joy. Her old father sat with the tears streaming down his cheeks, glad to his weak old heart's core that his little Ellen had turned out so beautiful and grand, able to talk as well as the minister. Her mother sat beside him, her lips very stiffly shut, her eyes drooping with humility and pride as if she thought all Summerton was looking at her in admiration that she had brought up such a child. She would not let them think she was over-awed by it, and so she tipped her neck back uncomfortably and her head forward, and would

not look up to watch her darling, though she
confided to her husband on the way home that
she was "jest all of a tremble, lest Ellen'melia
should break down and forget her piece."

It is needless to say that Summerton was
astonished and that the minister and his sister,
and his sister's future husband, and his sister
and brother were delighted and charmed beyond
measure, and greeted Ellen with overwhelming
joy when the meeting at last was over and they
had her to themselves. Joseph, it is true, was
not very demonstrative. He had shaken hands
cordially, and then stepped back to give the
others a chance, and while he waited had
watched.

At home, in his palm-surrounded room he sat
alone, later, upon his couch, and thought of the
words of the stranger back of him on the platform. At last he said, as he began to prepare
for rest, "I shouldn't wonder if that was good
advice. I'll follow it."

Knowing Joseph as you do, do you think it
was strange that he should stand, the very next
evening, at the Haskins door, seeking admission,
and asking for the daughter?

Ellen came in, the same and yet a new Ellen.
She greeted him kindly, not effusively. That
was new for her. She used to gush. Ellen's
time to thank her first helper had not yet come,

and until then she must bide behind a calm re-
serve. This she well knew.

Joseph told his errand at once. Perhaps his
language was a little more blunt than that his
brother had used some time before, on a similar
occasion. He had come to ask her to join hands
with him and go to the foreign field. And he
had not learned any better in all his two years
at college, and his many meetings, and his intensity, he did not know any better than to tell
her a part of the conversation he had heard on
the platform the night before. Ellen's color
came and went. Her heart throbbed painfully,
but she kept her self-control. She had not borne
this young man's stunning blows of truth several
times before in her life for nothing. Presently
she gained control of her voice.

"No, Mr. Benedict," she said in a clear voice
which seemed to herself to be speaking away off
in the clouds somewhere, "it is not necessary
for you to do that. We shall both work well
where we are put, and we shall not make mar-
riages of convenience, either, for the Master's
cause. You remember," and here her voice tried
to be light and playful, but there was a suspicious
tremble in it, "you remember I 'know you do
not care anything for me except for your sister's
sake, and the promise,' and this cannot possibly
affect either of those."

Joseph looked at her a moment in amazement and alarm, and then it all came over him what she meant, and he saw himself in just the light he was.

"I am a fool and a blunderer," he said, "and I must have been a boor. I ought to go down upon my knees and beg your pardon for that brutal speech I made in that long time ago. But you see, Ellen, I love you, though I don't seem to know how to tell you of it, and it *will* affect both my sister and my promise, for I couldn't possibly live and work unless you will work with me. Ellen, I believe in my heart I loved you then. I remember thinking it was queer I cared to go out of my way for you when I had never done such things before. I believe I loved you then and didn't know it. Can you forgive me? And will you love me just a little? Cannot we go out to some far land together and work for Him? You know we started the promise together, and we can surely, work better if we help each other. Will you, Ellen?"

And Ellen answered, "Yes, I will."

And the next day was the marriage of David Benedict and Louise Clifton.

CHAPTER XXVII

DAVID and Louise were married and gone on a year's trip to the Holy Land. It had been David's deep desire ever since he had been a Christian to wander over the places where the Master had trod, and Louise found that it was her desire as well. Indeed, she wanted nothing apart from what her husband wished.

Ruth was glad and sad together to see them depart. She was very happy over David's marriage, for she had come to love Louise dearly, and she saw they were well fitted for one another, but they were gone, and Joseph was still in college and was to go to the seminary, and she was alone in the great farmhouse. They had wanted her to go to Palestine with them, but she would not. She had a feeling that people who were just married needed to be by themselves for a while without any third person there to meddle, so that they might become adjusted to one another's ways of living and thinking. Moreover she loved her work in Summerton and could not be persuaded to leave it. Nevertheless, when she saw them depart she shed a few tears and wondered what the Lord would have of her now that she was again bereft of family and alone in the world.

What she did immediately was to ask a dear old lady who had been a mother in Israel to her ever since she came to Summerton, to come and live with her that winter, and so she made a pleasant home for one who was alone in the world and needed beauty and help and comfort, and who in turn was rich in Bible wisdom and good sound advice and a blessing to all who came near her. Her name was Mrs. Brown, just plain Mrs. Brown, but her face was a benediction in itself.

The minister closed and locked the parsonage door on the day after the wedding and started out on a walk by himself toward the country. His mother had left earlier in the morning for a visit to her sister near New York, and a rest to her soul after the various labors of persuading to wear this, and have that, and not do this or that fanatical thing at the wedding. The one servant left to care for the minister was out, telling her most intimate friend about the wedding and all the extra work, and the house seemed unusually desolate to the minister. His heart ached. He wanted something and he knew what it was he wanted. Was it any use to try? He had been reading the twenty-fourth chapter of Genesis, preparatory to his next

Sunday's sermon. It had seemed to affect him strangely. He had taken a sudden determination. "I will ask the Lord to show me," he said; "I will ask a sign of the Lord as the men of old did," and he had knelt beside his study table and prayed long and then had gone out. And ever there came to him as he walked these words: "The Lord will send his angel with thee and will prosper thy way."

Out beside the little wood road not far away from the Benedict place he saw her. She was picking flowers or ferns or some sweet growing thing, and he went to meet her. She smiled and held out her hand to him, and he thought, he was sure, there had been tears in her eyes. He asked her to walk with him and they went on into the woods and there they sat down upon a mossy log. "Is your name Rebecca?" he asked her, and then he told her all that was in his heart; how she had blessed him ever since he had first met her and how he had loved and feared to tell it because he felt sure his love was not returned; and now he had read the chapter and it had led him to seek a sign of the Lord, and he had come feeling that he would be led in some way and helped; and how he would like to take her back home to the parsonage as his wife just as soon as she would let him. And then he waited for an answer.

And Ruth looked up with glad tears shining in her sweet eyes and said, "I will go."

As they rose to leave the woods that afternoon Robert Clifton quoted the text which had led him out to find her. "I being in the way, the Lord led me." "It is strange," he said, "how true that is. Every time when I have made up my mind to surrender my own way and follow what seemed to be pointed out as his way, I have been led to something great and sweet and beautiful, something that I wanted very much. And now at last it is you."

And Ruth, looking into the eyes of the man she loved said, "That text is true of me also. I certainly have been led into brighter and better things than I ever dreamed. Let us take it for our life motto, '*I being in the way,* the Lord led me.'"

As they came near to the house they heard through the open window the quavering voice of Mrs. Brown as she sang to herself a hymn that was dear to her and to them:

> "His wisdom ever waketh,
> His sight is never dim,
> He knows the way He taketh,
> And I will walk with him."